THE DOCTOR

DOCTOR #1

E. L. TODD

PROLOGUE

PEPPER

There were two options.

I could refuse to cooperate, throw a tantrum, and kick and scream the entire way. With a broken heart and a delirious mind, it's what I favored in that moment. I didn't want to be reasonable or understanding. I wanted to sit behind my desk at the shop and never leave.

Colton's message popped up on the screen. *Babe, are you coming?*

Babe. He'd called me that every day for the last five years. Now that sweet endearment would disappear for good. When enough time passed, I might forget about that nickname altogether.

But I didn't want to.

Pepper?

I looked out the window to the darkness outside. A storm of clouds covered the sky, and raindrops pelted against the window, streaking down until they ran into the flowerpots outside on the concrete. The sound was comforting because it was loud enough to drown out my labored breathing.

Colton texted me again. *I hate this too... You have no idea.*

I wanted to hurl my phone at the wall and watch it smash. He had the audacity to say that? He hated this?

I hated it more.

I was the one who'd lost everything.

I stared at the wet windows a little longer, and that's when the second option came into my head.

I could walk in there with my head held high, my shoulders back, and finish this with the last bit of strength I had. Kicking and screaming wouldn't change what was about to happen. It couldn't erase the past. The only thing I had control over now was me. Maybe I had every right to stare at the rain and ignore him.

But that wasn't the option I wanted to take.

I texted him back. *I'm coming.*

I STEPPED inside the law firm and was ushered into the office where our attorney was waiting for us. My waterproof jacket had beads of water rolling down the material and onto the floor. My shoes squeaked against the tile with every step I took, audibly reminding me this was completely real.

Not a nightmare.

John sat behind his desk, the paperwork laid across the surface along with two fancy pens. All he needed were a few signatures, and that would end everything.

End my marriage.

Colton rose to his feet when I stepped inside. Concern was heavy in his body movements, and when he made eye contact with me, I was relieved to see the same pain I felt mirrored in his eyes. It wasn't pity just for me.

It was his own heartbreak.

He stilled in front of me, a moment of awkwardness because he didn't know how he should greet me. His arms rose impulsively, his instinct to hug me like he always did. Maybe the look on my face changed his mind, because he lowered his hands to his sides then sat down again.

I pulled my hood off the back of my head and sat down, indifferent to my soaking wet clothes and the water dripping all over the floor.

John didn't complain. He pushed the two sets of papers closer toward us. "Just a few signatures and we're done. Painless."

Because the painful part had already been completed. We'd divided our assets so we could walk away with equal shares of our wealth. We hadn't bought a house, so dividing our bank account in two was pretty simple. While that procedure was excruciating, this was worse. It was somehow worse than when I packed up my things and moved out of my own home.

Because this was final.

Colton, the love of my life, was no longer my husband.

He was my ex-husband.

I thought of my two options again, how I wanted to handle this particular moment. Bursting into tears was my natural reaction, but that would only make me weak. More importantly, it wouldn't change anything.

Colton didn't grab the pen first, as if that would be insensitive.

I took an extra breath before I picked up the thick ball-point pen and added my signature. I scribbled it at the bottom, writing my married name for the last time. I added my signature to the rest of the sheets before I pushed them toward Colton.

He didn't take the pen right away. Instead, he stared at

me, a thin film of moisture in his eyes. Signing our divorce papers seemed just as hard for him as it did for me, even though he wanted this to happen.

Even though he was the one who left me.

He sighed quietly before he grabbed the pen and added his signature.

It was done.

We were over.

Officially over.

~

WE SAT in the back seat of the taxi as we headed back to our apartment building. The rain was coming down hard in the darkness, and the windshield wipers were working furiously to throw the rain off the window. Downtown Seattle was lit up beautifully by the lights from the buildings, and the rain only added to its charm.

But right now, I was immune to it.

Colton glanced at me from time to time, looking for tears on my cheeks.

I'd cried enough. I couldn't do it anymore.

The ten-minute drive was spent in silence. The two of us could make a conversation out of thin air. We were so close, had a connection so deep, and it was strange that we didn't feel it now.

Colton reached his hand across the seat and grabbed mine. He squeezed it three times, telling me how he felt without actually saying the words.

I didn't pull my hand away. I waited a long time before I reciprocated.

I squeezed him back.

The cab arrived at the building, and we stepped out of

the rain and into the lobby. We ditched the elevator and took the stairs to the third floor, where our apartments now sat across from each other. When Colton had first told me the truth, I was in shock. The apartment across the hall happened to open up that afternoon, and since apartments were nearly impossible to find in Seattle, I just took it.

Now I lived across the hall from him.

Probably not the best idea.

Colton walked me to my door, his hands in the pockets of his jeans. With blond hair and blue eyes, he was a beautiful man. With his strong physique, nice cheekbones, and shoulders that made every woman swoon, he was absolutely perfect. But his physical attributes didn't compare to what was underneath.

That heart of gold.

His eyes lingered on the floor before they rose to meet mine. Several seconds passed before the moisture developed in his eyes, the heartbreak that rivaled my own. He took a deep breath as he stared at me, his nostrils flaring slightly. "I'm so sorry…"

It was impossible to be angry at him, even though I had every right to be. But I loved this man so deeply that I didn't feel an ounce of rage. "I know." I knew this killed him. Every time I broke down in tears, he did the same. He hated himself for hurting me, and he hated himself for losing me too. Before I knew it, the tears started to sting my eyes too.

Colton cupped my face with both of his hands and pressed his forehead against mine. His fingers pressed lightly into my skin, his touch warm and soft. He closed his eyes and breathed with me, holding me like nothing had changed. "I don't want to lose you. I can't live without you, Pepper. I just can't. You're my best friend. You're everything to me." He kissed my forehead and rested his lips there, tears streaking down his cheeks.

"I know..." Now the tears came full force, streaming down my face like two rivers.

He pulled his lips away so he could look at me, unashamed of the emotion he put on display. "I know we should spend some time apart. But after that...I want you in my life. I don't want that to change. I know we won't be spending the rest of our lives together...but I still want you there every step of the way."

I was still in love with him. I could feel it in my heart every time I looked at him. When we were this close together, my breathing came out uneven because I couldn't forget the way his lips felt against mine. My marriage had been perfect because I was married to the perfect guy. I never wanted it to end. I needed to get over him, but the idea of losing him from my life forever wasn't an option. He was too important to me. "You know I can't live without you, Colton."

He gave me a smile, but it was filled with so much heartbreak, it simply looked sad.

"Give me some time. I'm still..." I didn't want to say the words out loud, but since he already knew how I felt, it seemed pointless to hide it. "So in love with you."

His eyes watered even more. "I loved being married to you, Pepper. I really did."

"I know..."

"I wish...I didn't feel this way. I tried to fight it so many times—"

"Don't." I didn't want to go through this again. I didn't want him to feel guilty either. "It's okay, Colton. Even if I could go back in time, I wouldn't change anything. I would still do it all over again...even if I knew it was gonna end like this."

He closed his eyes for a brief moment. More tears fell. "I don't deserve you."

"Yes, you do. We deserve each other." I grabbed both of his hands with mine. "We're both going to marry other people...but that doesn't mean we won't spend the rest of our lives together."

He brought my hands to his lips and kissed each one. "I'll make sure the next guy is good enough for you. Not that I believe there's any guy out there good enough for you." He brought my hands to his chest and placed them over his heart, right where I could feel his steady pulse.

Even now, I saw how much he loved me, how much he hated making me suffer. He was still the same man I fell in love with, a man who was kind, compassionate, and loving. I should have known he was too good to be true. "I find it hard to believe there's a man good enough for you too. But I'm sure we'll both find them...in time."

1

PEPPER

SIX MONTHS LATER

I slipped on my heels then walked across the hall. My bag was over my shoulder and I was running behind, but I needed to make a pit stop before I headed to the shop and opened the doors.

Colton was standing in the kitchen with his open tie hanging down his chest. In a white collared shirt with black slacks, he was almost ready for work but not quite. He held a hot pan over the stove, and once he finished his scrambled eggs, he poured them onto a plate. "You're running late."

"I could say the same to you." I went to the counter near the door and sorted through the mail. My stuff still ended up here since I hadn't changed my last name. The fact that I lived across the hall didn't make it any easier for the mailman to figure out where to put my stuff. I found the banking paperwork I needed for my shop and slipped it into my purse.

"Do I look like a post office to you?" He carried the plate and silverware to the table, where his hot coffee and newspaper sat. A teasing tone was in his voice, but he was also grumpy because he'd never been a morning person. Thankfully, he worked his own hours at the firm. Otherwise, he wouldn't be employed.

"No." I took the seat beside him and shoveled half of his food onto my plate. "You look like a diner."

As if he wasn't the least bit surprised, he drank his coffee and looked at the newspaper.

I sorted through the rest of my mail to make sure there wasn't anything else important. Most of it was junk. There were a few bills too, but I would still classify those as junk. I ate the scrambled eggs then looked through my emails to see if one of my shipments was coming in. It seemed like it was going to be delivered today by noon. "How's work going?"

"You know, blah, blah."

"Blah, blah?" I asked, finishing my plate until it was just as clean as it was when it came out of the dishwasher.

"Yeah." He turned the page of his newspaper. "Sums it up."

I got the impression Colton didn't like his new law firm, but he never came right out and actually said it. He'd always been an outgoing guy who wore his heart on his sleeve, but it never seemed like practicing law resonated with him. He'd been pressured by his father, and now he was stuck in a career he didn't really care about. "What's new with you?"

"The girls are going out tonight. You guys wanna join?"

"Depends." He shut the newspaper and then worked his tie with his fingers. "Where are you guys going?"

"This new sports bar called Hopkins. It opened up near the market."

"Not a fan of sports bars. The food is garbage, and the beer is watered down."

"But you know who goes to sports bars?" I teased. "Fit men."

He finally got his tie together, but it was a sloppy job. "Spoiler alert, babe. Only straight men go to sports bars. Not much for me there." He abandoned his dishes on the table when he stood up and grabbed his coat from the rack.

He used to leave his dishes everywhere when we were married, but now that we were just friends, I ignored his bad habits. It wasn't my problem anymore. Now I also left my dishes behind so he would have to deal with them later.

Payback.

"So, are you coming or not?" I left the table and walked up to him with my mail tucked under my arm. His tie was sloppy, and normally he cared about his appearance to a meticulous level. It was only more evidence that he didn't care about his job. I undid the silk fabric and started over, making sure it was tight and crisp. I flattened my hand and smoothed out the material against his chest.

"Obviously. I'm not gonna pass up booze and friends."

"That's what I thought."

"Alright. See you tonight." He grabbed his satchel from the rack and pulled it over his shoulder. He opened the door and prepared to walk out.

"Eh-hem."

It took him a second to turn back and look at me, as if he knew exactly what I was gonna say based on my tone. His face was visibly tense, prepared to hear something he didn't want to listen to.

"It's been six months, Colton."

He held my gaze but didn't suppress his irritation.

"You need to tell them." We'd been playing house for the last six months, showing up to family dinners and putting on a show for his parents. For the first month, it was fine because Colton needed some time to prepare himself. But now, I suspected he was dragging it out as long as possible.

If I never pushed him, he would pretend we were married forever.

"Yeah, I know. I'll do it soon..."

"Soon? As in when?"

"Soon." He turned around and walked off, his shoulders tense from the provocative conversation.

I watched him walk away without calling him back. His parents adored me, so telling them we'd been divorced for six months would break their hearts. On top of that, he would have to explain why our marriage didn't work out.

I knew that was the part he was dreading the most.

STELLA HELD up a one-piece ensemble with an open crotch, the black lace leaving very little to the imagination. She held it up to herself and turned to the mirror, imagining how it would look on her bare skin. "You think this would look good on me?" She fluffed her hair, like that would miraculously make her look more gorgeous. She was a personal trainer, someone in high demand, and she had the kind of figure fit models possessed.

I sorted through the shipment that had arrived and hardly looked at her. "Everything in this store would look good on you."

She fished for the price tag and nearly gagged. "Who spends a hundred and fifty bucks to get laid?"

"A lot of people." Well, except me. It'd been a long time since I'd worn lingerie. The last time I did was for Colton, and now I felt stupid because I had been trying to impress a gay man.

"But who can afford this?"

"You'd be surprised..." A large number of my clients

were women with rich husbands. They didn't have anything else to do, so they came in here for a shopping spree. I also had a lot of bridal parties come in here for lingerie parties. They all bought the bride-to-be something special for her wedding night.

"I need to find a man who can buy me this stuff. No way in hell I'm paying that price." She returned it to the rack then gave me a guilty smile. "No offense."

"None taken," I said with a chuckle. "It's all higher-end stuff, designer quality shipped from France and Italy. You do get what you pay for." I believed in my products. I didn't buy mundane pieces and then jack up the price for profit. Maybe to other people I just sold sex clothes, but I really enjoyed what I did. I put women in the right bras, and I helped them overcome their self-esteem issues when they purchased lingerie. Some of them were too nervous to go for it, but I convinced them their man would love it.

Too bad my man didn't love it.

Stella came back to the counter and watched me sort through the new panties and bras that had arrived. "You seem like you're doing a lot better, girl." The topic change came out of nowhere, but since my well-being was always on her mind, it didn't seem as jarring. "Six months ago, you were a totally different person. But now you're smiling and seem to be in a good place."

"Yes...I am in a good place." It took me a long time to get here, along with many sleepless nights, but somehow, I got out of the depression and moved on with my life—while my ex lived across the hall.

"And I'm glad you and Colton could stay so close. Not very many people could do that."

If he were someone else, I probably would have moved somewhere else and started over. But Colton was way too important to me. He was the single constant in my life, the one man who had always been there for me...even when he left me. Maybe we weren't meant to be in love, but we were certainly meant to love each other. "We love each other too much. And love always finds a way."

She smiled. "That's sweet."

Colton and I had a special relationship, the kind that could overcome anything, even something as heartbreaking as our divorce. When he'd first told me he was gay, I refused to accept it. We were so happy that it didn't seem believable. I didn't handle it very well, and it took me an entire month to come to terms with it. "I'm glad we made it to this point. The first three months were hard, but after that, it got a lot easier."

"So, does that mean you'll catch some tail tonight?" She perked up with excitement, like me getting laid was just as good as her getting laid.

I hadn't slept with anyone new or even tried. Anytime a guy asked me out, I shot him down, regardless of how hot he was. It didn't seem right, sleeping with someone new when I'd only been divorced for six months. "I think it's too soon, Stella."

Both of her eyebrows shot up her face as if she couldn't believe what I said. "Too soon? Six months is a long time. Shit, a month is a long time."

"Maybe if I just had a normal breakup, it would be different. But I was married."

"So what?" she asked. "Your husband told you he was gay. You don't owe him anything, Pepper. You have every right to sleep with whoever you want. Don't hold back because of him."

I was holding back for another reason, but I didn't want to admit it out loud—not even to Stella. Once upon a time,

I was a very confident woman. I was never vain, but I also knew what I was worth. I threw on lingerie and did a strip-tease for the men I was sleeping with. I wasn't afraid to be open with my sexuality, to do things other women would be afraid to do. Men were always attracted to my confidence.

But being in love with a gay man changed all of that.

Had he always been gay?

Or did I make him gay?

It wasn't a question I wanted to answer. I didn't want Colton to answer it either. "When it's meant to happen, it will."

"But still, you must be dying. I can't go more than a week without getting some action."

"More like a weekend," I teased.

She shrugged, unashamed.

That was one of the reasons I loved her. She wasn't apologetic about who she was. She didn't care what anyone thought of her.

"I'm gonna find you a guy tonight." She smacked her hand on the counter between us. "And you better give him a chance."

"I don't need you to find me a guy."

"Fine. Then you find one, and let me approve."

"You would approve anything at this point," I said with a laugh.

"So not true. He's gotta be hot. Like, super-hot. You deserve an unbelievable night. Something that's gonna get you back in the game in the most fabulous way."

That was every woman's dream come true. "We'll see what happens."

She raised an eyebrow. "So that means you're open to it?"

I shrugged. "I'm not committing to anything. But I'm not opposed to it either."

"Good. That's exactly what I wanted to hear."

The door opened, and the bell rang overhead. My shop was small so I didn't really need the sound, but when I was measuring a bust in the dressing room, it was helpful to know someone else was in the store. I had all manner of clientele that came into the store, mostly women, but of all different ages.

It was rare for someone like him to walk inside.

Tall. Handsome. Sexy.

In a black suit and tie, he looked like a very important man with important places to go. With dark hair and green eyes, he was so pretty it seemed unreal. Within the span of a few seconds, I noticed his hard jawline, the absence of a beard because he kept up his grooming, his perfectly styled hair, and the way his custom suit fit his biceps like cling wrap.

Stella couldn't keep herself together at all. Her mouth dropped open and she mouthed, "Daaaaamn."

I was facing him head on, so I kept my composure, not wanting to lose my shit when I was in his line of sight. I gripped the edge of the counter and pretended everything was normal, but my blood definitely got hot under my skin. Pretty men like that didn't walk into my shop very often.

His footsteps sounded against the hardwood floor, and then seconds later, he was at the counter. His visage up close was even better, a hint of a smile on his lips. One hand rested on the counter, his expensive watch giving me a flash.

Stella turned and stared at him, her eyes trickling down his frame all the way to his big feet. She mouthed again. "Double daaaaamn."

I tried to ignore her and hoped he didn't notice. "Good

afternoon. How can I help you?" I didn't let this pretty man unnerve me. He would have to be an idiot not to be aware of his perfection, so he was probably used to women drooling all over him—just the way Stella was right now.

"I have a pickup. Should be under Lacey."

Lacey. I remembered putting together an online order yesterday. It was a two-piece lingerie set—made for a woman who was a size zero but had an incredible bust. She must have picked out her lingerie, then her boyfriend picked it up for her.

That was the most romantic thing ever—seriously.

I would love it if a man did that for me.

He continued to stare at me, and his head cocked to the side slightly when I didn't give him a reaction.

I got lost in my fantasy for a second, imagining a hot guy like him picking up lingerie for me to wear. "Oh, of course. I have it right here." I kneeled down and looked behind the counter until I found the bag I'd prepared the day before. It was already paid for, so I stood upright and placed the bag in front of him. "There you go. Did you need anything else?"

He didn't check the bag. "No thank you." He gave a charming smile, showing all of his perfect teeth, and then walked out.

My eyes moved to his ass.

That thing was as pretty as his face.

The second he was gone, Stella whipped around and nearly hissed at me. "What the hell was that?"

"What the hell was what?"

"You didn't make a move."

"Make a move?" A constricted laugh escaped my throat. "When? He was here for forty-five seconds."

"That's plenty of time."

"Stella, you're crazy."

"Oh, come on." She moved into the center of the counter where Mr. Gorgeous had just been. "The old Pepper would have been all up on that. You would have made him laugh right off the bat and then moved in within ten seconds. He would have a date with you and your lingerie tonight."

I knew I'd really bounced back from my divorce when the suggestion made my neck flush with heat. I could picture myself with another man, his hot, naked body on top of mine. I didn't feel guilty about it, not like I had in the past few months. After being with the same man for five years, it almost felt wrong to think of someone else that way. "You're forgetting something big."

"Trust me." She held up her hand. "I was looking for it in his slacks."

"No, not that." I rolled my eyes, still surprised by her audacity. "He was picking up lingerie for some other woman."

"So...?"

"He obviously has a girlfriend."

"How do you figure?" She placed her hand on her hip, copping an attitude. "She's probably just some chick he's screwing. You think a man like that just settles for one woman? No way. He probably goes from woman to woman. And you could be next."

I never thought I would want to be some random woman on a long list. "There's no way to know now, so let's forget about it."

She pointed her finger in my face. "But if he comes in here again, you better go for it."

"We'll see..."

"I mean it. Come on, Pepper. You're back on the market, and it's time to embrace it. It's time to ask out hot guys and not care if they say no. It's time to end up in a stranger's bed.

It's time to whip out the lingerie and dance around like the sexy little thing you are. You know how flattered he would be if a woman like you made a pass at him?"

Even when I hit my lowest point, I felt so grateful that I had people like Stella in my life. She reminded me I was worth something. And she reminded me I was loved. "That's sweet of you to say."

"And it's true. Don't you forget it, Pepper."

2

PEPPER

W hen I got to Hopkins, I left my heavy coat on the rack by the door and walked inside. I was in a black dress with purple heels, dressing up a little more than I had over the last few months. Stella, Tatum, Colton, and Zach were standing at a table close to one of the TVs. My eyes immediately went to Colton's tie, noticing the way he yanked it loose the second he was off the clock. I stopped by the bar and ordered myself a beer before I joined them at the table.

Colton looked me up and down and whistled loudly. "That is one hell of a dress."

I let his compliment wash over me and tried not to think of the way he'd looked at me when I walked down the aisle. There were so many memories of us stored in my head, and it was impossible for me not to think about them from time to time. "Thanks."

Zach's eyes roamed freely, taking me in with the same approval, but with an added dash of masculine lust. "What dress? All I see are curves." He motioned with his hands, mimicking an hourglass frame.

"He's right," Stella said. "You clean up good. If only you'd been wearing that when Mr. Gorgeous walked inside."

"Who's Mr. Gorgeous?" Tatum asked. "Sounds like a man I want to meet." She sipped her vodka cranberry. "Stella doesn't throw that name out lightly."

"Well, this man deserved it—big-time." Stella was drinking a glass of red wine, wearing a long-sleeved sweater dress that blanketed her curves but couldn't hide them. "He came into the lingerie shop this afternoon. He was in this sexy suit, and he had the nicest smile. I thought Pepper was gonna make a move, but she just sat there."

I was suddenly aware of Colton standing next to me at the table, the man I'd vowed to love for the rest of my life. We hadn't talked about our dating lives since we got divorced. It seemed like a subject neither one of us wanted to broach first. I'd come to accept our new relationship, but I didn't exactly want to hear about what he did in the privacy of his bedroom. I wasn't sure if he felt the same way.

Stella picked up on my unease then shifted her gaze to Colton.

Zach took a longer drink from his glass than necessary, drowning out his silence with his loud drinking sounds.

Colton didn't have a visible reaction. He was normally easy to read, but not today.

"Oh, sorry," Stella said. "I wasn't thinking…"

Colton set his glass down. "Nothing to apologize for. We knew this day would come, and it's a good thing." He turned to me, giving me his endearing smile that showed his sincerity. "A really good thing. Don't tiptoe around me. We're friends. Friends talk about this stuff."

Stella relaxed when she realized she hadn't done anything wrong. "Good. I think it's time Pepper got laid."

"I second that." Tatum held up her glass.

"If you want to take care of it now, I can help with that." Zach waggled his eyebrows.

Colton was cool just a second ago, but that comment hit one of his buttons. His head snapped in Zach's direction, and he gave him a formidable stare, an unusual look to give his best friend. "Don't cross me."

"What?" Zach asked, brushing off the insult. "Come on, I was just making a joke."

"Friends don't make jokes like that about each other's wives," Colton countered. "That broke the bro code, and you know it."

"Ex-wife," I corrected.

"You know what I mean," Colton said. "Don't cross that line again." He'd been protective of me when we were together, and even now, things hadn't changed.

Zach didn't apologize, but he wore a guilty look as though he felt bad about the comment.

Tension settled over the table, and no amount of alcohol could dispel it.

So Stella changed the subject. "This guy had a big package."

"Did he whip it out or something?" Tatum asked. "How do you know?"

"I have a theory," Stella said. "And it's never let me down."

Colton drank his beer and looked at the table.

I wasn't entirely sure if I was interested in this conversation, but it was better than the one we'd been having just seconds ago. "What's your theory?"

"If a guy adjusts his pants often, it's big." Stella made her statement with finality, as if she'd just proved a theory in court. "If it's constantly getting in the way, then that means he has something to move around."

"Could be his underwear," Tatum said.

"Or he could have a hard-on," Colton added. "Happens a lot throughout the day."

"No. I saw him adjust himself the second he walked in the door," Stella said. "No way he popped a boner that quickly. That tells me everything I need to know. And that's exactly why Pepper is making a move next time he walks in."

"Ooh, I hope he comes in soon," Tatum said.

"Why was he at your shop anyway?" Colton asked.

"He picked up lingerie for someone." I didn't make eye contact with Colton, thinking about the last time I wore lingerie for him. I'd surprised him when he came home from work. We had good sex right afterward, but now I wondered if he had been picturing someone else instead of me the entire time.

The blow hurt my ego a lot more than I wanted to admit.

"That's pretty hot," Zach said. "She picks it out, and he picks it up? Sounds fun."

It was pointless to think about it too much because I would probably never see him again. And even if I did, I doubted I would make a move. It was time to put myself out there and start seeing other men, but getting my feet wet was the hardest point. I hadn't been single in so long, I couldn't even remember what that life was like.

Stella and Tatum excused themselves to the restroom, and Zach headed to the bar to get another beer. That left Colton and me alone, which shouldn't have been strange because we spent time alone together all the time. But something in the air felt tenser than usual.

"You shouldn't be hard on Zach. He was just trying to make me feel better."

Colton finished his drink then wiped his mouth with the

back of his forearm. "Together or apart, you're off-limits. He knows that. Any man would know that." He looked into his empty glass, avoiding eye contact with me. "But I'm glad to hear you like someone."

I rolled my eyes. "Stella is exaggerating. I interacted with the guy for a minute. Probably even less than that."

"It's still something. A part of me knows I'll be jealous when you're with someone else, but another part of me will be really happy when that day comes. It's complicated..."

"It's not." I knew exactly how he felt. I wondered if he was seeing anyone, but I never asked because I wasn't ready to hear the answer. "What about you? Are you seeing anyone...?"

He straightened then met my look, ignoring the empty glass in his hands. "Not really. It's been hard to get out there."

"Why is that?"

"It's just...new. I know this is what I want, but I'm nervous to pursue it."

"You shouldn't be, Colton. You're a gorgeous man with a heart of gold. The second you put yourself out there, you'll have too many options to choose from. I know taking that first step is hard... I've been struggling to take the same first step."

A soft smile formed on his lips, reaching his eyes toward the end. "Thanks. That means a lot coming from you."

"Then put yourself out there and find what you're looking for." It would have been easy for me to be angry with him, to never forgive him and turn him into a stranger I never spoke to. But my love for him was too strong, strong enough to cut him slack he may not have deserved.

"I guess I need to tell my family first. If I put myself out there and become more open about it, my parents will find out in the worst possible way. I've been putting it off because I know it's going to open old wounds. I'm not even sure if they'll accept me. They'll be disappointed that I threw you away. Then they'll be even more disappointed in me for...the path I've chosen."

I really had no idea how his parents would react, but Colton's fear wasn't unfounded. They would definitely be upset when they heard the news. And there was a good chance these changes would affect his relationship with his family forever. "We can do it together, if that will help."

"You'd come with me?" he asked, not masking his hint of surprise.

"Of course." I rested my hand on his. "I'm here for you —always."

He turned his hand over and squeezed mine. "Thanks. That means a lot to me."

MR. GORGEOUS CAME in again a few days later.

This time, he looked even sexier than last time. He'd ditched the suit and wore workout clothes, a gray t-shirt that fit snugly across the muscles of his arms and chest. His shirt wasn't damp, so it seemed like he was going to the gym after he picked up his next piece of lingerie. His running shorts showed off his toned legs and nice calves. He was over six feet of masculine beauty.

The bell rang overhead, and he moved past the hangers of lingerie and the tables with lacy thongs and panties. He didn't stop to look at anything, probably trusting that Lacey had picked out the perfect thing to wear.

I was so obsessed with those green eyes and muscular physique that I nearly forgot to greet him when he stopped right in front of me. "Uh, hi." The words stumbled out of my mouth without a hint of confidence, and I wanted to smack myself right across the forehead. Shyness was not sexy at all.

"Hey." He made eye contact with me and flashed me that pearly white smile. He had full lips that I could picture right against my mouth. My lips could practically feel his softness without even touching him. My mind continued to slip away into erotic fantasies with unbridled freedom. It was probably because I hadn't been intimate with a man in so long, and even my last screw was questionable. Now, my body was going crazy.

"Hi." Ugh, I already said that.

Instead of brushing me off or rolling his eyes, he smiled wider. "Hi."

At least he was nice about it. "Another pick up for Lacey?" Now that I thought about it, I realized I hadn't seen an order for Lacey. I had an order for Brenda, but that was it.

He rubbed his hand across his smooth jaw, probably checking the closeness of his morning shave. "No. It's for Brenda." He lowered his hand, his soft smile stretching once more.

There was another woman? Then he definitely didn't have a girlfriend. He was the player Stella pegged him as, buying lingerie for different women and enjoying every moment of it.

And that meant he was single.

I could totally go for him.

All I wanted was sex anyway, so this was perfect. I could even bring my own lingerie.

I grabbed the bag from under the counter and placed it in front of him. "There you go. Did you need anything else?" How did I even ask a guy out? Did I just invite him over to my place? Did I just blurt out that I wanted to have sex with him? Man, I had no game at all.

"Thank you." He grabbed the bag by the handle and held it at his side, but he didn't walk out right away. He continued to stand there and look at me.

Maybe he would ask me out and I wouldn't have to worry about it at all.

"Is this your store?" he asked.

Not the question I was looking for. "Yes, it is. I've been running it for almost five years."

"That's awesome," he said with sincerity. "Do you offer any special events? Like bridal showers?"

Maybe I'd made the wrong assumption about this guy. Maybe he wasn't straight at all. The hot ones were usually gay, so that wouldn't be surprising. When it came to reading orientation, I already proved how bad I was at it. Maybe I was completely wrong about this guy. "I do, actually."

"Thanks." He spotted my business card sitting on the counter, so he placed it in his pocket before he turned away. "Have a good day." He walked to the front door, his rock-hard ass tight even in running shorts.

Whether he was straight or gay, nothing was going to happen with this guy. "Yeah...you too." If he was straight, he wasn't interested in me. And if he was gay...he still wasn't interested in me.

My return to dating life was getting off to a bad start.

A KNOCK SOUNDED on my door.

I was sitting on the couch with a glass of wine in my hand. My hair was pulled back into a bun, and I was looking over my bookkeeping while the game was on in the background. Instead of going out or to the gym, I decided to stay in—and forget about my uneventful afternoon. "It's open."

Colton opened the door. He was in his gray sweatpants and a white t-shirt, clothes I bought him for Christmas a few years ago. "What are you up to?"

"Watching the game, eating dinner, and working." I turned back to my notes.

He eyed the table and only noticed my bottle of wine. "So what are you eating for dinner?"

I held my wineglass. "This."

He chuckled. "I have some leftover enchiladas. You want some?"

I missed his cooking. He used to take care of all the meals when we lived together. The only thing I could cook with was a toaster, and even then, I burned everything. "No thanks. I had a big lunch today."

He stood behind the couch and watched the TV. "How are the Maroons doing?"

Maybe I should have figured out he was gay a long time ago since he had no interest in sports. He couldn't even remember the team names. I loved baseball, basketball, and football, so sports were on all year for me. Whenever I watched a game, he usually found something else to do. "The Mariners."

"Oh yeah. Sorry."

"They're winning, thankfully."

He helped himself to an empty glass in the kitchen before he filled it with wine. Then he sat beside me on the couch and put his feet on the coffee table.

I didn't mind because my feet were always on the coffee table.

"Brought work home today?"

"Yeah, I had a lot of customers today, so I didn't get this done in the office."

"Being busy is a good thing."

"It is. I'm not complaining." I took another sip of my wine then glanced at him on the other side of the couch. It seemed like there was something he wanted to talk about, but he was taking a long time to get to the point.

"Mr. Gorgeous stop by?"

"Actually, he did."

He turned his head my way, interested. "Did you go for it?"

"No. I chickened out."

"Why?" He ran his fingers through his short blond hair, naturally magnetic without even realizing it. I used to notice all those little movements he made when we were married. I still noticed them now, but I didn't want to jump his bones anymore. "Pepper, I know I'm gay, but trust me when I say you're gorgeous. If you throw yourself at any straight man, he's gonna say yes."

"That's nice of you to say, but I really don't have any game anymore. It's been so long since I've been single, I don't even remember how to be single."

"You don't need game," Colton said. "I'm serious. Just ask him out. You don't need to jump through any hoops like men do."

"I don't even want to ask him out. I just want sex." It was an awkward thing to say to Colton, since he was the man I used to sleep with, but he was probably just as frustrated with his dry spell.

Instead of being uncomfortable, he grinned. "If you say that, then he'll definitely, absolutely, say yes. That's every man's fantasy, listening to a woman ask for sex point-blank."

"I might have pulled that off years ago, but not anymore."

"Why not?" he asked. "You're even more beautiful today than the day I met you."

We got married when we were twenty-one. We were young at the time but in love...or so I thought. Now I was twenty-six, and I still had time to play the field before I really thought about having a family. "You're sweet, Colton."

"Well, I mean it." He scooted closer to me on the couch and rested his hand on my thigh. "I want you to have everything you want. I know you're going to get your happily ever after, and that guy is gonna be much better for you than I ever was."

My eyes softened. "I don't know about that..."

"I think so. And the nice part is, I won't be losing you. I'll be getting another friend, another family member."

I guess I felt that way about him, whenever he found someone he really liked. "That's a good way to put it."

He turned to the TV and watched the game for a bit, sipping his glass of wine as I returned to working on my books. "I don't see how you follow this. It's so boring. So much waiting around. At least with basketball, there's always something happening."

"Each sport has its perks."

"I guess," he said. "Baseball players wear those super-tight pants, so that's nice."

It was the first time I'd heard him say something like that, and surprisingly, it didn't feel strange. "Can I ask you something?"

"Anything." He didn't take his eyes off the TV.

"When did you know?" I didn't need to specify exactly what I meant. We'd never talked about this before because I didn't have the heart to ask. Now that I'd had enough time to get over Colton, I could finally ask these questions.

He shrugged. "I guess I kinda always knew. I just always felt like something was missing. I had the perfect wife and the perfect marriage...but it didn't feel complete. I found myself aroused in the locker room at the gym. It kept creeping up, and the more I fought it, the more difficult it became. Then I started having really vivid dreams, and there was no hiding it anymore. I wanted to make it go away because I was so happy with you...but I couldn't."

"I'm glad you didn't, Colton. Everyone deserves to be in love and to be happy. If you weren't in love...that's okay."

He turned to me, sadness in his eyes. "I wanted to be."

I grabbed his arm and rubbed it gently. "I know you did. But you're going to find exactly what you're looking for someday. And the same thing will happen to me."

He nodded. "You've been so easy on me, Pepper. Not very many women would be so understanding."

"Well, I really love you, Colton. No matter what."

A ghost of a smile formed on his lips. "I really love you, babe." He grabbed my hand and brought it to his lips for a kiss. "I really like what we have. I feel like we have everything we had before...and now we have a better relationship."

"Yeah, me too."

He released my hand and relaxed back into the couch.

"So, when are we gonna talk to your parents?"

"Well...I have some news on that front. My brother called me this afternoon."

I'd never met his older brother, not once. He didn't come to the wedding or a single holiday. He'd been in the military for the past decade. He was constantly overseas, working on things he couldn't talk about. Every time he was home, I'd managed to miss an introduction. "How is he?"

"Not really sure. He left the military, and he's moving to Seattle. He asked if he could stay with us until his place is ready."

"So you didn't tell him about us?"

He rubbed the back of his neck and sighed at the same time. "We don't talk very much, so I didn't want to spoil the conversation talking about that, you know?"

"Well, when he comes over, he's going to wonder why I'm living across the hall from you."

"I'll explain it then."

"The second he walks through the door?" I asked incredulously. "He just left a stressful life in the military, and you're going to drop this on him? Yeah...welcome home."

He chuckled. "My brother and I aren't super close because he hasn't been around much for the last ten years, but I think I can talk to him about this. It'll probably make it easier to tell my parents when he already knows. Have another person in my corner."

"Your parents aren't going to gang up on you, Colton."

He shrugged. "You never know..."

"Don't forget how much your parents love you. Nothing is gonna change that." I placed my hand on his muscular back and rubbed it gently. "So, when does your brother get here?"

"Two weeks. He's doing some therapy before he's officially discharged."

"Therapy?"

"He said it's mandatory."

Then he must have seen some pretty gruesome stuff.

"He said he already has a job lined up here. He just needs a place to crash until his new place is set up."

"That's nice he's going to stay with you. You guys can spend some time together."

"Yeah, it should be good." He turned his eyes back to the TV, but he really didn't appear to be watching it. His thoughts seemed to be elsewhere, thinking about the mound of issues he had to tackle when he couldn't procrastinate any longer.

3

PEPPER

It was only a matter of time before people who knew us figured out why Colton and I separated. I kept the information to myself because Colton was really private about his newly acknowledged sexual orientation, but I also just didn't want to talk about it.

I knew what people would say.

That I turned him gay.

That I wasn't good in bed.

Wasn't woman enough.

I didn't care what people thought of me. They didn't understand how much love there was between the two of us. They didn't understand how complicated it was. Being judged and ridiculed was difficult, but I refused to let it get to me.

I refused to let it define me.

But then I saw some terrible things on social media.

Candace, a woman Colton and I used to hang out with, had a few things to say about it. *She may have a nice body, but she obviously doesn't know how to use it. She made a hot man gay, like we don't already have enough hot gay guys in the world.*

A few other people chimed in, people who didn't even know me. *She must be bad in bed. Really bad.* The comments went on and on, and I was almost tempted to jump in and defend myself.

But that would just be an admission that I cared what they thought of me.

I shut my laptop and tried to erase the comments from my memory.

How could people be so cruel? I'd lost the love of my life. It wasn't something that should be mocked.

I did my best to control my emotions, but I felt the buildup of tears behind my eyes. I hadn't cried in months, and I didn't want to start the healing process all over again. At least when I was crying then, it was because I was heartbroken over Colton.

I wasn't gonna cry over them.

I took a deep breath and stilled my tears. Then I did what any other woman would do.

I told my friends we were going out for a drink.

"FORGET THAT CUNT." Stella got fired up the second someone crossed me. She was that loyal friend who wasn't afraid to rip someone's hair out of their scalp. She would even shove someone's head in a toilet. "Candace was always such a bitch."

I'd seen Stella do it.

"She wanted Colton's nuts," Tatum said. "She was pissed when you got him, and now she's using this as revenge. Sad people like that do whatever they can to make themselves feel better." Tatum had bright blond hair and gorgeous blue eyes. She was petite, several inches shorter than me, but possessed just a dash more sass. She wore a black cardigan over her dress, and her hair was pulled back in a bun.

"And she's a very sad person," Stella added. She had deep brown hair the way I did, but her figure was much more impressive. She did hundreds of crunches every day and trained both men and women in fitness. She had ink on her arms and along her back. It looked amazing on her because she had the body for it.

I considered myself to be tame by comparison. I didn't have any tattoos, but I did have a navel piercing. My shoulder-length brown hair had grown out over the last few months and now reached the top of my chest. It was the longest it'd ever been—due to neglect. "I know I shouldn't care—"

"You shouldn't," Stella pressed. "She's just a whore. Always has been and always will be."

"People are such assholes behind their computers." Tatum had ignored her drink for the last ten minutes, and her ice had started to melt and water it down. "But she wouldn't have the balls to say it to Pepper's face."

"Because I'd kick her ass," Stella snapped.

Stella really would. She had the stamina to run marathons and the strength to dish out black eyes.

"Forget her," Tatum said. "You're a gorgeous woman, and there's nothing wrong with you."

I believed them. I really did. But in the back of my mind, there was still a seed of doubt.

Tatum narrowed her eyes on my face, like she could see it. "Pepper..."

"I know you're right," I admitted. "But sometimes, I wonder..."

"No." Stella snapped her fingers. "No wondering. It's obvious Colton absolutely adores you. Love was never the problem. You were never the problem. He still follows you everywhere you go. He's just...not programmed that way."

"And that's not your fault," Tatum said. "Come on, you own a lingerie shop, for crying out loud. You're a very sexy woman. If Colton couldn't stay straight for you, then he couldn't stay straight for anyone. You were never the problem."

I was lucky I had my own personal cheerleaders to get me through this. "Thanks, guys. I'm in a much better place now, but sometimes...the darkness gets to me. I was really happy with Colton, and he seemed happy with me. It just makes me wonder if there was something I could have done."

"No." Stella snapped her fingers again. "Don't do that to yourself."

"We won't allow it." Tatum waved the bartender over and got me another drink even though I was only halfway done with my first one. "Don't forget who you are, Pepper. I've always admired you. You're confident, independent, and strong. You opened your own business entirely on your own and never cared what people said about you selling lingerie. I'll never forget when you spotted Colton in that bar and you marched up to him and asked him out on the spot. That's the kind of woman you are—you take charge. Don't forget that."

When my personal cheerleaders reminded me of my own qualities, it made me feel so good deep inside. It pulled me out of my funk of despair and reminded me of my value. They weren't petty compliments to boost my ego. Those were all facts. "Thanks, guys. I needed a pick-me-up, and that did the trick."

"We know what our girl needs." Stella raised her glass and tapped it against mine.

I did the same to Tatum before I finished off that drink and moved on to the next one.

"So, we're making a pact tonight," Stella said. "We're all going home with someone—including you." She pointed her index finger right at my face. "So find someone you like. Otherwise, you're sleeping here."

I normally wouldn't agree to that, but Candace's comments had really gotten to me. I wanted to prove her wrong—and prove my insecurity wrong too. I wanted to go home with a hot guy, have great sex, and prove to myself that I wasn't the problem.

As if the universe wanted that very thing to happen, I turned my head, and my eyes settled on someone familiar.

Mr. Gorgeous.

He was standing at a table on the other side of the room, two friends with him. He was drinking a dark beer as his fingers casually relaxed around the table. He didn't have a woman on his arm, and it didn't seem like he was shopping for lingerie that night.

That jaw was just as clean as the last time I saw him. He took care of himself, styling his hair and giving himself a close shave every single morning. When he glanced at his shiny watch, he did it with such grace, possessing enough confidence that all the women in the room turned his way. He turned back to his friends and continued whatever conversation they were having.

He was the first man I'd ever been seriously attracted to since my divorce. Any other time I saw a man I liked, there was too much guilt associated with it. It felt like I was cheating on Colton even though I was absolutely single. But when I looked at this guy, I didn't feel any hesitancy at all. I just wanted a hot night of sweaty sex. He didn't even need to tell me his name. All I wanted were a few hours of his time, a chance to prove myself and climax at the same time.

He had broad shoulders that were lean and toned like the rest of him. I wanted to push that jacket off his shoulders then unfasten every single button of his shirt until I could feel his bare chest. I wanted to yank his belt out of his loops and spank myself with it. My fantasies ran wild, and I didn't even notice that Stella was trying to get my attention.

"What the hell are you looking at?" Stella waved her hand in front of my face before she looked over her shoulder to see what I was staring at.

"Mr. Gorgeous." I took a big drink before I patted my lips with the napkin. "He's the man I'm going home with tonight." I smoothed out my dress and fixed my hair before I started to strut. "Don't wait up."

BY A STROKE OF LUCK, the two friends he was with both excused themselves to the restroom just before I reached his table. He took a drink of his beer as he turned his gaze to the TV, watching the Mariners game like a sports fan.

At least we had something in common.

I kept my confidence in check and refused to back down. Maybe he wouldn't be interested, but I couldn't be deterred by the rejection. Six months was a long time to hide from the world, and I was done hiding. It was time to put myself out there—for better or worse.

Before I reached the table, his eyes flicked to my face briefly, and he turned back to the TV. He did a double take then, either recognizing my face or liking my dress. He turned his head slightly back toward me, those green eyes now glued to mine. His hand slowly lowered the beer back to the table, and his complete focus was pinned on me.

That was a good sign.

It gave me an extra burst of energy, another reminder that I was a beautiful woman who had something to offer. Having a gay ex-husband didn't make me less desirable. I was one hell of a woman, and it was time to remind the world of that truth.

With perfect grace, I stopped at his table, the proximity enough to make anyone think we knew each other intimately. Any time I'd interacted with him, there had been a counter in between us, so I didn't have this close experience. I could smell his cologne, see the distant shadow of his beard, and could tell that his lips truly were soft.

He pivoted his body slightly toward me, the corner of his mouth rising in a smile. A brightness was in his eyes as he took me in, far more interested in me than the score on the TV. His arms rested on the table next to his beer, and it didn't seem like he cared about anyone else in the room. Maybe he bought that lingerie for the models he bedded, but he didn't seem to be thinking about them in that moment.

I wasn't looking for a date. In fact, I was steering far away from it. All I was interested in was sex, and not as a precursor to any kind of relationship. I was physically ready to get back on the horse, but I certainly wasn't emotionally ready to have a deep and meaningful relationship. I didn't give him my name, and I didn't ask for his. I didn't ask if he was a Mariners fan or if he preferred IPAs. I got right to the point. "There's a specific piece of lingerie I want to show you —at my place. Want to come along?"

Mr. Gorgeous actually had the humility to be taken back. His eyes narrowed with a hint of surprise, and he went absolutely still, as if he were repeating my spoken words in his head. He clearly had never expected me to be so bold, to cut right to the chase without even asking for his name. A second later, a handsome smile spread across his lips. "Only if you're wearing it." He opened his wallet and tossed cash onto the table before his arm circled my waist. Over six feet tall with a lean and muscular body, he was one major piece of eye candy. The other women in the bar who had been patiently waiting for him to make a pass their way frowned as we walked out together.

I passed Tatum and Stella on the way out and gave them a wink.

Stella mouthed to me. "Daaaaamn."

Tatum discreetly gave me a thumbs-up. "Get it, girl," she mouthed.

AFTER A SHORT CAB ride to my place, we walked into my apartment.

His heavy footfalls sounded behind me, his muscled frame making an impact against the hardwood floor. He stripped off his jacket right away and placed it over the armchair in the living room.

My heart was pounding in my chest because I was aware of what I was about to do. I'd been sleeping with the same man for the last five years, and now was officially a new chapter in my life. I was going to bed with this handsome stranger—and I was going to enjoy it. "Take a seat." I kept up my confidence, turning around and looking him in the eye as I said, "I'll be right back."

His eyes scanned my body without discretion. "I find it hard to believe you could look sexier than you already do."

He lowered himself onto the couch, sitting right in the center with his knees apart. A man had never looked sexier sitting on that couch, aiming that heated stare at me.

The compliment made the tension leave my shoulders and reminded me that Stella and Tatum were right. "You're in for a surprise." I walked into my bedroom and fished out my collection of lingerie. I had a one-piece bodysuit made of black lace with a snap crotch. It cut low in the front and barely hid my tits from view. It was so see-through that it showed the color of my skin as well as the diamond in my pierced belly button. I dropped my dress and pulled on the bodysuit, fluffing my hair and checking my makeup in the mirror. I slipped on my black pumps then walked back into the living room.

Mr. Gorgeous was already staring at the open doorway, his eyes waiting for the moment when I would appear. Instantly, his eyes narrowed into a heated stare, and the hard line of his jaw became even firmer with arousal. He cocked his head to the side slightly as he examined me up and down, the approval obvious in his stare.

My hand moved to the knob on the wall, and I dimmed the lights in the living room.

He whistled quietly under his breath. "Damn."

I crossed the living room and reached the couch, seeing him sit up eagerly and undo each button of his shirt. "Allow me." I straddled his hips, and my fingers took over the job, unfastening each one until I reached the bottom. More of his beautiful skin was revealed, along with the sexy eight-pack he was sporting. Once I saw his strong chest and the grooves along his stomach, I stopped thinking about my performance. I stopped wondering if I was sexy enough. I fell into the moment, locked my eyes on him, and felt my fingers shake in anticipation.

My hands moved to his belt next, and I unbuckled it before I pulled it through the loops. I folded it in half and then placed it in his left hand. "I wouldn't mind a spank or two." My hands moved into his hair, and I pressed my chest into his as I kissed him. I loved the feeling of those soft lips I'd fantasized about every time he walked into my shop.

He moaned against my mouth, either because of the kiss or because of the belt. His lips hesitated for a second, as if he were still processing the instruction I gave him. A moment later, his mouth reciprocated the affection, and he kissed me hard, kissed me like there was nowhere else in the world he'd rather be.

And then he whipped the belt against my ass.

My hands gripped his shoulders, and I moaned into his mouth. "Yeah…"

He hit me again.

I rocked my hips and ground against his hard-on through his slacks. I could feel the size, and I rubbed myself against it, eager to feel a man who was undeniably hard for me. Our kisses continued, and the belt lightly tapped against my ass during our foreplay.

The beginning was so good that neither of us skipped to the end.

He dropped the belt beside him and then moved his fingers between my legs. He must have known the crotch could be opened because he unsnapped it without even looking. His fingers explored me next, checked how wet I was with two fingers.

I was soaked.

My six-month dry spell was finally over.

He slipped two fingers inside me as he kissed me, gently pulsing as his skin became soaked with my arousal. He moaned into my mouth as he enjoyed it. "Such a nice

pussy." His free hand moved into my hair, and he deepened the kiss, not minding that his dick was still in his
pants.

My fingers worked at the fastening on his pants, and I
got them loose. His boxers were yanked down, and a long
dick was revealed, a size that rivaled Colton's.

Thank goodness.

He pulled his fingers out of my entrance then dug into
his pocket for a condom. A man like him probably didn't go
anywhere without his pockets lined with the foil packets.
Sex could happen anywhere, anytime.

"Allow me." I ripped into the packet and rolled it down
to his base.

He watched me with that same heated expression, like
he couldn't wait much longer for me to finish.

I enjoyed his girth in my hands, the way he was so hard
it seemed like he might explode. There was no hesitation,
no hint that he was thinking of someone else while he was
with me. I made sure there was plenty of room at the tip of
the condom before I climbed on top of him.

Then I lowered myself slowly, appreciating every single
inch.

"Oh...God...Yes." I hadn't felt this kind of penetration in
so long. Colton and I had signed our divorce papers six
months ago, but we'd stopped having sex two months before
that. In reality, it'd been eight months since I got laid...and
even longer since the sex was actually good. The sensation I
felt in that moment was nearly heavenly. I'd completely
forgotten how amazing this was, even with a man who didn't
have a name.

He gripped my hips and moaned under his breath, the
sound coming out masculine and deep. His fingers dug in a
little harder, and he gave me a searing expression that could

make a cold fireplace burst into flames. "You feel like a virgin, sweetheart."

Probably because I hadn't gotten laid in so long.

I gripped his shoulders and moved up and down his length, treasuring every single inch of solid masculinity. I bit my lip over and over because I couldn't stop moaning. I was visibly shaking in his arms, unable to process just how good this felt.

I went over six months without this?

Why the hell did I wait so long?

I pushed him back against the couch and rode him harder, pressing my face close to his. "Fuck, you feel so good."

He groaned in response. "You're something else..." He gripped my hips and guided me up and down as he thrust up. We'd started off slow and steady, but now we were fucking like rabbits in spring. He wanted me with the same desire that I felt, like he'd had a dry spell just as long...even though it couldn't possibly be more than a few days.

The greatest sensation was slowly creeping up my body. It was so powerful, I almost didn't recognize it. Searing hot like a pan right off the stove, it gave me third-degree burns. I kept slamming onto his dick, feeling the tingles creep up faster and faster.

And then it hit me so hard. "Jesus..." I squeezed his dick and the condom and burst like a lit firework. My fingertips went numb, and my ankles twisted into his thighs. Instead of issuing a sexy moan, I screamed like someone was murdering me, not fucking me. "Yes...yes."

He gave a few pumps before he followed right behind me, making a deep moan that made me tighten around him again. He thickened noticeably inside me before he released into the tip of the condom.

He had the sexiest expression as he did it.

I'd really missed this.

His pumps slowed, and his fingers stopped digging into me so hard. He rested back against the couch and stared at me with a heavy gaze, like he was still turned on despite the climax he'd just reached. "Woman...you know how to fuck."

And just like that, all my insecurities vanished. This man didn't know me, not even my name. He was a handsome playboy who could pick up tail whenever he wanted. He bought lingerie for his ladies and fucked them in it. A compliment coming from him carried a lot more weight than one from my gay ex-husband. "So do you."

I LEFT the note on his chest.

Had to head off to work. Last night was fun. Take care.

-P

My message was pretty clear that last night was just a hookup that meant nothing to me. I wasn't looking for a relationship or a second round. He probably didn't want that either, and I was fine doing the dirty work.

I went across the hall and let myself inside.

Colton was sitting at the kitchen table—with Stella and Tatum.

"What are you guys doing here?" I walked inside in my jeans and t-shirt, ready to head off to work once I had my morning coffee.

"Come on," Stella said. "We all know the first place you're gonna hit once your night is over."

"How was it?" Tatum clapped her hands like an excited cheerleader. "He make you come? Tell me he made you come."

Colton brushed off the conversation like it wasn't awkward. He sat back in his chair wearing his blue collared shirt and gray tie. A white coffee mug was in his hand, and he took a sip before he chimed in. "Let Pepper talk before you press her with inappropriate questions."

"Inappropriate?" Stella cocked her head and gave Colton a glare. "No. That question is completely appropriate."

"Yes," Tatum said. "I think your statement was what was inappropriate."

Colton rolled his eyes then pointed to the empty chair across from him. "Alright. I tried to save you from the hot seat. You're on your own."

I sat down and poured myself a cup of coffee.

Stella leaned forward with her mouth open, waiting for the silence to slip away.

Tatum spun a strand of blond hair, but her blue eyes were big enough to fit into a doll's head perfectly. "Spill it!"

I sipped my coffee, drawing it out as long as possible.

Stella shook her head, her eyes filled with poison. "You bitch."

"She's torturing us on purpose," Tatum said. "But that must mean some good stuff went down."

Colton set his mug back on the table. "Maybe Pepper is just too classy—"

Stella burst out with a laugh. "Yeah, right. Pepper? She wasn't always the good wife."

"She used to have a lot of fun before you came along," Tatum said with accusation.

I cleared my throat.

"Oh my god, she's ready." Stella gripped the edge of the table.

Tatum covered her mouth with her hands, her eyes still wide.

"Here's the dirt." I knew this was a big moment in our lives, and I wanted to savor it as long as I could. I'd taken a new step in the healing process, and now it seemed like I was a new person—in a good way. My confidence had strengthened, nearly returned to what it had been before. "I walked up to him and asked if he wanted to see me in lingerie."

Stella grinned from ear to ear. "Ballsy."

If Colton was uncomfortable, he didn't act like it. "No man would be able to turn that down."

"Hell no," Tatum said. "Then what happened?"

"We went to my apartment," I said, talking casually even though nothing about this was casual.

"What did you wear?" Stella asked, unafraid to cross the line into even more personal details.

"A black bodysuit made of lace," I said. "Snap crotch."

Colton whistled under his breath. "That'll do it..."

"There was no way that man could resist you," Tatum said. "With your hair and makeup done, you must have looked like a bombshell."

He'd seemed to view me as one. "We didn't even make it off the couch for the first round. We headed to bed afterward."

"And how was he?" Stella was dressed in her workout clothes, ready to meet her clients at the gym. She wore a pink sports bra with a tiny tank on top, along with her booty spandex shorts. She claimed her attire was to motivate people.

"Very skilled." I couldn't reflect on the night without wearing a smile. "Very sexy. He made this moan that was so irresistible."

Tatum melted right in front of me, her grin stretching wide apart. "So hot..."

"I came twice. That felt nice. It's been so long that I forgot how good it felt." The guilt washed over me, and I glanced at Colton to see if he was offended, but he still wore the same expression as before. It seemed like he was listening as my friend, not something more. He was nothing but supportive about my new adventure into single life.

"Excellent," Stella said. "I give this guy five stars."

"What's his name, by the way?" Tatum asked. "We can keep calling him Mr. Gorgeous, but I assume he has a name."

"I don't know," I said. "Never asked."

"Really?" Stella asked with a laugh. "Wow, so you guys really didn't talk."

"Nope," I said with a smile. "And that works for me."

"So he just left, and that was it?" Tatum asked. "Did he ask to see you again?"

"I'm not sure. I left a note on his chest before I came over here. Just said I had a great time and that was it."

Now Colton grinned. "Talk about hit it and quit it."

"So he's sleeping in your bed right now?" Stella asked in surprise. "You just left him there?"

"I'm sure he can find the way out," I countered. "I don't know anything about him, but he's gotta be somewhat intelligent."

"That's hot," Tatum said. "You got what you wanted without apology."

"I think it's pretty clear what I wanted." I'd walked right up to him and asked him back to my place. I never gave him any indication I wanted something more. If anything, I'd wanted him to be just a good memory that I could cherish. He helped me get back on the horse. His job was complete. "So, he won't be upset."

"Wow." Stella had a dreamy look in her eyes. "That's one hell of a night."

"He might want to see you again," Colton said. "After a night like that, he might want another round. Wouldn't blame him." He flattened his tie against his chest before he drank from his coffee, his blond hair perfectly styled for his day at work. He was a pretty man, and just from a look, it would be impossible to know he was gay.

"Well, hopefully, it doesn't come to that." I cupped my mug with both hands so I could savor the warmth as it spread through my fingers. It was a sunny day in Seattle, but that meant it would be a little chillier than usual. "Not interested. I just want that night to be what it was...a one-time thing. I'm not looking for a relationship right now. Being with him rejuvenated my confidence and helped me find the old me. But I want to play the field for a while and not force something with the first pretty man I see."

"That totally makes sense," Stella said. "You just got back on the market, and you should enjoy being single as long as you can. You've been stuck with a gay guy for the last five years. You need to make up for all that lost time."

Colton lowered his gaze but didn't voice his offense to the comment.

"That time wasn't lost." I looked at my ex-husband, my best friend, and showed him the same affection in my eyes that had always been there. "I wouldn't change those years for anything."

Colton responded with a slight smile. "Me neither, Pepper. Me neither."

4

COLTON

When I stepped through the door, the bell rang overhead.

Pepper was behind the counter of her boutique, her long brown hair pulled over one shoulder. She had green eyes that reminded me of tropical palm fronds, and when she wore deep red lipstick, it made her smile more apparent. She was the most beautiful woman I'd ever seen. It didn't matter that I liked men. Nothing could deny what was right in front of me.

Her little shop had a European design, carrying pieces made in France and Italy. Her items fetched a high price, but the craftsmanship made them worth it. Women loved to feel sexy, especially in expensive things.

She lifted her gaze to greet me. She always wore a smile when she greeted her customers, but when she recognized me, her smile widened even more. There was a hint of affection in her gaze, the same look she used to give me when I came home every day. "What a nice surprise. Are you shopping for yourself or someone special?"

I chuckled as I approached the counter. "Like anything would fit me."

She raised an eyebrow. "Do you want something to fit you...?"

"No. I'm not that kind of gay."

She finished making her note before she put her pen down. "How was work?"

"Eh. You know." I looked at the new display she had on the wall, along with the counter showing off new thongs. Being married to a sexy woman like Pepper had only made me realize just how gay I was. She was a perfect ten, on the inside as well as the outside. I tried so hard to pretend to be something I wasn't just so I could keep her.

"Actually, I don't." She looked at me with that knowing gaze, her intelligent eyes absorbent like a sponge. She had fair skin with a few faint freckles, and her delicate frame was beautiful with her tall height. She was just a bit shorter than I was, but she was tall for a woman. She had the body of a model, even though she denied it every time I mentioned it to her. "Sometimes I get the impression you don't like your job."

"Well, who does?" I said with a chuckle.

Her gaze softened in sadness. "I do. Stella does. If you don't like it, why don't you change it?"

Pepper always wanted the best for me. There were very few people in life who were so selfless. When I told her the truth and ended our marriage, she was upset but always supportive. She had every right to hate me and never speak to me again, but that wasn't her reaction. Now she was my best friend, and that relationship wasn't easy to maintain, at least in the beginning. But nothing ever stopped her from loving me. "Not so easy. I'm in too deep to change my career."

"But you could switch jobs or fields. There's a lot you can do with a law degree."

"I guess."

"The way I see it, you can keep doing the same thing and be miserable. Or you can take the chance and do something different. Odds are, you aren't going to be less happy, so you may as well go for it."

"Not a bad way to put it."

She smiled. "I'm very wise, I know."

"You really are."

"So, what brings you in? Other than getting a new thong."

"I'm meeting Zach for a drink. Wanted to see if you wanted to come along."

She glanced at the clock on the wall then surveyed her store. "It's been a pretty slow day, so I may as well close. Sometimes it's a hit or a miss. Today was definitely a miss."

"Not a lot of people need lingerie on a Tuesday."

"Well, a lot of people needed lingerie yesterday." She put her tablet and receipts away before she grabbed her coat and walked out with me.

"Heard from Mr. Gorgeous?"

She set the alarm and locked the door. "Nope. But that's how it's supposed to be. He seems like a playboy, so I don't think I need to worry about him."

"But you're a special woman. I'm sure he hasn't stopped thinking about you."

We walked down the sidewalk and headed to Hopkins for a drink. It was a chilly afternoon, but the rain was gone. We both wore black jackets to hide our bodies from the breeze in the air. Sometimes when it was just the two of us, I wanted to wrap my arm around her waist the way I used to.

But then I remembered those days were over. She was just my friend now—my best friend.

"You're sweet, Colton. But he gets tail all the time. I'm sure he's moved on to the next lady."

"You'd be surprised…"

We entered the bar and both ordered our beers. Zach was already at the table, his eyes glued to the game. We'd been friends since high school, so our friendship went far back. He was the first person I told when I came out of the closet, and he helped me reveal the truth to Pepper. Not once did he treat me differently because of it. "It's a close game."

I glanced at the score. "Then I'm not making any bets."

Pepper pulled out her phone and texted someone before she took a drink.

Zach yanked his eyes off the TV so he could look at her. Taller than me and with brown eyes, he'd always been a hot commodity with the ladies. "How's it going, Pepper?"

"Great. I had no customers today, but that gave me time to read." She pulled her jacket off her shoulders and revealed the teal blouse that hugged her curves perfectly. She hung the jacket over the back of a nearby chair.

"I'm doing great, thanks for asking," I said sarcastically.

Zach brushed off the comment. "I've been talking to you all day through texting."

"But a lot has happened since our last message," I countered. "Maybe I got fired or something."

"You wish you got fired," he said with a chuckle.

Ever since I'd opened up about my sexuality, most of the office disliked me. Maybe if I'd come in as a gay man at the beginning, it wouldn't be weird, but since I'd divorced a beautiful woman, they viewed me as strange. The work environment progressively became more and more hostile. I never told Pepper the truth because she'd probably march down there and stab my boss in the eye with a pen.

Zach turned back to Pepper. "I heard you got laid."

She couldn't hide the smile from stretching across her face. "The rumors are true."

Zach grinned. "Good to hear. It's hot when a woman gets some D."

I thought this conversation would make me uncomfortable or jealous, but it never did. Truth be told, I was relieved Pepper was finally making progress with her love life. I hadn't made much in mine, but I didn't want her to be miserable forever. She had been in love with me for a long time, and she had needed about three months to finally move on from those feelings.

Pepper turned to me. "Does this make you uncomfortable?"

It took me a second to process her question because it was unnecessary. "Not at all."

She turned back to Zach and continued the conversation.

I watched the game for a while before I directed my attention across the room. At another table was Aaron, one of the men who went to my gym. He was with two other guys, and I knew from watching him so much that he definitely swung the way I did. He had a hard body, nice cheekbones, and a boyish smile. I'd noticed him a long time ago but never had the balls to actually do anything about it.

I was out of the closet but with no game.

Pepper must have noticed my stare because she said, "You know him?"

"Uh, he goes to my gym." Like I hadn't been staring at him with longing, I turned back to the TV and pretended to be involved in the game even though I didn't give a shit about sports. My brother had always been into every kind of sport, even playing rugby when he was overseas, but I could never get myself to care.

Pepper kept watching Aaron, like she was putting the pieces together, before she turned back to me. "Go talk to him."

"Why?" I asked, a little too defensively.

"Because he's cute, and you clearly like him."

"I do not," I said in mock offense. "I just—"

"Come on, man. Grow a pair and pick up a dude." Zach continued to speak his mind, never being delicate with me even though my orientation had changed. He treated me exactly the same, giving me a hard time when I deserved it. "You've been single forever, and you haven't done anything about it."

"And he's very cute," Pepper said. "Just ask him out. What's the worst he could say? No?"

"Uh, yeah," I said. "And I just...I've never done this before."

"So?" Pepper asked. "Tell him that."

I knew I needed to put myself out there, but something was always holding me back. I didn't want to allow the truth out in the open because it would make its way back to my family, but the truth was I just didn't have any confidence. "Look, I just—"

Pepper walked off and headed right for their table.

Zach chuckled as she walked away. "I'm glad the old Pepper is back. She's a badass."

"Uh..." I watched her walk right up to Aaron and somehow make him laugh. "I kinda miss the old Pepper." Back and forth, their conversation went, and it seemed to be going well because he wrapped his arm around her waist. Then she pointed at me.

Oh god.

Aaron looked my way, a handsome smile on his face.

"Dude, you look like shit," Zach whispered. "Smile or something. Stand up straight. Be sexy."

"How do you be sexy?" I countered.

"I don't know, but looking like a pussy isn't the way to do it."

I straightened my spine and shoulders and smiled back, doing my best to seem confident rather than out of place.

Then Pepper and Aaron walked to our table.

"Oh shit, he's coming over here." I turned to Zach, like he would somehow know what to do.

"Isn't that a good thing?" he asked. "Just be you. See where it goes."

"Oh god..." This was my first time putting myself out there, and I had a feeling I was going to crash and burn.

Pepper reached me first, Aaron right behind her. "Colton, I want you to meet my new friend, Aaron. Aaron, this is Colton."

Aaron smiled at me then extended his hand for a shake. "Pleasure."

"Uh, yeah." I took his hand, feeling the spark immediately burn up my fingers and my arm. "You too."

"We go to the same gym, right?" he asked, still smiling.

"Yeah, I've seen you around a bit."

"You can bench like two hundred pounds, right? I've noticed you."

I felt the burn of my cheeks and the thump in my heart. I knew I was gay because I was currently addicted to gay porn, but this small conversation convinced me even more. "Yeah...about two hundred. And I've noticed you too."

Pepper moved into Zach's side. "You wanna get out of here?"

"I think that's a good idea." Zach left cash on the table then walked out with Pepper.

Before Pepper walked out, she turned back to look at me, a dazzling smile on her face. Then she winked at me.

I didn't know what I did to deserve such an amazing woman in my life. I was so lucky to have her, and I would never take her for granted. It must not have been easy for her to give me away like that, to push me out of my comfort zone so I could flirt with a guy.

But that proved how much she loved me.

I winked back.

5

PEPPER

A week went by, and I didn't see Mr. Gorgeous again.

I was afraid he would stop by the shop to see me, but he seemed to want to leave our night untarnished the way I did.

Now it was a perfect memory, something that would never be ruined. It was a night that changed my life, a night that put a spring in my step and a smile on my face. I had amazing sex with an amazing man.

Now I was ready to take on the world.

That Saturday I had a private bridal shower gig. It was usually the bridesmaids and close friends that gathered around and picked out the lingerie for the bride. I brought everything in her size with me, and sometimes she would try it on for the girls if she was comfortable.

Events like that tended to be my biggest moneymakers.

The house was in a quiet neighborhood near the coast. Two stories with a gorgeous front yard, it was a dream house. The perfect place to settle down and start a family. Only rich people lived over here, so I suspected this woman came from money. Or maybe she was about to marry into money.

I grabbed my box of lingerie along with my tablet and gear and headed to the front door. After I rang the doorbell, a pretty brunette answered.

She looked just as perky as she sounded on the phone. With dark hair and green eyes, she was a beautiful girl, someone who would look amazing in a mermaid gown as she walked down the aisle. Her sparkly engagement ring sat on her left hand, catching the light and creating rainbows all over the walls. "You must be Pepper. It's so great to have you here. Come inside." She gave me a quick one-armed hug before she escorted me farther into the house.

The entryway led to the large staircase that went to the second floor. Vaulted ceilings had immense windows that filled the house with natural light. A table sat in the center of the room with a large vase of fake flowers. "This is a beautiful home."

"I couldn't agree more. Too bad it's not mine." She took one of the boxes and helped me carry it into the living room. "It's my brother's place. He's letting me live here until the wedding. My fiancé is a doctor, and he's moving from Chicago."

"Wow, you have a nice brother."

"Yeah, he's not bad." She downplayed her affection for her brother, but she smiled as she said it. "The girls will be here in about an hour. I'm just finishing up with the appetizers. So you can set up everything right here in the living room. Give me a holler if you need anything."

"Thanks, Sasha."

She walked down the hallway and entered the kitchen on the other side of the house. When I was alone, I set up my tablet along with the pieces of lingerie I would be debuting. She said she had a large bridal party of ten girls, so chances were, I was going to sell a lot of pieces. I didn't take cash or checks, just debit and credit cards. It was a lot easier to keep track of things that way. Besides, no one used cash these days.

The garage doors opened, and three men let themselves inside. All dressed in workout clothes with sweat streaked across their foreheads, they looked like they'd had a good workout. One had a basketball tucked under his arm, so it seemed like they'd just hit the courts.

I eyed their muscled biceps and sexy arms, hardly paying attention to their faces. I assumed one of them was Sasha's brother, the guy who could afford this beautiful house. All the furniture was black leather, and the interior design was distinctly masculine. It didn't seem like a woman lived with him.

I walked toward them to introduce myself.

That was when I locked eyes with Mr. Gorgeous.

Wow, what were the odds?

He didn't seem surprised to see me, as if he expected me to be standing in his living room. That same sexy smile stretched across his face, the memory of our night together dancing across his eyes.

I was caught off guard a lot more than he was. It took me longer to recover, to plaster a smile on my face and pretend everything was normal. "Long time, no see." When I focused on that handsome grin, the nerves started to fade away. I had no reason to be nervous, so the thought made me relax.

"Couldn't agree more. Guys, this is my friend..." He cocked his head slightly.

I waited for him to finish the sentence.

"This is the part where you tell me your name," he said with a chuckle.

"Oh, sorry." That's right, I never told him my name. "Pepper." I shook hands with his two friends, who were both muscled and sexy. They didn't match his caliber, but they were pretty close. "Nice to meet you both. I'm handling the lingerie party for Sasha."

"Ooh…" One of the guys waggled his eyebrows. "Sasha in lingerie…I have to stick around for that."

Mr. Gorgeous dropped his playful banter and gave his friend a cold look that clearly said, "I will kill you."

His friend chuckled then walked off. "We'll be in the game room. We'll grab you a beer on the way." They both walked off and left us alone together.

The two of us stared at each other, filling the silence with more silence. It wasn't exactly awkward, but it wasn't comfortable either. If we were kissing and taking off each other's clothes, it would probably be a more satisfying environment. I would prefer it, at least. "Had a good game?"

"Just shot some hoops." If he hadn't wanted to talk to me, he could have just walked away, but he lingered behind, like we had unfinished business. "Now we're going to drink a few beers and watch the professionals down some shots."

"That's gonna be a good game. If I didn't have to work, I'd be watching it."

"Blow this off and join us."

I smiled because I assumed he was kidding. "I've got bills to pay."

"I'm sure they'll buy your stuff whether you're here or not."

"Hmm…not sure if that's a compliment or an insult."

"Compliment." His handsome smile returned. "For you, I only have compliments." His gray t-shirt was tight on his muscled arms and his strong chest. It was loose around his waist because he had a tight stomach and narrow hips. He was a beautiful man with an even more beautiful body. Even in his workout clothes, his sexiness couldn't be denied. "Let me introduce myself." He shook my hand. "Jax."

"Nice to meet you, Jax." When I shook his hand, I felt the same spark I'd felt last week. The chemistry was there, like two combustive chemicals that were meant to stay far away from each other. We were volatile, explosive. "I'm Pepper...as I mentioned."

"Pepper." He savored my name on his lips. "I like your name."

"Thanks. It's easy for people to remember."

"I certainly won't forget it." His eyes smoldered.

I tried not to melt into a puddle on the floor.

"You want to have dinner with me tomorrow night?"

I should be flattered. If I weren't good in bed, I wouldn't be getting this invitation. But if we were having dinner, we weren't having sex. And if we weren't having sex, then it sounded like the beginning of a relationship. "How about dessert at my place instead?"

He crossed his arms over his chest, his head tilting slightly to the side. His smolder was replaced with a faint look of surprise. "I admit, that does sound better."

"Sweeter, if you ask me."

"What time are you thinking?"

"Eight." We'd have sex, go to sleep, and then he would disappear in the morning.

"Right to the point, huh?"

I shrugged. "I'm a busy lady. Running a business isn't easy."

"A working girl. I like that. I'll see you tomorrow night, then." Just when he moved to walk past me, his arm gently brushed past mine. He looked down at me as he did it, purposely getting close to me before he walked off.

I was too weak to fight it, so I turned and got a glimpse of his ass before he walked away.

~

"SMALL WORLD." Colton sat on the other couch and munched on the chips and dip sitting on the coffee table. The game was on the TV, but that was for me, not him. "You do a lingerie party right at his house."

"Yes...it's a very small world."

"And he's coming over tonight?" He rested his ankle on the opposite knee, his fingers wrapped around his IPA.

"Yep."

"Two for two, huh?"

"I just hope it's as good as it was last time."

"Probably better, actually. He wants more, and you want more."

"I hope you're right. He asked me to dinner at first." Maybe he was just making the gesture to be polite, but sitting in a crowded restaurant dressed in nice clothes sounded unappealing to me. I didn't want to get to know him, to know his hobbies or his favorite sports teams. It seemed like I was a man who was only after tail, but it didn't change what I wanted. I wasn't going to fall for another guy until I knew he was the right one. Mr. Gorgeous was an obvious player—and he definitely wasn't the right one.

"What an asshole," he said sarcastically.

"I don't want dinner. I thought that was clear."

"The more you don't want him, the more he wants you. It's just how men are."

"You aren't like that," I countered.

He shrugged. "Well, that's how straight men are." He popped another chip into his mouth. "I made up the second bedroom for Finn. He's gonna be here for a few weeks, so I hope he's comfortable."

"You're still going to bombard him when he walks through the door?"

"No. I was hoping you would be here too."

I guess that made sense. "I've never officially met him, so I would like to give him a warm welcome. I've only seen a few pictures of him."

"He looks different from our past family photos."

"In what way?" I asked.

He swirled a chip through the salsa before he took a bite, the crunch more audible than the commercial in the background. "More rugged, I guess. Every year he's been in the military has made him a little harder."

"Harder?"

"You'll see what I mean."

I looked at the clock and realized my guest would be over in thirty minutes. "So, are you going to tell me what happened with Aaron, or am I gonna have to drag it out of you?" I'd given him plenty of time to fess up on his own, but it was obvious he was keeping his night to himself.

A slow grin crept into his face. "Nothing, really. We had a few more beers and just talked."

"That's it?" I asked incredulously. "You expect me to believe that? You're so into him." It was strange to see my ex-husband hard up for someone else, especially a man, but now that it happened, it wasn't so bad. I wanted him to be happy. I also wanted him to realize he could have whoever he wanted.

"We exchanged numbers. I haven't called him yet."

"Don't play hard to get."

"I'm not," he argued. "I'm just...a little nervous."

I rolled my eyes. "He obviously liked you, so there's no reason to be. You shouldn't drag your feet for too long because someone else might snatch him up."

"True..." He looked down into his beer bottle, his thoughts drifting somewhere else. "I know this is what I want, but it's still a rough transition. I feel like it's not really real until I tell my family. I know that doesn't make any sense, but without their approval, I just don't feel free..."

I could understand his vulnerability, but he shouldn't have to feel that way. "Colton, you never need anyone's approval to be who you are. Whether they accept you or not shouldn't matter. Live your life the way you want."

That tender look entered his eyes, like he loved me more today than he ever had before. "You always know the right thing to say."

"Because I'm saying the truth—which is pretty easy to preach."

He drank from his beer then set it down on the table. "I'll give him a call, then."

"Good. You should invite him out to hang with us sometime. Make it less tense."

"Yeah...good idea."

"What do you think Finn will say?"

He shrugged. "I really don't know. He's such a manly man, you know? But he's always had my back... I really don't know what to expect."

"Well, if he gives you a hard time about it, I'll kick his ass."

He laughed like that was ridiculous. "He's the strongest guy I know."

"Well, I'm the strongest chick you know. I could take him."

"If anyone else said that, I would think they're crazy." He shook his head slightly. "But with you...it's not that crazy."

WHEN JAX KNOCKED on the door, I was ready to go. In a black baby doll with a matching thong, my hair was fluffed high and my makeup was heavy. I was ready to get on all fours and feel him drill me from behind.

I opened the door and got the exact reaction I wanted.

He crossed the threshold as his hands dug into my hair. His full lips landed on mine, and the kiss he gave me was even better than the last. His foot kicked the door shut behind him, and he gripped my cheeks with his big hands.

It felt so good to be held by a man.

"Fuck, you look hot." He barely broke our kiss to whisper those words.

"You're about to look hotter." I yanked his shirt over his head and felt the grooves of muscle I'd missed. He had a prominent eight-pack that my fingers loved to cherish. I traced the deep V along his hips before I reached the top of his jeans and unfastened the button. "Dessert..." As I fell to my knees, I pulled his jeans with me.

He stilled above me, a heated look of surprise in his eyes. "Jesus."

WHEN WE WERE FINISHED, we both lay in silence as our body temperatures cooled down. I was fulfilled just the way I was last time, and my head was still slightly spinning because of the throbbing goodness between my legs.

I missed sex.

It used to be that good with Colton. Or maybe that was just my imagination.

Jax lay beside me with his hand resting on his hard stomach. His long legs stretched to the end of my four-poster bed. He had large feet, nice calves, and thighs that rivaled those of a lumberjack. He was sexy from head to toe, and for the night, he was completely mine.

His hair was messy from my anxious fingers, but when it was all over the place, it only added to his charm. He turned his head my way, a sleepy look in his eyes that was filled with satisfaction. "You feel like a virgin, but you fuck like a prostitute. And I mean that in a good way."

It was safe to say I wasn't the problem in my marriage. "Thanks. You're a good lover."

"That's what I am to you? A lover?"

"Unless you want to be my prostitute?"

A sexy chuckle escaped his lips. "I'd settle for that."

"And you can earn some extra money." Not that he needed it. He lived in a big, beautiful house, so he had to be a millionaire.

"Wow. Getting paid to screw a gorgeous woman like you. I must have done something right…"

I turned on my side and faced him, the straps of my top hanging down my arms. He hadn't taken off my dress because he went straight for my thong. "Well, it's getting late…" It didn't seem necessary for him to sleep over, especially since it wasn't the weekend. I couldn't just bail on him and disappear into Colton's apartment.

He grinned like I'd made a joke. "You're finished with me?"

"I'd say I'm satisfied."

He turned on his side so he could face me head on. His wide shoulders led to muscular arms, and he was one of the sexiest pieces of man candy I'd ever seen. "What if I'm not finished with you?"

I held his gaze as my pulse raced in my neck. He cornered me in a way I didn't expect, and I struggled to fire off a comeback. Just when I thought I was ready to kick him out of my apartment, he said something that got my engine revving again. "Then we're never going to get to sleep."

"I'm a bit of an insomniac anyway."

"I'm not. I like my eight hours of sleep."

He propped himself on his elbow then hiked my leg over his hip, bringing us closer together. We were practically snuggling, something I tried to steer away from. His searing-hot skin was comfortable against mine, and when his large chest expanded against my body, it felt like solid rock. "I've never met a woman like you."

"Are you sure?" I stared into his green eyes and felt my nipples harden in my bra. His jaw was developing a faint shadow, a hint of the beard that would sprinkle his face if he didn't shave every morning. "You don't know me too well."

"That's exactly why. You don't want me to know you." He studied my face, memorizing my features like he wanted to reflect on them later. His large fingers gently gripped my leg, digging into the muscle of my thigh. His fingertips were slightly callused, like he was a man who did hard labor every single day. "I've never been with a woman that tries so hard to get rid of me." He moved himself farther over me, our bodies becoming tangled together as he held himself on top of me. His hand glided farther up my leg until he gripped my cheek.

"I have only one thing on my mind. I'm sure you do too."

"What makes you so sure?" When he pressed his face close to mine, his cologne drifted into my nose, the scent mixed with sweat and sex.

"You come into my shop and buy lingerie for different women...that's kinda a giveaway."

My answer made him still, and then his features hardened into a playful look. "That's what you think? That I buy lingerie for my ladies and ask them to wear it?"

"Unless you're buying it for yourself..."

He gave a deep chuckle. "I like you."

My playful attitude died away, surprised by the sincerity of his words.

"My sister had already picked out a few things for the wedding. Her friends from out of state are buying it for her as a gift, and I'm picking it up. Lacey and Brenda are two of her friends."

"Ohh..." I hoped my cheeks wouldn't turn red in embarrassment from the completely inaccurate assumption I'd just made.

"But I'm flattered you thought otherwise."

"I feel a little stupid right now."

"Don't." He leaned down and gave me a soft kiss. "So, now that we've had dessert, how about we have dinner?"

"Honestly, I'm not hungry."

"Neither am I. How about tomorrow?"

Why was he obsessed with taking me to dinner? "I'm gonna be straight with you, Jax. I'm just looking for a booty call. No dinner, no dates."

"Yeah, I picked up on that. I was looking for the same thing."

"You've changed your mind?"

"Yes." His hand glided farther up my body, underneath my baby doll and to the skin of my belly. "And I don't change my mind too often. I like you, Pepper. Let me buy you dinner. You can have your way with me afterward."

It was a tempting offer and I almost said yes, but then

the pact I made with myself came back to me. "I'm not looking for something serious."

"It's dinner, not a marriage proposal."

"Even so…"

"Come on, sweetheart." He gently ground against me, pressing his hard-on into my body. "Don't make me ask again. I'm not the kind of guy that asks in the first place."

I thought I should tell him the truth, that I was newly divorced and still rediscovering myself. But I didn't see the harm in a single dinner. We would have sex afterward, and after enough time had passed, we would both lose interest and move on. One dinner couldn't hurt, right? "Alright. But I get to pick the place."

He smiled. "Perfect. Where did you have in mind?"

"Mega Shake."

6

PEPPER

J ax didn't seem like the kind of guy that would order a greasy burger and fries, not with that ripped body, but he sat across from me in the booth and took an enormous bite out of his burger. "Damn. Forgot how good that was."

"You probably don't eat stuff like this too often."

"No. It doesn't look like you do either." With both elbows on the table, he gripped his burger and took a few more bites. When the sauce caught in the corner of his mouth, he quickly licked it away, making the mess look sexy.

"No, I do. I just lost a bit of weight recently." I was never heavy, but I had a lot more curves than I do now. Moping around the apartment and not eating for three months made me drop a dangerous amount of weight. I'd started to recuperate, but it would take me a while to gain back the twenty pounds I'd lost.

"Workout regimen?"

"No, I just..." I didn't want to unload my personal life on him so soon, especially when I didn't see this relationship going anywhere. We were just having fun, so I decided to focus on only positive aspects. "I cut out carbs, and it just happened."

"Sounds about right." He placed a few fries in his mouth and chewed as he watched me, more interested in my face than the feast sitting on his plate. "I've never taken a woman to a hamburger joint for a date before. It's a nice change."

"I'm not a fan of fancy places. You spend a lot of money to have pretentious food and sit around for twenty minutes waiting for the bill to finally arrive. This is more my style."

He chuckled. "And I think you're my style."

"You're just saying that because I sell lingerie and eat burgers."

"No," he countered. "I'm saying it because you wear lingerie, and you're a cheap date." He returned his burger to his tray and crossed his arms on the table, giving me his intense focus. "How long have you had that shop?"

"Almost five years now."

"And what made you pursue that business?"

I shrugged. "It's difficult for women to find quality underwear."

"Uh, have you heard of Victoria's Secret?" he asked, his eyebrows raised.

"But that's mass-produced stuff. The products I sell are direct from the designer, and they're specifically made for every body type. With popular stores, they expect every single woman to fit into one design...which isn't possible. When you come into my shop, you work with me on a personal level so you get a much better experience. Besides, a lot of women are self-conscious about wearing lingerie, and I boost their ego a bit." After my husband told me he preferred men, I needed an ego boost too. Wearing lingerie helped with that—and so did Jax.

He listened to every word I said, a handsome smile on his face.

"What?"

"You're cute."

"Cute?" I asked.

"Yeah. It's obvious you love what you do. Running a business isn't easy, especially a small boutique place like that. But if you've been in business for so long, you obviously have loyal customers. They must like you as much as your lingerie."

Now that I had given Jax a chance, I saw the sexy qualities underneath his sexy exterior. He was charming, sweet, and attentive. "Well, thanks..." I looked down and picked up a few fries before I placed them in my mouth. "What kind of business are you in?" I'd never planned to ask him because he was obviously wealthy. Rich people didn't usually like to be asked how they earned their living. But it would be even more awkward if I never asked.

"Real estate."

That was too vague of a response. I wasn't sure what he meant, but I didn't want to press him on it. That could mean he invested in real estate, or maybe he was just a real estate agent. "Do you enjoy that?"

"I love it. I love finding people the right home. It's rewarding and exciting."

So he was a real estate agent. To live in a big house like that, he had to be one of the best in the area. "Well, whenever I'm ready to buy a house, maybe you could help me out."

"I'd love to. Instead of giving me a commission, you could give me something else." He sent me a quick wink.

I was pinching my pennies so I could afford to move out of the apartment across the hall from my ex, so I would take any discount I could find. "You've got a deal. So, how long has your sister been living with you?"

He released a quiet sigh, like the question stirred up resentment. "Too long. She's been living with me on and off for a few years now. She's much younger than me, so she stayed with me while she went to college. Now that she's getting married, she and her fiancé are moving in to a place in my neighborhood, but it's not ready yet. That means I'm stuck with her until I hand her off to her husband." He spoke about her like she was a pain, but in my limited inter- action with her, she seemed really sweet, so I doubted he disliked her that much.

"Do your parents live in another state?" I kept eating, interested in the way he discussed his relationship with his sister. As an only child, I couldn't relate to that situation at all. I'd always been alone.

"No." He suddenly grew quiet and cleared his throat. "They passed away almost ten years ago." He shifted his gaze down and looked at his fries before he placed a few into his mouth. He brushed it off like it was nothing, but his eyes held a moment of sadness. Whenever he smiled, he looked even more handsome. But when he frowned, he seemed empty. "Car accident. Drunk driver."

"I'm so sorry..." My hand immediately darted across the table and rested on his. My heart broke for his parents, people I didn't even know. Losing one parent must have been hard enough, but losing two was unbearable. It resonated with me down to my core, stirred up heartbreak that I tried to forget. I'd never had parents either, so I knew his pain—all too well.

"Thank you." He didn't pull his hand away from mine. "I was in my early twenties, and Sasha was still in high school. I became her guardian, and she lived with me through college. After she graduated, she moved out for a short time, but rent became too much and she didn't like living alone, so she came back."

"That's really sweet of you."

He pulled his hand away and shrugged it off. "She's my sister, so I didn't mind. But I'm glad to have my space once she gets married. Her fiancé is a good guy, so that's a relief. I'm happy to hand her off to him."

"You sound like her father."

He shrugged. "I kinda am, honestly." He picked at a few more fries before he lifted his gaze to look into mine. "I didn't mean to bring down the energy. Tell me something about yourself."

He'd shown a side to himself that I didn't know existed. When I saw him walk into my lingerie shop, I'd just assumed he was a playboy who got whatever he wanted. As I peeled back the layers, I realized I was completely wrong. This man was kind, compassionate, and loving. "I lost my parents too..." It was easier than the whole truth.

He stilled at my words, his eyes softening into a deep look of sadness.

"And I know exactly how you feel."

COLTON PLACED the chips and salsa on the coffee table, along with a bowl of pretzels. It seemed like he was having a small get-together rather than inviting his brother to live with him for a few weeks.

"Trying to make a good impression?" I teased.

He handed me a cold beer before he twisted off the cap of his own. "I haven't seen him in three years. If we don't have anything to say, at least we can eat to make it less awkward." He grabbed the remote and turned on the TV. "What game do you think he'd want to see?"

"Depends. What kind of sports does he like?"

He shrugged. "I don't know. I think anything."

"Well, the Trail Blazers are playing the Rockets right now."

"Alright." He started flipping through the channels. "What channel is that…?"

How did I not know he was gay? "ESPN."

He kept hitting the button on the remote, flipping through reruns of *Seinfeld* and *Friends*. "That doesn't help me. Give me a number."

"Oh my god." I snatched the remote from his hand and hit the guide button. "Look, the name of the station is to the left. All you have to do is scroll down until you find it. And then, boom." I hit the button, and then the game was on. "You can pass the bar, but you don't know how to use the TV."

"I'm sorry I don't have the ESPN channel memorized like you," he said as he rolled his eyes.

"Well, if you want to impress Aaron or anyone else, you should try to get this down."

"What makes you assume he even likes sports?"

Sometimes I worried Colton wouldn't survive out there in the real world. "You met him at a sports bar…"

"Well, I was there too, and I don't like sports."

"If your brother is a fan, then you're going to have to learn if you want him to be comfortable here for a few weeks."

"When I tell him I'm gay, I'm sure that will lower his expectations for his visit." He sat back in the cushions and took a big drink. "Man, I'm so nervous. Finn has won like a million medals for his service, and he's such a…macho man.

He might storm out once I tell him." He rubbed his fingers across his forehead as he massaged the muscles around his eyebrows.

"That doesn't matter. He's your brother—your blood. Don't assume he's going to judge you."

"Well, most people do judge me." He sat up and set his beer on the table. "Do you know how many people have given me shit for leaving you? Like, I'm a superfreak for not being attracted to you?"

"Well..." I pointed to myself, trying to break the tension with a joke. "Look at me."

Thankfully, it worked, and a smile spread across his face.

"Your brother loves you, Colton. He wouldn't have asked to stay here unless he wanted to be here. You being gay isn't going to change anything."

"I really hope you're right."

"If he gives you a hard time about it, I'll set him straight. You've always got me in your corner."

"Thank god," he said. "I wouldn't be able to survive without you." His sincerity always touched me because he was so honest about it. He still relied on me the way I relied on him.

"And I wouldn't be able to survive without you."

Before I finished taking another sip of my beer, a knock sounded on the door.

Colton tensed in trepidation all over again, his shoulders straightening in fear and his eyes widening to the size of marbles. "Shit, that's him."

"Don't act surprised. You knew he was coming."

He stood up and smoothed out the front of his t-shirt, not that his brother would care how he was dressed. He fixed his hair too, like he was nervous to meet the Queen of England instead of his own flesh and blood.

"Jesus, stop being dramatic." I grabbed his elbow and walked to the door with him. "You're overreacting. So just chill out and be yourself. Even if he has a problem with it, that's his prerogative, not yours."

"Yeah, okay." He took a deep breath before he opened the door.

Finn stood on the threshold with two heavy bags over his shoulders. He was taller than Colton, with arms thick like tree trunks. Cords of veins ran from his biceps down to the tops of his hands. His sun-kissed skin suggested he spent more time outdoors than indoors.

He was not what I was expecting.

Rugged, tough, and dangerously handsome, Finn had the hardest jawline I'd ever seen. As if someone placed a knife to his throat and chiseled out his perfection, he was carved from marble. His chin was blanketed with a layer of hair from not shaving, the shadow adding to his rough exterior. The only soft aspect of his appearance was his eyes.

Crystal blue.

They examined his brother from behind a façade of mystery. Shifting back and forth slightly, he studied his flesh and blood like he was taking in his features. He wore a gray t-shirt that fit snugly over his thick arms and shoulders, and the way the fabric stretched over his huge chest made it look like a second skin. The clothing stuck against his stomach like a curtain clinging to the wall, and a faint outline of his eight-pack was noticeable. His dark jeans hung low on his hips, and his muscled thighs stretched out the fabric of his jeans. Even though his luggage must have been heavy, he didn't sway under the weight.

It didn't affect him at all.

One of his most prominent characteristics was his tattoos. Black ink stretched up and down his arms, various images woven together into a single canvas. There were numbers, pictures, bullets, and countries permanently written into his skin, like his body carried the story of his life in the military.

Colton seemed just as surprised by his brother's appearance because he still didn't speak.

I was frozen to the spot, shocked that this undeniably sexy man could be related to Colton. Colton was a beautiful man too, but he was much softer than his brother. His skin was fairer, and while he worked out, he wasn't bursting with strength the way his brother was. Just from examining Finn's facial features, I could tell his personality was nothing like Colton's.

He was hard, cold, and blunt.

The silence didn't affect Finn at all. He seemed to thrive on it, holding his brother's gaze like he refused to speak first. His eyes were the same color as Colton's, but since his other features were so strongly different, they didn't look anything alike.

Colton finally found his footing. "Wow...you look big."

Finn finally relaxed his aggressive expression, letting a ghost of a smile enter his lips. He wasn't warm or welcoming like his brother, and that was the extent of his affection. "Nice to see you too, Colt."

"Let me take one of your bags." Colton pulled one off Finn's shoulder and nearly fell to the ground under the weight. "Do you have rockets in there?"

Finn picked it up again and placed it back over his shoulder, unaffected by the weight. "Something like that." When Colton and I stepped out of the way, Finn walked inside. He set his bags down against the wall away from the living room.

Colton knew his brother better than I did, but he

seemed shocked by his transformation. "What are they feeding you over there? A cow a day?"

Finn turned back around, and this time, his eyes settled on me. Clear as a summer day, his blue eyes hinted at a beautiful sky right at noon. His gaze drilled into mine harder than a jackhammer, and he seemed to see all my secrets with just a single look. He examined me with the same intensity that he looked at his brother, but my silent interrogation seemed even more intimate. He stepped closer to me, his heavy footfalls audible on the hardwood floor. "Finn." He extended his hand to shake mine, his eyes still glued to my face. "This moment is five years in the making."

His hand lingered between us, but I didn't take it. A strong instinct was telling me to keep my hand away, not to touch his large hand and feel that warm skin. His persona unnerved me in ways I couldn't explain. A handshake felt too intimate, even though it was a common gesture between strangers.

He kept his hand extended, his gaze unreadable as he waited for my reciprocation.

I glanced at his hand again, seeing the ink that made it all the way to his wrist. My confidence had returned in the last two weeks, but now that I was standing in front of this tattooed behemoth, all of that growth had gone out the window. I finally placed my hand in his, dwarfed by his size and power, and we shook hands. "Pepper." This was Colton's flesh and blood, and I expected to connect with him instantly just the way I had with his parents. I expected to make a joke and hug him, but instead, I felt ice-cold and searing hot at the same time. "It's great to finally meet you."

He finished the handshake but continued to grip my palm, holding all the weight so I could relax in his embrace. What felt like an eternity passed, and he didn't blink that entire time. I felt like I was a target and he was a sniper, studying my behavior so when he pulled the trigger, he wouldn't miss. His gaze wasn't threatening, but it was so intense that it felt like a stampede right into my private thoughts. "I'm sorry I missed the wedding."

"Oh...don't worry about it." It didn't matter anyway. We didn't even last three years before we signed our divorce papers. My wedding was the happiest day of my life, but now it was the most ignorant day of my life. Finn didn't miss anything, except the beginning of a marriage that was never meant to last.

He finally released my hand, and when he did, it was as cold as the first day of winter.

Colton watched the entire exchange but didn't seem alarmed by it. He must not have picked up on the intense feelings in my chest, the strange sensation that was coursing through my blood. I couldn't tell if I was afraid of Finn, aroused by him, or something else entirely. "Let me show you your room," Colton said.

Finn didn't greet him with a handshake or a hug. He didn't seem like the affectionate type, not one to walk into a room and greet everyone he knew warmly. He didn't seem like an asshole, but he didn't seem hospitable either. "Couch is fine, man."

"I have a guest room," Colton answered. "No point in wasting it."

"In that case..." He picked up both of his bags and followed his brother down the hallway.

Now that I had a second to myself, I could recover from what I'd just experienced. It was spiritual, packed with mild adrenaline, and it made me feel so many things at once that I wasn't entirely sure what I felt at all.

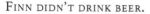

Finn didn't drink beer.

He drank scotch—a lot of it.

He didn't touch the snacks Colton put on the table, and most of the time, he directed his stare to the basketball game on the TV. Colton and I finished our beers in about half an hour, but Finn had three glasses of scotch—and seemed unaffected by it. He turned back to his brother but didn't say anything, preferring silence over conversation.

He was definitely the strong and silent type.

He made me uneasy, but I couldn't put my thumb on why. He was confident in his skin, confident in awkward silence. He stepped into a room with his brother and a stranger but still retained all the power.

Colton attempted to make conversation. "How does it feel to be back?"

Finn swirled his drink slightly before he took a drink. "Not sure yet."

We both waited for him to elaborate, but nothing was forthcoming.

"Are you home for good?" Colton asked.

"My service is finished." He set the glass back on the table, making sure it sat on a coaster even though Colton didn't care if he used one or not. "I'm a civilian now."

Maybe Colton was right. Finn might not be as open-minded as I thought. He was so tough and cold that he might not accept the truth.

Colton nodded but exhausted his attempt at making conversation.

So I tried. "Colton mentioned you have a job lined up. Where will you be working?" I had no idea what he did in the military, so I didn't know what kind of skills he had.

Veterans were usually desirable in the workforce, so he probably had an easy time finding work.

He turned his gaze on me—and that intensity was back. "Johns Hopkins."

"The hospital?" I asked, unable to keep the surprise out of my voice.

Finn gave a slight nod. "The ER."

"Are you a medic? A nurse?" Maybe that was his discipline, treating soldiers on the battlefield. It would explain why he was so withdrawn, after all the things he must have seen.

"Physician." He took another drink of his scotch, nearly finishing his third glass.

"Oh, that's great." So his job was even more stressful than I assumed.

"Mom mentioned you were getting your medical license in the military," Colton said. "That's awesome."

"My training is a little different from traditional education." He held the glass between his large hands, shifting it back and forth. "I specialize in procedures in the field, working with whatever I have at the time. Mainly traumas. Johns Hopkins offered me a position in their emergency department when I left the service."

I already respected people in the military, but now I respected this man even more. His coldness was excused, and his silent hostility seemed natural. After spending ten years in that line of work, it was expected for him to be closed off. "Now you can be close to family, so that's nice."

"Yeah," Colton said in agreement. "I've only seen you a few times in the past few years. Almost didn't recognize you on the doorstep. Mom and Dad will be really happy to spend more time with you—me too."

"About that..." He set his glass back on the coaster.

"They don't know I'm here yet. They think I'll be here in a few weeks. Keep that to yourself."

Colton cocked an eyebrow. "Why?"

"Just want some time to decompress. My house is still in escrow, but once that's finished, I'll be able to move in." He rested his elbows on his knees and rubbed his palms together. He had short brown hair, a color much darker than Colton's.

"Whatever you want, man," Colton said.

"Where's your place?" I asked.

"Over on Escala," Finn answered. "Close to the water."

That was close to where Jax lived. It was a swanky neighborhood with prime real estate. His salary from the army must have been pretty competitive if he had the down payment for a place like that. "That's a nice area."

"Super nice," Colton said. "I can't wait to see it."

"Me neither," I added.

Finn watched the game again, seeing the next three-pointer made by the Rockets. He turned back to us a moment later. "How are things with you two?"

Colton and I were both silent. We were sitting on opposite ends of the couch, not looking like a married couple at all. Colton had agreed to tell his brother the truth, and now seemed like the best moment.

Colton looked at me, as if he needed some encouragement.

I knew I had to give him a shove. "Actually, we have some news..."

Finn watched us with that stern expression, his jaw chiseled and his cheekbones prominent. His hands rested together, and he kept his gaze locked on to mine, patiently waiting for whatever revelation I was about to make. Other people would give some kind of reaction, visibly tensing in preparation for good news. But Finn was fearless, remaining calm regardless of what would come next.

Colton was quiet for a long time before he finally shared the truth. "Pepper and I split up six months ago."

Finn looked at his brother for a few seconds, but his eyes shifted back to me.

"We haven't told anyone in the family yet," I said. "We've been dragging our feet for a bit."

Most people would have asked a million questions about what went wrong, but Finn didn't do that. Colton's mother would be in tears, and his father would be in shock. Finn didn't have a visible response, which wasn't too surprising because he'd just met me for the first time. "Are you separated? Or divorced?"

"Divorced," Colton said.

Finn didn't ask why. He shifted his gaze back to his brother, his thick body in the same relaxed position as before. "It seems like you're on good terms."

"We are." Colton patted my hand as it rested on my thigh. "We're still best friends. We're still in each other's lives. And of course, we still love each other."

I gave my ex a soft smile, returning his affection.

Finn sat back against the couch, his knees apart and his large chest taking up the entire half of the couch. He glanced back and forth between us, trying to connect the dots but unable to make a picture. "What am I missing?"

Divorced couples didn't sit on a couch together and say they loved each other unless they were talking to their kids. I wanted to take the lead and relieve the pressure from Colton, but this was something he needed to do on his own.

"There's no easy way to say this..." Colton looked at the table as he fidgeted with his hands. His movements became faster the longer he built up to the dreadful moment.

Finn was still like a statue.

Colton finally let the words break free from his chest. "I'm gay." He still couldn't look at his brother, as if he was too ashamed to make eye contact. "When I couldn't deny it anymore, I told Pepper the truth. She's been so supportive this entire time and made it so easy on me. Now we're just friends...best friends."

I watched Finn's expression, waiting to see the critical judgment creep into his gaze. He didn't blink as he stared at his brother, but his thoughts were blank. He was impossible to read because he was so still and silent.

When Finn didn't speak, Colton looked up to meet his gaze. "So...that's it."

Still, nothing.

I knew Colton was looking for a more concrete response, needing to know if his brother was disgusted by the truth. He feared the worst and prepared for it by gripping his hands together. "Finn?"

"Yes?" He continued to stare at his brother.

"You haven't said anything..." Colton clearly didn't know how to interact with his brother because they'd drifted apart. Only seeing each other once every three years had practically made them strangers. But I couldn't blame Colton for not knowing how to read a statue.

"What am I supposed to say?" Finn countered.

"You just don't seem to have much of a reaction." Even I couldn't tell if he was annoyed or pleased by the news.

"What kind of reaction should I have?" He grabbed his scotch and took a drink. "The two of you seem to be in a good place. You both seem happy. There's not really much to say."

"Finn," Colton said. "Your brother just told you he was gay. Does that upset you?"

It was the first time Finn raised an eyebrow. "Why would it? You basically just told me you liked apples yesterday and now you like oranges. Why should I care what you like? It makes no difference to me. Love who you want to love. Be who you are. It doesn't change anything."

Now I finally understood his reaction. He was indifferent because there was no reason to have a reaction. Gay or straight, it didn't make a difference to him. He didn't just have an open mind, he was extremely progressive, not judgmental or critical of someone who was different from him. "I told you, Colton."

Finn watched his brother. "What did you think I was going to say?"

"I don't know," Colton said with a shrug. "You're a military man. I wasn't entirely sure..."

Finn finished his glass before he set it on the table. "I've spent the last ten years of my life in the service of my country. I fight for the rights of all Americans, regardless of your religion or sexual orientation. Next time you think of me as a military man, think of that."

My eyes softened for this hard man, a man who was clearly selfless and compassionate. His exterior wasn't warm like an open fire in the midst of winter, but it was obvious he had a warm heart under all those muscles.

"Thanks, Finn," Colton said. "That means a lot to me."

"I don't care for the way you've treated Pepper, though." He turned his gaze back to me. "You should have had the courage to be honest about who you are instead of wasting her time. That's five years she can't get back, Colton."

Colton bowed his head in shame.

"I loved being married to Colton, so I don't consider it to be a waste of time." I defended Colton even though Finn had a valid point. "I'm still young, and I'll find the man I'm supposed to be with. If anything, being with Colton has taught me exactly what I want in a husband."

"You don't have to defend me," Colton whispered. "He's right."

"You're loyal." Finn spoke the words while looking into my eyes, the comment jarring and unexpected. "That's a rare trait. It's like a diamond in the rough. You can keep digging and never find it. But when you spot it, it shines so brightly, there's no mistaking it." He'd barely said a few words the entire night, but once the subject of loyalty had been broached, he practically recited a poem. "You're a very lucky man, Colton. To have a woman who has your back like that."

7

COLTON

My alarm went off then I got ready for work. I showered, put on my collared shirt and tie, and then walked into the kitchen to have my morning coffee and bagel.

Finn was already there, in the middle of the kitchen, doing push-ups in his sweatpants. His breathing was even and slightly labored, and with perfect form, he lowered himself to the floor then pushed up again. His back and chest were covered with tattoos as well.

I wondered if Mom knew about this canvas.

I filled a mug with coffee and watched him continue his workout. Just watching him exert himself was a workout for me. "You're up early." He didn't start his job today and he wasn't used to the new time zone yet, but that didn't stop him from rising at seven in the morning.

He ignored me and finished his set before he stood up, sweat making the muscles of his chest glisten. His body showed his fatigue, but he still didn't breathe deep and hard like he had done a serious workout in the middle of the kitchen. He wiped his forehead with the back of his forearm. "I slept in, actually." He got up and poured his own cup of coffee.

I grabbed a bagel slice and placed it in the toaster. "Want one?"

"No thanks." He carried his mug to the kitchen table and sat down. He pulled his phone out of his pocket and seemed to go through his emails.

I sat across from him and opened the newspaper.

His eyes were downcast as he scrolled through his phone, his large torso covering the entire back of the chair. He was built like a brick house and looked dangerous, like a criminal in a dark alleyway.

We looked nothing alike.

Our facial features were similar and we had the same blue eyes, but other than that, we were starkly different. My body was toned and in shape because I worked out often, but my physique was nothing compared to his. "What are you doing today?"

"Hitting the gym in a little bit."

I stopped reading the newspaper and gave him an incredulous look. "Didn't you just work out?"

"Warm-up." He typed a message on his phone before he set it on the table. "Mom and Dad know?"

I knew he was referring to the news I shared with him last night. "No."

He tilted his head slightly, his eyes narrowing a smidge. "You told me first?"

"Yeah...I thought it would be easier."

"So they won't gang up on you?"

I nodded. "They're going to be disappointed. I know they are."

"They will," he said without sugarcoating it. "But I think their disappointment will be over Pepper, not your sexuality.

Mom never has anything bad to say about her. Whenever she mentions her, she talks about Pepper like she's a queen."

"Because she is."

The corner of his mouth rose in a slight smile. "Letting her go must have been difficult."

"Extremely."

"You're lucky she stands by you."

"She loves me…" I didn't know what I did to earn her loyalty and devotion, but I would gladly accept it.

"I can tell you love her too."

"With all my heart."

He grabbed his mug and took a drink, the perspiration on his chest slowly evaporating.

"Are you happy to be back in Seattle?"

He shrugged. "I'm not sure how I feel about it. Every morning when I wake up, I try to remember where I am. I'm used to moving around so much that staying still feels odd to me." He didn't talk about his service very often, and I knew he would never give me any details. "I haven't kept in contact with anyone around here, so I'll have to make some friends."

"Well, you already have me and Pepper."

He took another drink of his coffee, cold to my comment. "It's a start."

"What made you leave the military?" He'd seemed to be completely invested in his career, and pulling out when he was so young was confusing.

He held his mug by the handle, the steam slowly rising to the ceiling. "It was time." He dismissed the conversation by taking a drink of his black coffee. He'd never been open with me before, and it was unlikely he would start now. "Are you still at the same firm?"

"Yes." Unfortunately.

"Do I detect resentment?"

"No. Just indifference."

"You don't have a mortgage or a family. May as well take a risk and leave—if you don't like it." Finn had never been tied down to anything. As far as I knew, he'd never had a girlfriend or aspired to have a family. Mom stopped asking him about it because she knew Finn wouldn't change his attitude.

That made telling her I was gay so much harder. "Pepper told me to leave too."

"Then do it."

"I'm thinking about it..."

"You could always start your own firm."

"That's a lot of work." I would be working nonstop because all the load would fall to my shoulders. I would also have to handle the business side of things. If the business went belly-up, so did I.

"The best things in life are hard to seize."

The door opened, and Pepper walked inside. She was dressed for work, wearing black skinny jeans and a purple blouse. Her hair was curled and stretched down her chest, and she wore a gold necklace my mother had given her for her birthday. Black pumps were on her feet, and they made a tapping noise throughout the apartment. Pepper was naturally beautiful, not requiring much maintenance. The second she woke up in the morning, she was ready to go.

Finn turned in her direction the second he heard the door open. His eyes took her in, starting from her long hair down to the black shoes on her feet. He didn't seem to care if I noticed or not because he continued to stare at her.

"What's for breakfast?" she asked. "I smell something good."

"Coffee and bagels," I answered, taking my eyes off my brother and looking at Pepper.

She stuck out her tongue and made a disappointed face. "No pancakes? Bacon?"

"Not unless you're making it," I countered.

"You know I can't cook," she said. "Why do you think I come over here every morning?"

Finn held his mug in his hand but didn't take another drink. Now all he did was examine Pepper with an unreadable expression. He was tense like usual, his eyes two dark shadows. "Do you live nearby?"

She joined us at the table, and just before she sat down, her eyes flicked to his bare chest. She stilled for two seconds, caught off guard by his near-nakedness. She tried to hide her hesitance by sitting down and looking into her coffee. "I live across the hall."

"So, when you moved out, you moved ten feet across the hall?" If Finn noticed the way she looked at him, he acted as if he didn't. He was probably used to women staring at his physical perfection. The dog tags hanging around his throat and the tattoos only made him more interesting.

"Not on purpose." She crossed her legs and sat upright, showing her elegance through her posture. "At the time, I just needed somewhere to live, and that apartment was available. Finding a decent place in this city is harder than it seems."

"I'm not judging you." He stared at her just as intently as he did last night, abruptly stern.

"I wouldn't care if you were." She blew her breath across the surface of her coffee before she took a drink.

Finn's mouth softened into a faint smile.

"Colton, I have a package coming today. Would you

mind picking it up?" Pepper turned back to me, her elbows resting on the table.

"Why can't you pick it up?" I countered, even though I didn't mind doing something for her.

"I'm working late tonight. And then I have a date..." She turned her gaze away quickly, like she didn't want to look me in the eye as she said it.

"A date?" I asked. "Are you talking about Jax?"

Finn watched our interaction and ignored his phone every time it lit up with a message.

"We went to Mega Shake the other day and had a good time," Pepper explained. "He's not the kind of guy I thought he was. His parents passed away when he was young, and he had to take care of his sister. He's actually very sweet."

Pepper had told me she wasn't ready for a relationship, but maybe now that she put herself out there, she realized she was wrong. Once she got her feet wet, she waded further and further into the depths until she was completely submerged. "That's great. You'll have to bring him out with us sometime."

"Yeah, maybe," she said. "I don't know. We'll see. I keep trying to keep it physical, but he keeps wanting something more."

"That doesn't surprise me at all." It didn't matter how gay I was, I knew Pepper was stunning. On top of that, she was the most compassionate and badass woman I'd ever known. "I'll pick up your package for you."

"Thanks." She finished the rest of her coffee before she left the mug on the table. "I'll see you later."

"You aren't going to clean up after yourself?" I demanded, eyeing her dirty dish on the kitchen table between Finn and me.

"Nope. You were a pig when we lived together. This is payback." She walked to the front door. "Bye."

Now Finn grinned wider. "I like her."

I called to her as she walked out the door. "Bye, babe."

She shut the door behind her.

"Listening to her talk about her love life doesn't bother you?" Finn asked the second she was gone.

"Not at all. She kinda set me up with this guy, actually."

"So you guys really have moved on from each other." He didn't phrase it like a question, more of an observation.

"The first months were hard. We stayed away from each other so we both had space. But after about three months, we started to be friends again. Here we are now..."

"That must have been hard for her."

It was, but I would never share her darkest moments with anyone, not even my brother. That was between her and me. "But she's the strongest person I know. There's nothing she can't overcome."

8

PEPPER

J ax and I had dinner together, going to another casual diner like Mega Shake, before we headed back to his place. His sister wasn't home, so we had our privacy to go upstairs to his bedroom and do what we did best.

After a rendezvous that made my toes curl, I lay beside him in his large bed, the sheets so soft against my skin they felt like rose petals. I lay in my own sweat as Jax lay beside me, his chest glistening with exertion.

I stared at his ceiling and felt my eyes grow heavy. It would be so easy for me to fall asleep and worry about getting home in the morning, but I wasn't looking for a sleepover. That would make the relationship more serious —and that was the last thing I needed right now. "You have a really nice place."

"Thanks." He turned on his side and looked down at me. "You have a really nice body."

"Thanks, but it's still not as nice as your house."

He dragged the backs of his fingers down my arm, his eyes taking in my naked frame on his mattress. "I disagree."

His fingers moved down my belly and over my hip, tracing my hourglass figure.

Lying there as a beautiful man touched me was a small piece of heaven. My eyes could close and I could slip away, sexually fulfilled and physically comfortable. I loved the way he smelled and the way his callused fingertips gripped my tits when he fucked me. "I should get going…"

His hand clutched the inside of my thigh, grounding me in place so I couldn't slip away. "Or you could stay here."

"I have work in the morning."

"Regardless of where you sleep, you still have work in the morning."

"Why do you want me to stay?" Tomorrow wasn't the weekend, so we wouldn't have any time together anyway.

"Because I want to see a beautiful woman beside me the second I open my eyes."

"Well, there is porn…"

He smiled as he moved on top of me, using his heavy frame to keep me in place. His thighs separated mine, and he brought our bodies close together. It was the same position he'd just screwed me in. "You're much better than porn."

"Why, thank you. I try."

He pressed his lips to my neck and kissed me, blanketing my hot skin in delectable kisses everywhere. They started off soft and sweet, but slowly escalated into aggressive embraces. He moved to the hollow of my throat before he placed his face above mine. "Stay."

It was tempting to say yes, but I already felt myself falling into a relationship I wasn't ready for. "Jax, I'm really not looking for something serious." Jax was a sweet guy and I didn't want to offend him, but I had to be honest.

"Sleeping over makes it serious?"

"More serious than I want it to be."

His hand slowly slid into my hair, and he brushed his lips past mine, teasing me. "And why don't you want anything serious? I think I'm a pretty good catch. Most of the women I bed want more of me, not less."

"You are a catch, Jax." My hands slid up his back and into his hair. "You aren't the problem. I'm just not...there." I didn't want to dump all my personal baggage on him, but the more he tried to keep me, the more I had to confide in him.

His brilliant green eyes looked into mine with concentration, like he was trying to read the truth before he pulled it out of me. "What aren't you telling me, sweetheart?" He rubbed his nose against mine as his fingers touched my neck.

I held my silence, unsure if I wanted to come clean.

"What are you afraid to tell me?"

"I'm not afraid."

"Then tell me. We've only been seeing each other for a few weeks, but honestly, I like you. I want to keep seeing you. If there's something I need to know, you should just tell me now. Might save me some heartache down the road."

The guilt burned my throat because the idea of hurting him made me sick. Colton had hurt me so much, and the last thing I wanted to do was hurt someone else. "Alright." My palm glided up his chest and stopped over his slowly beating heart. "I got divorced six months ago. You're the first man I've been with since...my ex-husband. It's the first time I've put myself out there, and I've been taking it slow."

Jax didn't give me a judgmental look or ask a million questions. He didn't even seem disappointed. Like I was talking to a friend, he seemed understanding. "Now I see..."

"So I'm really not looking for anything serious...at least

right now. I'm in a good place, but having anything more
than a fling is just too soon. You're right, I should have been
up front about that in the beginning."

His fingers started to play with my hair again, and when
he rubbed his nose against mine, it made my heart throb.
"Thank you for telling me."

I was relieved he didn't ask any questions, like why I got
divorced. No woman wanted to admit her husband was now
gay and seeking other men. It didn't make me look the least
bit desirable.

"I can take it slow."

"Thanks…"

His cock had hardened during the conversation, and
now it was pulsing right against my clit. He started to rock
into me, grinding right against my most erogenous zone.
"I'll let you leave," he said in a husky voice. "Once I'm
finished."

I STOPPED by Colton's apartment on the way back to mine.
I'd ordered some toiletries from Amazon, and thanks to my
Prime membership, getting the essentials shipped to my
door was easier than stopping by the store on the way home
—especially since I didn't have a car.

I walked inside the apartment without knocking
because that was how Colton and I were, stopping by
randomly without giving any notice. But now there was a
roommate living with him, and I didn't have the manners to
knock.

Finn was sitting on the couch watching the basketball
game. He was in just his black sweatpants, his shirtless back
covered with black ink. One image that caught me by

surprise the most was an image of a black tank. The ink was so heavy that it covered the fair color of his skin, but it couldn't mask the prominent muscles of his frame.

He was built like a brick house.

He didn't have a single ounce of fat on his body. He was all muscle and masculinity.

I'd never seen a man like him in person.

When he heard me walk inside, he looked at me over his shoulder, that same stern expression on his face as last night.

His stare was so intense, I nearly forgot why I was there.

He held my gaze for several seconds before he set down his beer and rose to his feet. Six foot three of pure masculinity, he was the prime example of what testosterone looked like in physical form. I'd always considered Colton to be manly, but his brother put him to shame—as well as all other men.

He walked around the couch and came toward me, his sweatpants dangerously low on his hips. He had tattoos across his chest and stomach, but the details couldn't hide his extreme eight-pack. A silver chain was around his neck, and at the end hung his dog tags. He slowly walked up to me as he slid his hands into his pockets.

I'd just been in bed with another man, but now I couldn't even remember his name.

Finn stopped a few feet in front of me and stared at me with those blue eyes. His gaze was so hostile, it seemed like I was his enemy rather than his friend. He always seemed to look that way, but when he stared at me it was particularly potent.

Now would be a good time to say hello, but the words refused to form on my tongue. I couldn't think of anything logical to say, so I let the tension escalate between us, the intimate eye contact and the rising heat.

What was happening?

Finn seemed to thrive on tension. It didn't matter how awkward or uncomfortable he made me, it didn't affect him at all. He appeared to be immune to human emotion, relishing heated discomfort.

Was he like this with everyone?

I finally broke the ice because I couldn't take it anymore. "Who's winning?"

He didn't glance at the TV, keeping his gaze focused on me. "The Warriors. Basketball fan?"

"Basketball, football, and baseball."

He gave a slight nod. "Ironic. Colton hates sports."

"Yeah, it's strange. I never should have married him."

"Not because he was gay?" He didn't smile, but it seemed like he was teasing me.

"No. I'm okay with the gay thing, not the sports thing."

A slight smile crept onto his lips, but it was so faint, I wasn't sure if it was real. But there was a gentle brightness to his eyes, as if he was responding to my humor. "How was work?"

"Long, but enjoyable."

"What do you do?" He stood perfectly straight, his shoulders so broad, he looked like a billboard. It didn't seem like he'd shaved that day because the shadow on his jaw looked darker than it had that morning. His biceps were so prominent, it seemed like he had a tennis ball sewed inside each arm.

"I own a boutique lingerie shop."

His playful attitude died away immediately, his eyes darkening noticeably. His body tensed slightly, his powerful muscles flexing even more. The muscles of his eight-pack clenched, the images on his body shifting with his subtle movement. "Really?"

"I'm surprised Colton didn't tell you that."

"Yes...I'm surprised too."

I'd stopped by here to see Colton and collect my package, but now that I had been cornered by Finn, I didn't think about much else. It seemed like it was just the two of us in the apartment, like there was no Colton at all. "Where's your brother?" Talking about my lingerie shop had only seemed to intensify the situation.

Finn pulled his left hand out of his pocket and rubbed the back of his neck, keeping his gaze on me without blinking. Any subtle move he made was sexy, practically pornographic. He moved to a new place and was starting a new job, but he would have no problem scoring tail left and right. All he'd have to do was take off his shirt, and he would get pussy. "In the shower. Your package is on the table."

I would have noticed if I hadn't been staring at him so hard. "Thanks..."

I grabbed the box off the table then moved back to the door. "Well, good night—"

"How was your date?" He joined me by the entryway, his large feet thumping against the hardwood floor. When he came close to me, I could smell his cologne. It was pine needles mixed with soap.

I forgot I'd mentioned it that morning. "We got Chinese then headed back to his place."

"That's not what I asked."

My eyes shifted back and forth as I looked into his, my heart racing as he asked his questions so bluntly. "We had a good time. I told him I'm recently divorced... He seemed okay with it."

"Why wouldn't he be?"

"Most men don't want a woman with baggage."

He towered over me with his height, and even though there was some distance between us, it felt like he was infecting all of my space. "A real man doesn't care. He'll carry her baggage for her."

Just when I thought this man couldn't surprise me more, he did.

"I'll tell Colton you stopped by." And as if the conversation only ended when he decided to end it, he walked away. "Good night, Pepper."

I watched his muscular frame shift and move as he headed back to the couch. It was such a nice view that I almost forgot to head back to my apartment. "Night, Finn."

9

COLTON

We slid into the booth at the bar, Finn taking the side that faced the TV because he cared about the game more than I did. Zach sat beside me, still in his work clothes because he'd headed here right after work. I was in my suit and tie. Finn was the only one dressed in street clothes. He wore a black t-shirt that fit his sculpted muscles perfectly, and his silver chain hung down his chest. Ever since he arrived on my doorstep, I'd never seen him remove that necklace. Even when he walked around the house shirtless, the tags rested against the center of his chest.

"What did you do in the military?" Zach asked Finn, making conversation since this was the first time they'd met each other.

"Trauma physician." He rested one arm over the back of the booth and kept his gaze on the TV.

"Whoa, that's sick." Zach spat out his thoughts without thinking twice about them. People who didn't know members of the military didn't know how to behave, what kind of questions and comments were appropriate.

Finn turned his gaze to Zach, and the coldness of his stare suggested he didn't appreciate the comment. "You think it's sick?" He lowered his arm and slowly sat forward over the table.

I learned a long time ago to steer clear of this topic. Finn didn't like to talk about it, and if anyone said something insensitive, he didn't refrain from turning hostile.

"One of my boys stepped on a mine and lost his leg. Out in the middle of the desert with just two nurses, I had to give him a blood transfusion and stop the bleeding. Do you have any idea how difficult it is to give orders when a soldier is screaming at the top of his lungs?" He stared Zach down with a slightly crazed look in his eyes. "No. It wasn't *sick*." He sat back against the leather booth and looked at the TV again.

My brother and best friend weren't off to a good start.

Zach sat quietly, unsure how to follow up that comment.

"Finn, Zach wasn't trying to be insensitive," I said gently.

"Then don't say insensitive shit." He returned his arm over the back of the booth and stared at the TV. "Men play *Call of Duty* in front of their TVs and think war is some glorified game. War is not a game. It's real—and people die."

Zach cleared his throat then apologized. "Sorry."

Finn gave a slight shrug, like that was the most forgiveness Zach was going to get.

The waitress walked over to our table, finally ready to take our drink orders. She had a beer in one hand, and she placed it on the coaster in front of Finn. "A beautiful woman sent this over."

Finn lowered his arm from the booth again and turned to her, his eyes changing from hostile to smoldering. He was used to being the center of female attention anytime he walked into a room, so he didn't seem surprised by the free drink he was getting now. "Tell her thank you for me."

With thick blond hair and green eyes, she was a pretty woman who probably got hit on all day at work. She had an hourglass frame, a busty chest, and long legs that were unmistakable in her jeans. "You just did." Her hand moved to his wrist on the table and gave it a gentle squeeze before she turned around and walked off.

Finn stared at her ass as she walked before he turned back to me. "I've been meaning to ask you something."

Zach shook his head slightly, his eyes full of disbelief. "I'm a good-looking guy, but that shit doesn't happen to me."

Finn turned to my friend. "It's much easier to let tail chase you than it is to chase tail."

"Uh, easier said than done," Zach said with a laugh.

"I'm telling you, it works." He twisted off the cap of his beer and took a drink. "What's the policy on bringing dates back to the apartment?"

"There's no policy." I didn't care if Finn brought women back to the apartment. They probably wouldn't hang around very long, so it wouldn't affect my life too much. Besides, he was only staying for a few weeks. So far, he'd been meticulously clean, making his bed every morning, always doing the dishes, and picking up after himself so well it didn't seem like he was there in the first place.

"Good to know." He took another drink.

"Does that mean she's coming to the apartment tonight?" I asked.

"That's what the forecast predicts." He turned his gaze to the TV again. Even though a beautiful woman had just made a pass at him, not once did he look at her or show any real interest.

"Are you going to talk to her?" I asked, unsure what his

game was.

"Eventually," he said with indifference. "I'll get to it."

"What if she's a weirdo?" Zach asked.

Finn shrugged. "It doesn't make a difference to me. I'm not a picky guy."

Zach stared at him with obvious envy. "I hate you, man."

"Why?" Finn took a long drink of his beer then addressed him.   •

"A beautiful woman just brought you a free beer, asked to have sex with you, and then she didn't even take our order," Zach said. "And I suspect we aren't going to get free drinks."

"Women respond to confidence. You could go home with any woman in this bar tonight if you played your cards right. Give them a reason to say yes, and they will." Maybe Finn didn't realize that he was the best-looking guy in the room, so his experiences with women were much different from ours. Just his arms alone were distracting. Not only were they muscular, but so ripped it seemed like a slender layer of skin was the only thing keeping his muscles together.

"I think you're oversimplifying it," Zach said. "But thanks for the tip."

I spotted Pepper walk inside with Tatum and Stella behind her. They were all dressed to impress. Stella was in dark jeans with heels and a top that cut so low her cleavage was noticeable. Tatum was in a long-sleeved dress with tights underneath. Pepper stood out from the rest because she was in black jeans that were so skintight, they showed every sculpted muscle of her legs. Heeled boots were on her feet, and she wore a black V-neck with a brown leather jacket on top. Her hair was in large curls and her makeup a little heavier than usual. There was no doubt in my mind that I liked men, but there was also no doubt in my mind that Pepper was the most beautiful woman in the room. "The girls are here."

Zach followed my gaze. "And Stella looks damn hot."

Stella was the obvious beauty in the group because her body was so perfect, but I still didn't think she could outshine Pepper.

Finn looked over his shoulder and watched the girls walk inside. He'd never met Stella and Tatum before, so hopefully, he would make a better first impression than he did with Zach.

When Pepper spotted us, the three of them walked over. "You got the best booth. Perfect."

Finn rose to his feet and stared down at Pepper, that same weirdly intense look on his face. He didn't greet her with a hello like a regular person. He seemed to think his tense energy was welcoming enough. "Why is it the best booth?"

She nodded to the TVs. "No matter where you sit, you have a prime view. Plus, it's equal distance between the kitchen and the bathroom. The two things that dictate my life are eating and peeing."

He didn't introduce himself to the girls. Instead, he kept looking at Pepper. "Can I get you something to drink?"

"Uh, sure," Pepper said, caught slightly off guard. "I'll have what you're having."

He turned to the other two. "What about you?"

Tatum reacted to Finn the way all other women did, with wide eyes and a gaping mouth that practically drooled.

Stella immediately straightened, making her already tight body even tighter. She wore a wide smile that was highlighted by her red lipstick. "Cosmo."

Finn turned back to Tatum, who hadn't given him a

selection.

Stella nudged Tatum in the side. "What do you want, girl?"

Tatum finally recovered from my brother's handsome good looks. "Uh, cosmo is fine."

"You got it." His eyes shifted back to Pepper before he walked away and headed to the bar.

"Uh, I'll take a beer too, asshole," I called after him.

"Make it two," Zach called out too.

All three women had their necks craned as they stared at Finn's hard ass.

I wasn't the least bit surprised by Tatum and Stella, but Pepper's reaction surprised me. We weren't married anymore, but he was my brother. My family was still her family.

Stella turned to me, accusation heavy in her eyes. "How did you not mention that you have a hot piece of ass for a brother?"

"Yeah," Tatum said. "We're both single over here, and you've been holding out."

"He's a player, so don't bother," I said honestly.

Stella still wore the same dumbfounded look. "Who cares? I'm a player too. Not all men have asses that chiseled, alright? He's one hell of a hunk." She scooted into the booth. "I'm going for it."

Tatum scooted in after her. "Uh, what about me?"

"You can go when I'm finished," Stella said.

"Ew," Tatum said. "That would just be weird. We need to flip a coin or something."

I was grateful Pepper wasn't taking part in this. "He's just a guy."

"He's, like, the sexiest guy I've ever seen," Stella said. "I mean, look at him."

"Ouch," Zach said. "I'm man candy too, aren't I?"

Stella patted his hand like it was the snout of a dog. "Of course, sweetie. He doesn't make you any less beautiful. But he's just so..."

"Rugged," Tatum answered. "Those shoulders and that jawline..."

Pepper finally said something. "You guys are treating him like a farm animal you're about to slaughter, trying to find the best cut of meat."

"Your point?" Stella asked seriously. "Isn't that all guys ever do to us?"

Pepper didn't have an argument against that, so she shrugged. "Good point."

"Let's flip a coin before he comes back." Tatum opened her clutch and fished out a quarter. "Colton, you do the honors."

I didn't want to take part in this. "This is too weird."

"Fine, I'll do it." Zach grabbed the quarter. "Loser gets me." He flicked the quarter into the air, and it landed with a thud on the table.

Finn returned to the table at that moment and handed the drinks around. He got Zach and me the same kind of beer he was drinking. He took a seat beside Pepper, the four of them cramming together on one side so their arms were touching.

"Heads!" Stella threw her arm in the air. "I win."

Tatum stuck out her tongue. "Damn."

Zach waggled his eyebrows. "Hey, you still got me."

Now she blew on her tongue, making a loud farting noise.

"What are you guys flipping for?" Finn held his beer between his fingers, his eyes casually shifting back and forth between us and the TV.

Stella covered up the truth surprisingly well, not skipping a beat in her lie. "We just settled where we're going to dinner tomorrow night."

"And where is that?" Finn asked.

"Mega Shake," Stella blurted, our favorite place to visit.

"I'm Finn, by the way." He didn't extend his hand to shake theirs, probably because Pepper was in the way. "I'm Colton's brother, and I'll be staying with him for a few weeks."

Stella waved with her fingertips. "Stella."

Tatum beamed. "Tatum."

He gave a nod before he turned back to the TV. "Nice to meet you."

"Right back at ya." When he was turned away, Stella studied his profile even more. "Are those dog tags?"

He seemed like he would rather watch the game, but he turned back to Stella to be polite. "Yes. I was in the military for ten years."

Stella looked like she was about to fan herself at any moment. "Wow…"

"That's amazing," Tatum whispered. "Did you just get out?"

He nodded. "I start my new job in a couple days."

"Where are you working?" Stella asked.

"The hospital," Finn said. "I'm a doctor."

Stella looked like she was going to melt right on the spot.

Pepper seemed to get bored of the conversation because she started talking to me. "How was your day?"

"It was alright. I'm working on this real estate case, and it's a bit boring." I worked at a firm that specialized in real estate suits. It wasn't the most eventful job in the world, but it was better than other gigs. "What about you?"

"I booked two lingerie parties this Saturday—back-to-back."

"That's good."

"It is," she said in agreement. "But there goes my Saturday. The Mariners are playing too."

Finn finished his conversation with the girls and seemed to listen to ours instead.

"When are we doing that double date?" she asked me.

"You're going to bring Jax?" I asked in surprise. "I thought you weren't doing serious."

"It's not." She pulled her hair over one shoulder, in Finn's direction. "I told him I'm divorced."

"You did?" I asked in surprise. "How did he take it?"

"Really well, actually. Didn't seem to care at all…"

"Because he shouldn't care," Finn interjected even though he wasn't part of the conversation. "A real man shouldn't be intimidated by a woman's past. If he really thinks less of you for it, then he's not man enough for you." He said all of that while his eyes remained glued to the TV.

Pepper stilled at his speech, but she didn't seem surprised by it. "He said he was fine taking it slow. Now he understands I really don't want anything serious. He said he likes me and wants to keep seeing me."

"Well, that's great," I said. "Sounds like a nice guy."

"So, are the four of us going to go out tomorrow night?"

Aaron and I had been texting back and forth, but nothing had come out of it. "I'll ask Aaron."

"Good. I'll let Jax know." Pepper watched the TV just the way Finn did, heavily absorbed in the action going on.

Zach was staring at Tatum, who was making eyes at Finn.

Stella was doing the same thing.

I was the only one at the table who managed to keep his eyes to himself.

Like every weekday morning, the alarm went off, and I slammed my hand on top of the clock, silencing the annoying screeching noise. We were out later than I wanted to be last night, drinking while they watched the game.

I rubbed the sleep from my eyes then made my way into the kitchen. I usually had my morning coffee after my shower, but today I needed my caffeine hit before—not after. I made a pot and poured it into a mug before I sat at the kitchen table. I had a briefing today with my boss, another member of the anti-gay bully club.

The more I considered it, the more I wanted to start my own firm. If I hated going to work this much, maybe I should find another job. Pepper was usually right about these things. Since she'd owned a business for many years, she might be able to help me.

Footsteps sounded behind me, and I assumed Finn was up early, ready to have coffee and do his "warm-up" in the middle of the kitchen. The man was committed to fitness the way I was committed to coffee—he never took a day off. "I went to the store yesterday, so there's a carton of egg whites in the fridge."

"Uh, thanks," a feminine voice sounded from the counter behind me.

I immediately turned in my chair and locked eyes with the blonde from the bar. Most surprising of all was what she was wearing.

Almost nothing.

She was in a black thong and a matching push up bra.

What was even more disturbing was it didn't seem like she cared that I could see her. She poured a mug of coffee, popped a half of a bagel into the toaster, and then walked back to Finn's room like everything was normal.

Alright.

I showered next and got ready for my day, and by the time I returned to the kitchen, Finn's lady friend seemed to be gone. He was sitting at the kitchen table scrolling through his phone, just in his sweatpants like any time he was home. "She seems nice."

He didn't look up from his phone, his eyes scanning from left to right like he was reading something. "Yeah? I'll take your word for it."

I sat across from him and gave him the stink eye. "She walked around nearly naked."

He set his phone down and met my gaze. "I told her you were gay."

"What does that matter?"

He shrugged. "That's probably why she didn't bother putting clothes on."

"Just because I'm gay doesn't mean I want to see a naked woman in my apartment."

A slight grin stretched across his face. "I think it livens the place up."

"Well, it's not *your* place."

"I asked if you were okay with it, and you said yes."

"Again, I didn't expect to see her parade around here like it's fashion week."

"Whatever." He grabbed his mug and took a sip. "She's gone, and you won't see her again."

"Didn't hit it off?" I opened my newspaper again.

He shrugged. "We didn't talk much."

Of course they didn't. "You aren't going to see her again?"

He shook his head. "If I bump into her again, maybe. But I'm not planning on it."

Finn had never been a one-woman kind of man. He wasn't even considered a player because he didn't pretend to be charming or interested. He was abundantly blunt about his intentions. He probably hadn't taken a woman to dinner in the last ten years. "Can I ask you something personal?"

"You can try. I probably won't answer." He sipped his coffee again then held the mug in both hands. With his ankle resting on the opposite knee, he watched me with a slightly tilted head.

"You're thirty now. Is marriage something you'll ever be interested in?"

"Wow...girl talk." He chuckled then drank his coffee again.

"Not girl talk. Just trying to get to know you."

He held the mug in his hands as he stared at me, his features giving away nothing of his thoughts behind his eyes. "My future will be identical to my past. I've always been a drifter, and I always will be."

"That didn't answer my question."

"Colt, you already know the answer."

He wanted to be alone for the rest of his life, but being handsome and mysterious wouldn't last forever. "Any reason why?"

The steam erupted from the surface of his coffee and drifted toward the ceiling. "I've been around, Colt. I've met beautiful women in all parts of the globe. They're all equally gorgeous, interesting, and wonderful. But it doesn't matter how remarkable they are. I just don't feel anything. I'm incapable of it. If I ever met a woman that I loved, I would change my tune. But not once have I ever met a woman I kept thinking about when she was gone. I'm not going to force it if it's not meant to be. I would much rather be alone than pretend to love someone when I don't." He drank from his glass then licked his lips. "Girl talk over yet?"

"I was just curious. We've been apart for so long, I feel like I hardly know you. I want to make that right." We'd been living together for a few days, but there was still this distinct distance between us. He was cold and difficult, but in time, he might warm up to me. When I told him I was gay, he didn't care in the least. That formed some kind of connection between us, but I wanted to expand that further.

He held my gaze for a long time, carefully considering his words before he spoke. "I'd like that too."

My brother wasn't as cold as I thought he was. When I put affection out there, he reciprocated—in his own way.

"When are you going to talk to Mom and Dad?"

"Hmm...that's the million-dollar question."

He gave a slight chuckle. "Don't worry about it. Regardless of what their reaction is, it won't change your life."

"Uh...it will change my life."

"Then don't let it." He simplified everything, but somehow, there was wisdom in his words. "If they really have a problem with it, that's their issue. Move on and forget about them. If they turn their backs on you, then you should do the same to them. As long as you control your emotional response to any situation, nothing can affect you."

"Meaning?"

"Think of it this way." He set his mug on the table. "You're the thermostat. The temperature will rise and fall, but your setting will always be the same. Walk in there, tell our parents the truth, and then stand your ground. Regardless of how loud they scream or how deep their disappointment, it doesn't change the way you feel—because you set the temperature."

In a complicated way, that made sense.

"I'm not a very likable guy—at least in the civilian world. You think I give a damn?"

No, not in the least. "Not really."

"You're right, I don't. Take me or leave me. There are some people who will always dislike you no matter what you do, and there are some people who will always think the world of you no matter what you do. Stick with the second group. It'll make your life much easier." Despite my brother's usual silence, he had a lot to offer. He was smart, reasonable, and loyal.

"I didn't realize you were so wise."

He rubbed his fingers across his chin. "When you've been in life-and-death situations, you filter out all the bullshit. You realize it doesn't matter. Nothing really matters." He rose from his chair and carried his mug to the sink. "I'm headed to the gym. You want to get a beer later?"

I wanted to accept his offer right away, but then I remembered I had plans. "I already have a double date tonight."

He turned off the faucet and stared at me for a few heartbeats. It seemed like he was going to say something, but then he quickly changed his mind. "Then I'll see you when you get back."

PEPPER and I walked together down the sidewalk toward the bar where we were meeting. She looked beautiful in a black dress with heels, along with her long coat with gold buttons. "All Stella and Tatum can talk about is your brother."

"Well…he makes quite an impression."

"Stella said she's gonna make a move next time she sees

him. You think he'll go for it?"

I felt Pepper wrap her arm through mine as we walked together. When we were married, we used to hold hands, but now this was the kind of affection we shared. "He's not picky, if that's what you're asking. He brought home some woman last night, and she walked into the kitchen half naked."

"She didn't know you were there?"

"No. She knew."

"She's ballsy," she said with a laugh.

"So, I'd be surprised if he said no."

"Well, that's good news for Stella. She can't stop talking about him."

"You think he's hot too?" I asked.

Pepper looked straight ahead and slid her left hand into her pocket. She didn't answer right away, probably handling the situation delicately. "He's your brother, so it's kind of a weird question, don't you think?"

I grinned. "So that's a yes."

"Well, come on," she said incredulously. "Only a gay woman would think he's not hot. I didn't know men could even be that fit. He almost looks fake."

"He works out a lot. Does a hundred push-ups first thing in the morning."

"Ooh...what time?"

I laughed. "Okay, you're right. It is a little weird."

"Then don't ask me about your brother...because you aren't going to like what you hear. I will admit he's pretty intense, though. I came by to pick up my package the other night, and it was just so..."

"Awkward? Uncomfortable?"

"No...I can't really explain it. He's just intense."

"I know what you mean. He's been that way since we

were young."

"You two are nothing alike. It's hard to believe you're related."

I shot her a glare. "What's that supposed to mean?"

"Nothing bad," she said quickly. "You're just more... approachable. He's more...scary."

We rounded the corner and approached the bar where we were meeting our dates. "So, does Jax know I'm the one you were married to?"

She paused before she answered. "No. Does Aaron know?"

"No. We barely know each other, and I didn't want to lead with that..."

"Yeah, Jax was understanding too. But I really don't want to tell him because...you know. We aren't serious, so I don't see why I have to. If it goes somewhere, I'll tell him."

"So then we're just best friends? That's the story?"

"Yeah. Cool with me."

When we walked inside, Pepper spotted Jax right away. He was standing at the bar, looking fit in a gray V-neck and dark jeans. He wore a nice watch, and his short hair was combed back. His eyes were on the TV, so he didn't notice us right away. "That's him."

I'd never met him before, so this was my first time seeing the guy. "Wow. You guys weren't kidding with the Mr. Gorgeous nickname."

"I know, right?" She led the way and walked up to her date, showing her rediscovered confidence. "Hey."

It was nice to see the old Pepper come back to life. For the last few months, her shoulders weren't straight and she slouched. She didn't have that sass that made me fall in love with her in the first place. But now all those wonderful qualities were back.

The second Jax turned to her, his eyes lit up with excitement. "Hey, sweetheart. I like that dress." His arm circled her waist, and he pulled her in for a kiss, a soft embrace that was barely appropriate for a bar full of people.

I thought it would make me uncomfortable to see Pepper kiss another man, but it didn't bother me at all. It made me happy to see a man appreciate her, blanket her in the affection she deserved.

"Thanks." She pulled away even though he wanted to keep the kiss going. "Jax, I want you to meet someone very special." She turned to me and hooked her arm through mine. "This is my best friend, Colton."

Jax must have already known I was gay because he didn't seem jealous at our affection. He gave me a handsome smile and extended his hand to me. "It's a pleasure. Pepper has told me so much about you."

I shook his hand. "Trust me, she's told me more about you." I winked.

He chuckled and dropped his hand. "So, where's your date for the evening?"

"Not sure yet." Just when I turned to the door, I saw Aaron walk inside. He was my height, and he wore a blue scarf around his neck. He shed his outerwear and placed it on the coat rack, revealing the chiseled body I'd noticed at the gym for the last few months. "Right there. And...wow."

Pepper moved back into Jax's side and ran her hand up his chest. "So, you want to get me a drink?"

"I'll get you whatever you want, sweetheart," he said as he looked down at her.

I watched Aaron glance around the bar until he noticed me. Then he gave me a brilliant smile, the kind that reached his eyes. "Hey. That shirt looks great on you." He reached for my arm and touched my bicep.

My heart rate spiked the second he touched me, that butterfly feeling millions of people described when they found love. The gesture was innocent, but the sensation was so thrilling, I couldn't wipe the smile off my face.

I was so gay.

"Thanks," I said. "Can I get you a drink?"

"You can get me a few. I had a crazy day at the salon." Aaron was a hair stylist at his own shop downtown.

Now that I knew that, I always had an excuse to see him —if my hair grew back quickly enough. "Me too. But let me introduce you to Jax." I turned back to them at the bar. "Aaron, this is Jax. Jax, this is Aaron."

Aaron shook his hand. "It's so nice to meet Pepper's boyfriend. You know, she's the one who introduced us. She's quite the lady."

Pepper made a slight face at the term boyfriend.

Jax didn't seem to care. "Yes, she's a very special woman. I couldn't agree more." He squeezed his arm around her waist and pulled her close. "You guys want to get a table? The game is on, so I know Pepper is gonna want to watch."

"Like I'm the only one," she teased.

They walked away and picked a booth.

I stood with Aaron at the bar so we could get our drinks.

"Man, Jax is a hot piece of man." He watched him at the table before he turned back to me. "And Pepper is gorgeous. They're a perfect couple."

"Yeah...I think they are." People used to say the same thing about us, that we were a match made in heaven. Sometimes when I thought about our failed marriage, I felt the regret and pain in my chest. I really had been happy with her. But now things were the way they were supposed to be.

And we still had each other.

10

PEPPER

Jax lay beside me in bed, my one-piece lingerie hanging from the corner bedpost. After he yanked it off my body, I kicked it away, and it happened to land there. His tight stomach rose and fell with his even breathing, and his slender happy trail disappeared under the sheets where the rest of his body was hiding. "That was good aim."

"Thanks. It's not about how you put the lingerie on, but how you take it off."

He rested his arm behind his head and turned his head slightly my way. "Well said, sweetheart."

He called me by that name more frequently, using it several times when we were together. I'd warmed up to the nickname since a man had never called me that before. Colton always called me babe, and I couldn't picture another man getting away with the endearment. "I need to buy some new lingerie. I'm running out of surprises for you."

"Ooh...you should borrow my credit card. Max it out."

I turned toward him and tucked my leg between his.

My arm rested in the center of his chest, and my face found a home on his shoulder. "Be careful what you wish for..."

"Trust me, there's no better way to spend my money." His large arm circled my waist, his fingers slowly moving against my back. He watched me with his pretty green eyes, a slightly playful look in his gaze.

"What about retirement? Your mortgage?"

He shrugged. "Who needs it? I'll live with my sister."

"Talk about payback."

"She deserves it." He gripped the back of my knee and hiked it up farther. "Speaking of my sister...she wants to know who my mystery woman is."

"Couldn't it be several women?"

"Nope. She figured it out."

"And how did she do that?" I lifted myself up so I had a better view of his handsome face.

"My friends ratted me out."

"Betrayal."

He shrugged. "She has a way of getting information out of people, so I wouldn't be too hard on them."

"Imagine if she knew it was me...the lingerie girl."

"She told me she liked you."

"Well, yes, as the girl who handled her lingerie party. As the woman dating her brother...I don't know about that."

"What's there not to like?" His hand glided up my leg until it rested on my ass.

"My job. I'm sure she doesn't want to picture her brother's girlfriend in lingerie."

"That's her problem, not ours. I really think she'd like you." He gave me an expectant look, like he was hoping I would offer to have dinner with her.

I definitely wasn't there yet.

He didn't press it. "I really liked Colton. How long have you two been friends?"

Technically, only about six months. "I've known him for almost six years."

"You two have a connection. I can tell by watching you together."

Because we shared everything, from our home to our bed. "He's a good guy."

"He seems to like Aaron."

"He's had a crush on him for a long time. I finally pushed them in the right direction."

"You're his coach."

"And he's mine." I rubbed my hand up Jax's chest, feeling the dissection of muscle between his pecs and stomach. He had a small patch of hair at the top, fluff that felt good against my chest when he moved on top of me.

"So, you think he likes me?"

"Yes. Very much." I knew Colton just wanted me to be happy. Seeing me move on probably gave him a great sense of relief.

"Awesome. I got the approval of the best friend."

"My other two friends like you too—even though you haven't met."

He made a thumbs up. "I'm hitting it out of the park."

I chuckled. "I guess so." I leaned over him slightly to check the time on my nightstand. It was half-past eight, and I needed to get to sleep.

Before I had to ask him to leave, he picked up on the gesture. "I should get going..." He barely hid his disappointment as he got out of bed. When he was on his feet, his entire body was visible, from his sculpted torso to his tight ass.

So pretty.

He pulled on his t-shirt then grabbed his boxers. "Can I ask you something?"

"Sure." I scooted out of bed and pulled on my silk robe. I tied it in the front then ran my fingers through my hair.

He pulled on his jeans then faced me, his handsome face full of concentration. He took a moment to think about his words before he finally said them. "Seeing anyone else?"

The question was so unexpected that I couldn't keep the surprise off my face. I'd barely started to see him. I couldn't imagine seeing another guy on top of that. "No."

"Neither am I."

We weren't exclusive, so it wouldn't matter if he were seeing someone else. I might be a little jealous, but not jealous enough to complain.

"Maybe we could keep it that way."

It seemed like my conversation about keeping our relationship light had fallen on deaf ears. "I told you—"

"You don't want anything serious. I got it. But I want you to know that I'm not seeing anyone else if you want to...skip the condoms." He fished into his pocket and pulled out a folded piece of paper. He set it on the bed then pulled on his shoes. "Just a thought." He walked into the living room to let himself out.

I eyed the paper but didn't open it, already guessing what it said.

I followed him into the living room and walked him to the door. "I'll think about it."

He turned around to kiss me goodnight before he walked out. "Goodnight, sweetheart." His hand cupped my cheek, and he kissed me softly on the mouth, his affection deep and throbbing.

Whenever he kissed me like that, I forgot about all my insecurities. I forgot that I was newly divorced and starting over. I just kissed this beautiful man and felt good inside. "Goodnight."

He opened the door and walked out.

I stayed in the doorway and watched him go, seeing the way his jeans hung low on his hips. He had a perfect butt, the kind I liked to claw when he was on top of me. When he was out of sight, I turned to step back into my apartment.

But then I spotted Finn.

Shirtless and barefoot, he moved down the hall slowly with his arms hanging by his sides. He came from the direction of the trash chute, so he'd probably just made a drop-off before getting ready for bed. He eventually stopped in front of me, his hands resting near his pockets. He had the perfect figure, enormous shoulders, long arms, and manly hands. His tattoos couldn't disguise the complicated webbing across the surface of his hands. Thick cords were in his neck too because his body was so phenomenally tight.

Just looking at him made me feel out of shape.

Like any other instance when we were in the same space together, it became eerily quiet. Packed with enough tension that could reach every corner of the room, we seemed like two opponents on the battlefield. He had no reason to dislike me, so his heated intensity came from somewhere else.

He was a man of few words, and it didn't seem like he was going to say anything now.

It was still so hard to believe he was Colton's brother— they were nothing alike.

When he knew I wasn't going to speak first, he said something. "Colton had a good time tonight."

"It seemed like it." He and Aaron had fallen into quiet conversation, sticking to themselves instead of conversing with Jax and me. There was subtle touching and a few laughs. Colton seemed nervous, but as the night progressed, he loosened up.

"I admire you." The compliment fell out of the sky without warning. It struck the earth and made me slightly unbalanced. He said it with such sincerity in his blue eyes that there was no mistaking how much he meant it. He rarely spoke, so he made every word count. "Going through all this couldn't have been easy for you. Most women would have hated Colton for what he did—and no one would have blamed you for it. You've got a big heart and a fiery resilience."

It was a sweet thing to say, and I didn't realize how much it meant to me until I heard it from his lips. "Thanks..."

"Now you're still friends... That's even more impressive."

"Love is love, right? Whether we're married or just friends, I'm spending the rest of my life with him. I hope I don't live across the hall from him forever," I said with a chuckle. "But I hope we're always this close."

"You will be." He slid his hands into his pockets and stepped closer to me, standing in front of my door exactly where Jax had been moments earlier.

I tried to focus my eyes on his face, but my gaze wanted to drift over that inked body, to see the art as well as the muscle. "Do you ever wear a shirt?" I blurted, my mind working quicker than my rational brain.

The corner of his mouth rose, creating a boyish smile. He never grinned the way Jax did, showing all of his teeth in a true smile. He seemed incapable of it. But the partial smiles seemed more endearing. "No. Not really."

I finally lowered my gaze and stared at his military tags. There were two of them on a single silver chain. His name, ID number, and address were chiseled into the metal. Behind that was the canvas of ink he displayed. Everything seemed to have a military theme, from soldiers in battle to the red cross symbol. His body was a historical record of everything he'd endured. I lifted my gaze back to his. "You never take them off?"

His hand reached up and gripped both tags in his fist. He squeezed it gently, his knuckles stretching with the moment. "Night and day, this chain has hung around my neck for the last ten years. I couldn't imagine taking it off." He released the tags and returned his hand to his pocket.

I glanced at the necklace again before I met his gaze. "Your tattoos are beautiful."

His eyes dilated slightly, like my compliment meant something to him. "You really think so?" Maybe he was challenging me, expecting me to find the depiction of war to be despicable.

Maybe it was an insensitive thing for me to say, but I wouldn't take it back. "Yes. It's who you are." I was in my lilac silk robe, my hair probably messy and my makeup smeared from rolling around with Jax, but I didn't feel awkward standing in front of him. My arms crossed over my chest, and I was suddenly aware of how naked I was underneath the material. My nipples pressed into the fabric even though I wasn't cold.

"A lot of people don't like who I am."

"Why?" I whispered, finding this man to be utterly fascinating. His withdrawal made me want to pull him closer. His coldness made me want to warm him.

"They think I'm selfish. Think I'm an asshole."

"You don't seem like a man who cares what other people think."

He tilted his head slightly, examining me deeper. "I'm not. But I know they're right."

"I don't know about that..."

"I do," he whispered. "But when you've seen what I've seen...it's just easier to stop caring."

My eyes softened when I heard his confession. He was a strong man, but he was clearly broken on the inside. He was speaking to me openly, a complete stranger, because whatever weighed on his mind was so heavy. "You were good to Colton when he told you the truth."

"Because I'm loyal. But loyalty doesn't make me a good man."

"Compassion, love, and friendship do—and you have all of those qualities."

When he took a deep breath, his shoulders rose slightly as his chest expanded. His eyes narrowed further, his expression darkening to the point where he looked angry, but the rest of his body implied he was touched instead. "Baby, you don't know me."

The endearment washed over me, and I didn't stop it. It felt like the warm water of a bath, so soft and inviting. If any other man spoke to me that way, I would shut it down and walk back into my apartment. But coming from him, a man I hadn't even known a week, it felt normal. "I know you well enough."

I WENT across the hall in the hope I would find dinner.

As if I'd had a sixth sense, Colton pulled the pan of enchiladas out of the oven. "You have the nose of a bloodhound."

"No. Just a hunch." I pulled the plates out of the cabinet and set them on the counter with the utensils. I purposely tried not to look for Finn, but it seemed like he wasn't in the apartment. "Will your brother be joining us?"

"He's at work. I'll save him some."

"Ohh...he started at the hospital today?"

"Yeah." He served the enchiladas onto the plates, and then we sat at the kitchen table.

"Did he seem nervous about it?"

Colton chuckled in response. "If my brother gets nervous, he doesn't show it."

I told Colton everything, but I didn't mention my conversation with Finn last night. It seemed too intimate to share with someone else. There was an unspoken connection between us, an energy that I couldn't describe. It was borderline supernatural because it was inexplicable. "I'm sure he had a good day."

"After taking care of soldiers in the field, working in the ER is probably boring to him."

"Maybe." Or maybe it reminded him of his time in the military—and haunted him. "So, anything happen with Aaron last night?"

Colton's grin was answer enough. "He came over."

"Ooh...details."

"We went into my room and fooled around. Then he left this morning."

"Did you have him walk around naked as payback? Since Finn had that naked girl over?"

He chuckled. "No. But that's a good idea."

"So...how was it?"

"Well, I told him this was new to me, so he took it easy. There was kissing and some clothes came off."

"Wow. Sounds hot."

"Yeah...it was." A redness burned in his cheeks. "I hope that doesn't make you uncomfortable."

"Not at all." I scooped a cheesy bite of the enchiladas

into my mouth. "I'm with Jax like three days a week now, and things are going well. Don't even worry about that."

"Great, I'm glad to hear that." He took a few big bites before he drank his soda. "Looks like good things are happening for both of us."

"Yes...good things."

~

I WAS JUST ABOUT to head back to my apartment when the front door opened.

In blue scrubs that were loose-fitting around his body, Finn walked through the door. A black stethoscope hung around his neck, and the deep V in the front of his shirt showed his muscles and tattoos. Despite working a twelve-hour shift, he didn't seem the least bit tired. A satchel made of brown leather hung over his shoulder.

"How was your first day?" Colton asked. "I saved you some dinner."

Finn carried his stuff to the counter, where he fished out his wallet and keys and set them down. "Thanks." When he turned to give us his attention, his eyes fell on me. When he wore all blue, it brought out the brilliant color of his eyes even more. "And it went well." He marched into the kitchen and pulled out a bottle of scotch before he filled a short glass.

I'd hardly ever seen him drink beer. He usually went for the liquor right away.

"That's all you're going to give us?" Colton asked with an attitude.

"Do you give me a more detailed answer when I ask about your day?" He downed the glass as he watched his brother, his ink moving all the way down his arms to his wrists. The metal of his necklace could be seen along his neck, but the tags disappeared under his shirt.

Colton made an angry face. "But my job is boring."

Finn returned the bottle to the cabinet. "So is mine."

"Yeah, right," Colton said sarcastically. "You save lives."

"And I also don't save lives." He opened the fridge and pulled out the plate Colton had saved for him. He popped it into the microwave, pretending his last statement wasn't as heartbreaking on his ears as it was on ours.

I was in my pajama bottoms with a loose-fitting t-shirt, so I didn't exactly look my best. But when I crossed the hall to spend time with my gay ex-husband, I didn't bother making myself look nice.

Finn heated up his food before he joined us at the table. "This looks good."

"I got the recipe from Pepper," Colton explained. "She used to make it all the time."

"And I think your version is better," I said with a smile. It was the only thing I knew how to make, and of course, he improved it.

"So, did you like it at the hospital?" Colton said. "You want to keep working there?"

Finn rested both arms on the table and ate quickly, like he hadn't gotten dinner that night because he was so busy. "We had so many patients that people were parked in the hallways. The doctors couldn't see people fast enough. There wasn't much time for chitchat."

"Well, you don't like chitchat," Colton teased. "So you must have loved it."

Finn kept eating, practically inhaling his food. "Pepper, this is good."

"Thanks," I said, even though I didn't deserve the compliment.

"I'm the one who made it," Colton said in offense. "And you're welcome, by the way."

"But she invented it." He wiped his mouth with a napkin. "You thank the scientist who discovered the antibiotic, not the doctor who gave it to you." His plate was wiped clean, and all that was left were a few streaks of sauce. He crumpled up the napkin then carried the plate to the sink. He washed it and placed it in the dishwasher like the perfect roommate.

It took me years to train Colton to do those simple tasks, and even then, he still chose to disregard his training.

Colton rose to his feet and left his empty beer bottle behind. "I guess I'm going to bed. I'll see you tomorrow, Pepper."

"I should hit the sack too." I rose to my feet and pulled my hair over one shoulder, suddenly feeling Finn's gaze on my skin. When I glanced at him, his stare was focused on my face. Instead of looking away, he kept up his stare, his eyes unblinking. I refused to back down, so I held his gaze, unsure what kind of stare-down we were having.

He turned his gaze back to his brother. "I have someone coming over. I'll make sure she wears clothes this time."

"Who's coming over?" Colton blurted.

"A nurse from the hospital." He washed his hands in the sink then stepped out of the kitchen.

"I thought you didn't have a chance to talk to anyone at work?" Colton questioned, behaving like a parent interrogating their son. He even put his hands on his hips.

Finn shrugged before he headed into the hallway. "I didn't."

"So Colton and Aaron are heating up?" Stella sat across from me in the booth at the bar, still in her workout outfit because she just got off work. Her usual attire was spandex shorts, a bright-colored sports bra, and a loose tank top that revealed most of her skin. Her hair was pulled into a tight ponytail, and even though she didn't wear makeup, she looked stunning.

"That's what he said. They headed to his place after our double date."

Stella watched me with her hand resting under her chin, giving me that pitiful expression full of concern. "Are you okay?"

"Yeah, I'm fine," I said weakly. I'd known this day would come, and now that it was here, it was hard to believe we had been married at all.

She cocked an eyebrow. "Are you really?"

"I guess now that it's happening, it truly feels real. But really, I'm okay with it."

"It's gotta be hard...seeing your ex move on."

"Yeah, but I have Jax. So I shouldn't care what Colton is doing."

"How's it going with him?"

"Good." The last time we spoke, he suggested us ditching the condoms. I hated latex as much as everyone else, but that seemed like a more serious relationship...even if it was just about comfort.

"You like him, right?"

"Of course I do. I just feel like he keeps wanting to move our relationship faster."

"Because he's so into you," she said. "There are worse problems than a beautiful man wanting you."

"Yeah, but I don't want to jump into another relationship so soon after my divorce."

"Girl, it's been like seven months now."

"Even so, it just seems strange. I go from being married into another relationship? Shouldn't I date a few guys in between?"

"Maybe. Or maybe you can skip all that. Jax seems like a great guy."

"He is..." He truly was wonderful, but all I wanted to do was hit the brakes. There wasn't that pull that I felt with Colton. I assumed it was because I just wasn't emotionally ready for a commitment. Maybe if I were in a better place, I would feel differently. Or maybe I only liked guys who were wrong for me—gay men in particular.

"He's gorgeous, rich, affectionate...what more do you want?"

"I don't know. I just haven't felt that feeling."

"What feeling?" she asked, taking a drink of her cosmo. "He doesn't make you climax?"

"No, not that feeling," I said as I rolled my eyes. "He gives me that feeling all the time. I'm talking about that big crescendo in your chest, those butterflies in your stomach, that cheesy I'm-falling-in-love feeling."

"Well, it's only been a few weeks," she countered.

"I felt that the first night I met Colton."

"And he turned out to like dudes." She squashed my confession with her hard words. "Just because you don't feel that way with Jax right this second doesn't mean you won't feel that way eventually. You're still recovering from a very painful divorce. Give it some time."

"You're always right, Stella." I tapped my glass against hers.

Stella's eyes wandered around the bar, and when she saw something she liked, she stilled, like a leopard about to strike its prey. "Ooh...I spy something sexy."

I turned around and spotted Finn standing alone at the bar, a scotch in his hand. He looked at the TV in the corner, his dark jeans fitting snugly over his tight ass. His shirt stretched across his shoulders, highlighting the beautiful muscles that framed his spine.

"He's alone, so I'm gonna make my move." She straightened her shirt and fixed the flyways that came loose from her tight ponytail. "Do you mind if I ditch you? You know I'm all about hoes before bros—"

"Unless there's an orgasm in sight," I said with a chuckle. "Yes, you have my permission. But I should warn you, that guy is one hell of a ladies' man. He's only been staying with Colton for a few days, and he's already brought two women back to the apartment."

That information didn't bother Stella at all. "That just means he knows exactly where everything is—and that's exactly what I'm looking for." She rose from the booth and left her drink behind. "Wish me luck."

"You aren't going to need it." When Stella threw herself at Finn, he would take the offer immediately. No guy would say no to Stella. She could have any man she wanted, not just because of her looks, but because of her confidence and intellect. I watched her approach Finn at the bar then engage him in conversation.

He pivoted slightly her way, his drink still in his hand. One hand slid into his pocket, and he listened to whatever line she fed him. A slight smile formed on his lips, and he said something in response.

I felt like I was spying, so I pulled out my phone and texted Colton. *Stella is throwing herself at Finn right now. Don't be surprised if you see her walking around your apartment naked tomorrow morning.*

I'll let Zach know. He'd love to see the show. Where are you right now?

Hopkins.

If she's putting the moves on him, what are you doing?

Drinking. I didn't prefer the fruity drinks the girls got. At the end of a long day, I always liked the taste of cold beer against my tongue. It wasn't too strong, and I thought the foam was the best part.

A guy is gonna start hitting on you any minute.

You flatter me. Colton thought I was a beautiful woman, but not every man in the world agreed.

I'm serious. A woman like you can't be alone in a bar for more than five minutes without getting a free drink.

Well, I paid for the one I'm drinking now.

"Ugh."

I looked up at the sound of Stella's voice. My eyes had been glued to my phone because I'd been talking to Colton with so much focus. The last thing I'd expected was for her to come back so quickly. "Ugh, what? What happened?"

"He turned me down." She grabbed her glass and took a long drink, nearly finishing the whole thing.

Not possible. "Are you sure?"

"No doubt."

Finn didn't strike me as a picky guy. If a beautiful woman wanted to jump his bones, he was at their service. "What did you say to him?" Maybe she didn't make it clear she wanted something casual. Maybe she made it seem like she wanted a relationship—and he definitely wouldn't be into that.

She slammed her drink down. "That I wanted to get on all fours so he could screw me from behind. He smiled and said he was flattered, but he didn't take the bait. I can't believe he turned me down. He didn't seem even slightly interested."

"That is weird..." Why would Finn turn down easy sex? He had a woman at his place last night, but I doubted that would change anything. "What exactly did he say?"

"That he had plans for the evening." She rolled her eyes. "Yeah...okay."

"Maybe he did have plans for the evening."

"Well, I asked if he was free any other time this week, and he said he wasn't."

Ouch. So he really did turn her down. "Don't let it bother you. His problem, not yours."

"I know. It's just a bummer because he's sooo hot. Men aren't built like that around here."

"You could still find someone better."

"Maybe." She pulled a ten out of her clutch and set it on the table. "I should get going. I've got a shower to take then a date with my vibrator."

"You could get a date with a real man if you wanted." The room was packed with men watching the game. She could have her pick of the crop.

"Nah. I can't handle another disappointment." She rose from the booth then patted my hand. "Thanks for trying to make me feel better. You've always got my back, girl." She blew me a kiss before she walked out. She walked right past Finn, who had his back turned to her as he watched the game. She flipped him off without him seeing then walked out.

I chuckled then looked back at my phone again.

Colton had texted me. *You turned quiet. That must mean you're enjoying a free drink right now.*

Finn turned her down.

Say what? No way.

Couldn't believe it either.

Strange. Maybe he's seeing that nurse again.

Maybe. Wouldn't Finn have just told Stella that if that were the case?

"Looks like you need another drink." Finn sat across from me and placed the frosty glass in front of me. It was the same IPA I'd been drinking. Mine was nearly empty, the foam long gone and the liquid nearly at room temperature. He'd refilled his glass of scotch, and now his fingers were wrapped around it like he couldn't let it out of his sight.

I locked my phone without taking my eyes off the beautiful man across from me. The shadow on his jaw was gone because he'd shaved that morning. His tanned skin stretched over his nice cheekbones, and his full lips looked soft like two rose petals. The sleeves of his t-shirt stretched over the large muscles of his arms, a beautiful compilation of biceps, triceps, and sexy skin. His ink matched the color of his shirt, making him look like the ultimate bad boy every good girl should stay away from. "You made a mistake. Any man would kill to be with Stella."

There wasn't a reaction in his eyes, an agreement or disagreement. "She's a beautiful woman. Just not my type."

"Not your type?" I couldn't stop the laugh from escaping my throat. It was the most ridiculous statement I'd heard all day. "What's not your type? Her perfect body? Her tight little shorts? Her long brown hair? Her confidence? Her good heart?" Maybe I was biased because I'd known her for so long, but she was definitely a catch.

His eyes stayed with mine as he brought his glass to his lips for a drink.

I waited for an explanation.

It didn't seem like I would get one. "What's your type?"

The question caught me off guard. "Uh...I don't know."

He took another drink before he set his glass on the table. "I wanted to ask you for a favor."

"After you turned down my friend?"

His eyes narrowed. "I don't hand out pity fucks."

I laughed again. "She definitely doesn't need a pity fuck."

"Why do you want me to screw your friend so bad?" He turned more aggressive than before, his face so stern, it seemed like he was on the brink of war. I could easily picture him in the military, wearing a uniform and barking orders with pure authority.

"Why don't you want to fuck my friend so bad?"

"Maybe because she's my brother's friend, and that would be inappropriate."

"Well, trust me. Colton doesn't care. I texted him through the whole exchange." I half expected Finn to rise out of his seat and chase after Stella, but he still didn't take the bait.

"I don't want her." He ended the conversation with the finality of his tone. He had so much power in his silence, so much unquestionable authority that I didn't challenge him. "Can I ask for that favor now?"

I masked my unease by taking a drink of the new beer he'd brought me. This man unnerved me, whether he was calm or aggressive. It didn't matter what his attitude was, he always had the same effect on me. "Sure."

"I'm getting the keys to my new place soon. Want to help me pick out furniture?"

I hadn't been sure what he was going to ask me, but that was the furthest thing from my mind. "What makes you think I'm qualified?"

"You're my only girlfriend."

"Girlfriend?" I asked, immediately confused by the label.

"Yes. A friend who's a girl."

Why did I assume otherwise? "Colton is gay. He has good taste."

"I disagree with that." He rubbed his forefinger around the rim of his glass, lightly touching the vessel with his callused fingertip. His eyes were on me, so he was unaware of the two women at the bar that kept looking his way. "I prefer you. But if you aren't interested, that's fine with me."

I worked with lingerie and designed my own store. I also put everything together at my new apartment, picking out the furniture and painting the walls myself. I even built my own cabinets. Perhaps Colton had mentioned that to him. "I would love to. And I would also love to see your new place."

"We can swing by now if you want. Unless you have plans tonight."

I hadn't contacted Jax since our last conversation, and he hadn't contacted me either. Perhaps he realized I needed space. "No plans."

"Alright. Let's go." He downed the rest of his glass in one gulp before he rose to his full height, six-three of pure masculinity.

I couldn't down my IPA like he did, so I settled for a sip before I left the cash on the table. To every woman's dismay, I walked out of the bar with Finn beside me, the ruggedly handsome and perfect man standing so close, I could feel his arm against mine. The first time he brushed up against me, I felt the warmth of his skin, how smooth it felt when it swept past me. I got a hint of his cologne, the scent of pine needles that made me think of the forest. I had enough exposure to him to feel how hard he was, how those muscles formed concrete because they were so tight and thick. I felt him in a way I hadn't before.

And I somehow felt closer to him.

THE TAXI DROPPED us off in front of the house.

I found it ironic that Jax lived just down the street. Finn would drive right past his house every day on his way to the city. It was a nice neighborhood, the ideal place to raise a family away from the bustling sounds of the cars, pedestrians, and canneries. Finn wasn't the family kind of guy, so maybe he was looking for the peace and quiet.

The house itself was gorgeous. Two stories with a manicured lawn, it had three large trees, a two-car garage, and a nice porch out front. The house was settled back away from the road, so the plants and trees kept it somewhat secluded. And if you were quiet enough, you could actually hear the waves from the bay. "Finn...this place is beautiful."

"Thanks." He walked past the SOLD sign and headed to the front door. He greeted his real estate agent and introduced me before we were allowed inside.

The double doors opened into a nice foyer, a staircase that led to the second floor. To the left was the living room, surrounded by a solid wall of glass that showed the large backyard. It must have been remodeled because it had a sleek and modern look to it. The kitchen had a space big enough for a dining table, and the kitchen itself was huge, having an island and lots of counter space. Not to mention, there were two ovens. "Uh...I'm in love with your house."

Finn took me upstairs and showed me the bedrooms. There was the master, an office space, and two bedrooms.

This house must have been insanely expensive. I wasn't sure how he could have afforded it, even as a physician. He must have been given a big bonus from the military...or he had another trick up his sleeve.

Finn followed behind me as he watched me take it all in. "Have any ideas?"

"Well, for starters, it's so beautiful that you could probably get any furniture you wanted and it won't matter." I examined the freshly painted walls and the hardwood floors. "And anything will go with these floors. You found a really great place, Finn. I might have to move in."

He came to my side and flashed me a half smile. "Not the worst idea I've ever heard."

I headed back downstairs and into the living room. "You can fit a lot of couches in here. Perfect for having a ton of people over for the game." I turned back to him, watching him stand near the fireplace with his arms crossed over his chest. With those jeans that hung low on his hips, he looked like a man who belonged on a billboard more than in a uniform.

"Where should we start? Don't say IKEA."

I chuckled. "No. This place needs something more elegant than that."

"Not Pottery Barn either," he said. "More masculine than that."

"We can make that work." When we were finished looking around, we walked out and the real estate agent locked the door behind us.

"When will the place be yours?" I asked as he waited for the Uber to pick us up on the sidewalk.

"Not for another two weeks. I'm waiting for a few more inspections, like mold and the integrity of the trees surrounding the property."

"You must be anxious. That place is so beautiful."

"I'm glad you like it."

"Has Colton seen it?"

"Not yet." He slid his hands into the pockets of his jeans

as he looked down the road. "I was planning on having him over when the furniture is ready, my parents too." It had been a sunny day in Seattle, but the lack of clouds made it even colder. Finn didn't seem bothered by the weather, even in his light t-shirt and jeans.

I wore a thick sweater, but I was still cold. "Excited to see your parents?"

He kept his gaze focused down the street even though our Uber was still two minutes away. "Yes. My mother will be really happy when I tell her I'm settling down here. She's been worried about me since the day I left for the military. Now she'll sleep better at night."

"Yeah...I can't even imagine."

"My dad has been more supportive about it, but he'll be happy too."

"Having your whole family within a twenty-mile radius is exciting. I know Colton loves having you home."

"Really?" He turned his head toward me, his complexion even more beautiful under the direct sunlight. "I assumed he was getting tired of me."

"Not at all. He hates that he really doesn't know you that well, that for the last ten years he's only seen you three times."

Finn kept staring at me, his gaze impossible to read but his intensity clear. His words indicated how detached he was, but when he looked at me like that, it had to mean he cared—at least a little bit. "It's crazy how quickly time passes. I was always so busy, so it passed even quicker for me. I grew apart from the people I used to know. Marriages, kids, birthday parties...I missed everything." Instead of looking away once he admitted his vulnerability, he continued to look at me, not the least bit ashamed of everything he'd just said.

My heart ached for him. "Why did you decide to join the military?"

"It's what I was meant to do." He kept it vague, only sharing a very small part of himself. "It was where I belonged."

"Then why did you leave?"

He showed a sign of hesitance, like he didn't want to answer. "It was time."

"What does that mean?" I had no right to press him on his answer. I'd only known him for a week, but I treated him like he'd been friends much longer. As if I had some kind of special leverage over him, I used it to my advantage, just the way a girlfriend would pester me about my mood until she finally got her answer.

He gave a slight shrug of his massive shoulders. "I've seen a lot of things. When you're exposed to that world for so long, it starts to mess with your head. Dreams turn into nightmares, and innocent gestures somehow seem hostile. Some men are too ashamed to admit when they've had enough, but they pay the price later. I thought it was best to step down...when I was still sane." He turned his gaze to the sidewalk beneath his large feet. Now he wore his heart on his sleeve, but he didn't seem to be uncomfortable doing that with me. We hardly knew each other, but we were standing outside his new house talking about something extremely personal.

I wished I could tell him I understood how he felt, but that would be an insult to his experiences. Someone like me, who sold lingerie out of a boutique store, had no grasp of warfare, death, and terror. "You made the right decision, Finn. You served your country for a long time, and we're all grateful for it."

He lifted his gaze again and looked at me, those blue

eyes so pretty, it was amazing how intense they could appear. "Thanks, baby." Again, he used that endearment, a nickname spoken between lovers. A man had never called me that before; it was always sweetheart or babe. It rolled off his tongue so easily, like he couldn't imagine calling me by anything else.

"Why do you keep calling me that?"

His strong physique didn't cower at the question. He pivoted slightly toward me, his body facing mine head on. With one step, he was closer to me, directly in front of me so a whisper would be audible on my ears. He kept his hands in his pockets, but his proximity was so intense, it seemed like his arms were wrapped tightly around me. He was nearly half a foot taller than me, so he had to bend his head down to share his whisper. "Feels right."

*Z*ach and I were playing a video game while Finn was at work.

"Take that, bitch." Zach stomped his fingers against the controller, making his character slam his fists into my face.

I used my special boost power to throw him off me. "You'll have to do better than that, *bitch*."

We didn't take our eyes off the TV until the match was won.

Zach raised his controller into the air then dropped it like a mic. "That's how it's done."

"Hey, don't drop those. They're like sixty bucks." I picked it up off the floor and set it on the table.

"Oh, sorry. So, how's it going with Aaron?"

"It's going." We texted back and forth, but nothing serious had happened.

"Sex?" he asked.

No. I still hadn't gotten laid. "Not yet."

"Does he know this would be your first time?"

I nodded. "I mentioned it."

"Well, hopefully, you get laid soon. You must be going crazy."

We did other things when Aaron came over the other night, and that would definitely hold me over until the time was right. "Stella made a move on Finn, but he turned her down. She was pretty ticked about it."

Zach looked so shocked, he couldn't even speak. His mouth hung open like a dog waiting for a bone. "Finn is gay?"

"Wait...what? That's not what I said."

"A man would only turn down Stella if he was gay. Come on, she's gorgeous. Those curves and that smile..."

"You're forgetting all the other women he brings back to the apartment."

"Oh yeah..." He finally shut his mouth and rubbed his chin. "That's a good point. Then he must just be stupid."

I shrugged. "I was surprised too."

"If Stella wanted to fuck me, no way in hell would I say no."

"I don't get it either."

"Have you asked him about it?"

I shook my head. "He's been working a lot, so I haven't seen him."

"Well, you should ask him because maybe he's in the middle of a serious breakdown or something. The only reason a man would say no to Stella is if he were in the middle of something really tragic."

Zach had always told me how hot Stella was. They'd been friends for a long time and Stella wasn't immune to his attraction, but nothing ever happened. They were either too good of friends, or she wasn't attracted to him—even though other women thought he was hot. "I'll ask him when he gets home."

"You should do that. I kinda want to punch him in the face for being so stupid...but I'm also glad he didn't sleep with her."

"Why don't you just ask her out?"

He laughed loudly, as if the suggestion were ridiculous. "Like she'd say yes to me."

"You don't know until you try."

He finished off the rest of his beer before he stood up. "I guess I'll get going. Do you know if Finn plays basketball, by any chance?"

"No. Why?"

"Was thinking of getting people together for some friendly games. You know, since the weather has been so nice."

"I could ask him."

"Cool." He gave me a high five then left.

About an hour later, Finn walked in the door. Wearing blue scrubs, he stepped inside and removed his shoes by the door. He removed his stethoscope and placed it in his satchel before he hung it by the door. "How's it going?" He pulled his shirt off right away and let it hang over his shoulder.

"You hate wearing clothes, don't you?"

He chuckled as he opened the fridge and scoured for leftovers. "Is this spaghetti taken?"

"All yours." I left the couch and joined him at the counter.

He put it in the microwave then moved to his stash of scotch in one of the cabinets. He added a single large ice cube to the glass then filled it with liquor.

"I've never met anyone who drinks that much hard liquor."

He brought the glass to his lips and took a drink as he

stared at me. He finished, licked his lips, then released a satisfied sigh. "You should join the military, then. People would call you a pussy if you drank anything else."

"I think they would call me a pussy for another reason."

He smiled slightly then took the spaghetti out of the microwave. He dug for a fork in the drawer then stood at the counter and ate it. My apartment had been a lot cleaner since Finn started to live with me. Not only did he clean up after himself, but he did all the household chores. There were never dishes in the sink, dust on the tables, and the laundry was always done.

"Just because you're staying with me doesn't mean you need to clean the apartment all the time. You're my guest. Let me clean up after you."

He finished chewing his bite before he released a quiet chuckle. "That's not why I do it, Colt."

"Then why do you do it?"

"Habit. I was trained to be clean all the time. When I see a dirty apartment, I have to tidy up. It'll nag at me if I don't."

"Then you should live with me forever."

Finn chuckled again. "Not enough money in the world, man."

"I don't know...you get free food."

"I know how to cook." He kept eating as he stood beside me, his physique so fit that it seemed like he hadn't eaten pasta in his entire life.

"I have yet to see it."

"I've been working a lot."

"You have time to clean but not to cook?" I crossed my arms over my chest.

He set his fork down and looked at me. "You got me. I'll make something tomorrow night. Invite Pepper over. We'll make it a family affair."

"She's my best friend, not my wife."

"She still has our last name, right?" He dug into his spaghetti again.

"Yeah, but that's because she's too lazy to change it."

"Or maybe she doesn't want to change it. It's a good last name." He finished his plate of spaghetti then started washing the dishes in the sink. "I know I'm not gonna change mine."

I watched him put everything in the dishwasher before he wiped down the counter, his shirt still hanging over his shoulder. "So, you turned down Stella?"

He grabbed his glass and took another sip as he faced me. "Another round of girl talk, huh?"

"Or just two brothers talking."

He shook the ice cube in his glass. "She's not my type, man."

I laughed because it was ridiculous. "I'm a gay man, and even I know she's a hot lady. How can she not be your type when you don't have a type? You'll bring any woman back to the apartment who hits on you."

"Not any," he corrected. "Stella is a perfect example of that."

"I'm just shocked. You know I don't care if you sleep with her. She's a big girl and can make her own decisions."

He drummed his fingers against the counter. "Look, I just wasn't into her, okay? Let it go." He finished his scotch then dumped the ice cube into the sink. After he rinsed out the glass, he added that to the dishwasher.

"I just find it strange." I crossed my arms over my chest and stared him suspiciously. "Unless you have a girlfriend?"

He grinned as if the suggestion were absurd. "No girlfriend."

"Then—"

"This conversation is over." He walked around me, his muscular shoulders shifting back and forth as he moved. He wasn't venomously angry, but his aggression shut down the conversation. "I'm gonna take a shower. You need to get in there first?"

"I'm good."

He disappeared down the hallway.

A moment later, Pepper walked inside. She glanced at the floor and noticed Finn's shoes and satchel before she came farther into the apartment. "Hey, how'd that big case go?"

"It went well." My boss usually picked me last for assignments because he didn't like me. Since we billed clients based on the number of hours we put in, when I didn't get work every day, it affected my paycheck. I really should just leave and find another job.

Pepper's eyebrow was slightly raised, like she didn't believe me but she wasn't going to harass me about it. She joined me in the kitchen then opened the fridge. "Ooh...spaghetti."

"Yes, you can have some," I said in a bored voice.

"I didn't ask." She piled it onto a plate and popped it in the microwave just as Finn had a few minutes ago. "Finn asked me to help him decorate his new house."

He asked Pepper? "He did?"

"Yep." She grabbed a fork from the drawer then watched the plate spin in the microwave. She looked like an impatient child, too anxious to wait the final thirty seconds before she could eat.

When did that happen? "That's random."

"He said he doesn't have any girlfriends."

"But he can hire a decorator."

"Maybe," she said. "But I suspect he's looking for human

interaction. Made it sound like that's something he's been missing."

My brother hardly said a few words to me, but he confided all of that to her? "I'm good with decorating...and I'm easy to talk to."

She gave me a sad look before she rubbed his arm. "He thinks the world of you, Colton."

"He said that?"

She squeezed me before she let go. "Pretty much."

"I'm just surprised that the two of you kinda have your own relationship now."

The microwave went off, so she retrieved her food and started to eat it with a fork. "It just happened. Maybe he's trying to get to know me because he didn't have a chance when we were married. We're divorced now, but since we're so close, maybe he sees me as still part of the family."

"You are part of the family, Pepper. Always." Regardless of what happened with our love lives, we would always be together. We would always spend the holidays together, take vacations together, and even have our kids play together. I would have a husband and so would she, but we would be as united as ever.

"I know." She smiled before she took another bite.

Finn came back into the room wearing his sweatpants, while drops of water still sprinkled his chest from the shower. His hair was damp, and he ran his fingers through it.

Pepper stopped eating for a second, her eyes moving to his wet body.

"So you want Pepper to help decorate your house but not me?" I demanded.

He grabbed a glass from the cabinet then filled it up with water from the refrigerator. It was a miracle he was drinking that instead of scotch. "Do you want to help?" He took a long drink, his throat shifting as he got the water down. When he was finished, he wiped his mouth with the back of his forearm.

"Well...no. But it would have been nice to be asked."

He came to my side and set down the glass. "Alright. You wanna help me move?"

"No."

"There we go." He took another drink again then looked at Pepper. "I'm cooking dinner tomorrow night. Join us."

She'd stopped eating the second he walked into the room, so now her attention was completely focused on him. "I would love to, but I already have dinners plans with Jax..." She lowered her gaze back to her spaghetti.

Finn kept up his stare, but it somehow turned darker, more intense. He didn't just seem disappointed with that answer, but furious with it. "Bring him along."

Okay, maybe he wasn't mad.

"Really?" she asked, turning back to him with surprise.

"Yeah," he said. "As a thank-you for helping me with the house."

"Wow." Since it was late in the evening, her makeup was already gone and her hair was pulled back in a loose bun. She wore a loose-fitting sweater and black leggings, looking ready for a yoga class. Whether she was dressed up to hit the town or dressed for a night in, she always looked pretty. "That's generous. I was gonna help you for nothing." Not only was she easy on the eyes, but she was the easiest person in the world to talk to. I could tell her anything. Even when I broke her heart and told her I wanted a divorce, she was selfless and understanding. That's what I thought every time I looked at her, that she was the perfect woman.

"I'd like to do something for you anyway," Finn said.

"After all, you've put up with my brother all this time. Now you're putting up with me."

"There's nothing to put up with. You guys are both wonderful." She finished her food then placed the dishes in the sink. "Finn, don't touch these. This is Colton's problem." She poked me in the shoulder before she left the kitchen. "I'll see you guys tomorrow."

"Night," I called after her.

Finn watched her go, his eyes following her closely until the door was shut behind her.

"So what are you making for dinner?"

Finn kept staring at the door, like it might open again and Pepper would return. "Is it serious?"

I glanced at the door then turned back to him, having no idea what he was talking about. "The dinner? It can be casual. It doesn't need to be—"

"Pepper and Jax. Is it serious?"

"Uh…I don't think so. She wants to keep it casual, but he keeps trying to make it more serious. He seems pretty into her."

"And is she into him?" Finn turned back to me, his stare hostile and his body language cold.

Finn rarely expressed interest in anything, so this conversation was even more peculiar. "Why?"

"Just curious."

This still was completely unusual. I had an assumption in my head, but it seemed so crazy, I almost didn't voice it. "You don't…have a thing for Pepper…do you?" That would be the most uncomfortable situation in the world, having my brother hook up with my ex-wife. I wasn't jealous of her with Jax, but I certainly wouldn't like to imagine my brother being in places that used to be mine. Plus, he was the kind of man you wanted to have stay away from the woman you loved, not get closer to her. I held my breath as I waited for the answer, praying my brother wouldn't turn my world upside down by crossing a line that should never be crossed. There were millions of beautiful women out there. She was the one woman off-limits. "Finn?"

He finally answered. "No. But I respect her a great deal. She's been through a lot and deserves a great man, not some dipshit pussy."

"Well, he seems nice to me."

"Women aren't looking for nice. They're looking for a man—a real man." He dismissed the conversation by walking away and heading back down the hallway. Even his walk was full of aggression. I couldn't see his face, but I imagined it looked similar to his body—pissed off.

12
_____

PEPPER

As soon as Jax walked inside, he scooped his hand under my hair and kissed me softly on the mouth, greeting me like it'd been a long time since we'd seen each other. We hadn't spoken in four days, and that was because I was busy working and researching furniture for Finn. But I was also avoiding Jax because of the last conversation we'd had.

He wanted to skip the condoms.

If we were both clean, I didn't have a problem with that. But then that would make us monogamous, and monogamy in any form was serious. Serious was the last thing I was looking for. It seemed like he was trying to rush me into a relationship indirectly.

He rubbed his nose against mine before he pulled away. "I started to get worried there."

"That I dropped you?"

"Yes."

"If I did, I would have the courtesy to tell you."

"Well, that's a relief...I guess." His hands gripped my hips as he stood in jeans and a long-sleeved maroon shirt.

The fabric fit his sculpted body well, covering him like a glove. "But I hope you never have to tell me at all." He looked into my eyes with his green ones, his affectionate words heavy with their implication. "My question didn't scare you off?"

"No. But I do have my answer."

"Please be yes..." He closed his eyes for a second. When he opened them again, he grinned.

"My answer is no." I didn't want to put him down, but I didn't want to mislead him either. He couldn't be upset with me when I'd been forward about my demands from the beginning.

He sighed in disappointment.

"That would mean we were monogamous. Monogamy is too serious for me right now."

"I'm not sleeping with anyone else, and neither are you."

"Be that as it may..."

"Do you want to sleep with someone else?" he asked. "Because I think I'm doing a pretty good job in there." He nodded toward the bedroom. "So you could keep being satisfied by me until you're ready for something new. In the meantime...we could make it more enjoyable."

I hated condoms as much as the next person, but I believed in my principals too much. "I'm sorry."

Instead of showing his disappointment again, he let the conversation die. "Alright. So, where are we having dinner?"

"Colton's place."

"And his brother is making us dinner?"

"Yeah. I've been helping him decorate his new home. It's his way of saying thank you."

"Well, that's nice of him. Where does he live?"

"He's staying with Colton until his place is ready."

"Alright. I like Colton, so it'll be nice to see him again."

"As long as you're with me, you're going to be seeing a lot of him." Like every day. I walked out of my apartment, and Jax came with me. When we stood side by side, he grabbed my hand and held it during the immensely short walk across the hall.

I tapped my knuckles against the door before we stepped inside.

Finn stood in the kitchen as he worked over the stove. Hot pans were sizzling, and a delectable smell wafted our way. His back was turned to us, and surprisingly, he had a shirt on. It might have been the only time I'd ever witnessed him clothed in the apartment.

Colton was on the couch, so he stood up to greet us. "Hey, babe." He hugged me then kissed me on the cheek. "You look really nice. I like this dress on you." He referred to the olive-green sweater dress I wore. It had sleeves and reached to a spot right above my knees. I wore black pantyhose underneath with my black boots. A black scarf was around my throat even though we weren't going outside.

"Thanks, Colt." He used to say things like that to me every day when we were married. It was one of the reasons I never figured out he wanted to sleep with men instead of me. Now I realized he was just being affectionate, admiring my clothes more than the way they fit my body.

"She looks great in everything she wears," Jax said. "And doesn't wear."

I slapped him on the wrist playfully. "Jax."

"What?" he said with a laugh. "You do."

Colton made an awkward face, probably because he had seen me naked, but Jax had no idea. "Finn won't let me help in the kitchen, but he must be doing fine because it smells great."

"It does smell good." I crossed the living room and

ventured into the kitchen where Finn was working. There were spices in the air, along with the scent of tender meat cooking on the stove. "I hope it's not going to be much longer because I don't think I can wait."

Finn washed his hands then dried them with a towel. He turned to me first, but instead of giving me a hug the way Colton had, he just looked at me. We'd never embraced each other with more than a handshake. For some reason, the idea of touching felt inappropriate.

He looked at Jax next, and his inviting gaze quickly clouded over. "Finn." He extended his hand to shake Jax's.

"Jax." Jax took it, and with his real estate agent persona, he smiled and shook Finn's hand. "Thanks for having us over. I'm glad Pepper is helping you with your house. I get a free meal out of her hard labor."

I smiled at the joke. "I guess dating me comes with serious perks."

"A lot of *perks*." Jax smiled at me, exchanging an inside joke that wasn't difficult for everyone else to decipher.

Finn abruptly dropped his hand. "Hope you like tacos."

"Are you kidding me?" Jax said. "We have taco Tuesday every week at the office. I wish every day was taco Tuesday."

Finn seemed to get bored with Jax and turned to me. "What can I get you to drink?"

"Water is fine."

Finn didn't look at Jax when he addressed him. "What about you?"

"Beer is good with me," Jax answered.

Finn poured the glasses and handed them over. "Just a few more minutes."

Jax and I moved to the kitchen table and sat down with Colton. I sipped my water and watched the guys drink their beer. They fell into a conversation about Jax's job as a real estate agent. I studied Finn for a while, watching him move around the kitchen and prepare everything.

"I'm gonna ask if he needs a hand." I excused myself from the table.

The guys kept talking about an apartment that sold in Seattle for a whopping twelve million bucks.

"Can I help with anything?" I spotted the sliced limes on the cutting board, the hot tortillas the bowl, and the garnish he already had ready to go. There was homemade guacamole, along with rice and beans. "Damn, this looks really good."

Finn flipped the steak in the pan before he grabbed the plates from the cabinet. "Do you actually want to help me? Or are you just coming in here to sneak a bite?" His tone was much more playful than it had been a second ago, so I knew he was teasing me.

"Both?"

He gave me a faint smile before he set the plates on the counter. "Put four tortillas on each plate and add the side garnish. I'll bring the steak in a second."

I scooped the rice and beans onto each plate before I set the tortillas on one side.

Finn came back a moment later with the diced meat and scooped it into every tortilla. "You know what to do next."

I put the cheese, salsa, sour cream, and guacamole on each one, along with a pinch of lime.

Finn placed the hot pans and dishes in the sink before he washed his hands again. "You want to serve the plates? I'll be there in a second."

I carried two plates to Jax and Colton.

Colton's tongue practically fell out of his mouth. "Holy shit, Finn can make this? He's been living here for a week and didn't bring this up until now? I've been cooking every night when I could have been eating like a king?"

"I wouldn't have cooked for you anyway." Finn carried the last two plates into the kitchen, setting them down at our chairs. "I made this for Pepper."

"Even though I let you live here rent-free?" Colton challenged. "Let you bring a bunch of babes to my apartment?"

Finn had a glass of scotch with him, the only drink he ever seemed to enjoy. The arguments his brother made didn't appear to affect him. "I can just take those tacos back, if that's what you prefer. I'm sure Pepper will eat them."

"I'm on it." I grabbed Colton's plate and started to drag it toward me.

"Whoa, let's take it down a notch." Colton took it and put it back in front of him. "You won't be able to fit into your dress if you eat these."

Jax waggled his eyebrows. "That works for me."

Finn's mood dived noticeably. His eyebrows furrowed, and he stared at Jax with annoyance.

"I can't believe I didn't know you could cook like this," Colton said. "You continue to surprise me."

"You haven't tried it yet," Finn said. "So you may be disappointed."

Colton picked up a single taco, placed it into his mouth, and took a big bite. He chewed slowly, and after the flavor exploded in his mouth, his eyes rolled to the back of his head. "Shit, this is good."

"Yeah, I know." An arrogant smile emerged on Finn's lips.

"Is this how you score chicks all the time?" Colton asked.

Finn took a bite of his food and never answered the question. He didn't even look at his brother as he chewed, looking at me across the table instead. "Any selections yet?"

"Actually, yes." I pulled out my phone and pulled up the pictures I'd saved on Pinterest. "What do you think of this?" Since he smelled like pine needles, I found a line of furniture that had earthy tones and an outdoor feeling. It didn't resemble something you would find in a cabin, but it was still pregnant with the outdoors. Finn seemed like a manly man, someone who liked to hike outside and be close to nature. His home was near the bay, along with the trees and the quiet. Seemed like the perfect design. I slid the phone toward him.

He picked it up and flipped through the pictures. His eyes were focused, and he ignored his food as he swiped through. He was impossible to read, so I couldn't tell if he liked anything or hated everything.

Colton kept eating, seeming to forgive his brother for ignoring him.

Jax addressed Finn. "Where's your new place?"

Finn didn't take his eyes off the phone. "Near the bay. Off Clover."

"No way," Jax said. "I live just down the street from you. What a coincidence."

Finn lifted his gaze, but he didn't share Jax's enthusiasm. He turned back to the phone then handed it back to me. "I like it."

"Really?" I asked, not expecting to solve this problem so quickly. I had spent a lot of time thinking about what he might like. There were a lot of different themes he could have used in that house, but I tried to find something that reflected his personality as closely as possible.

"Yes," Finn answered. "We should order it soon since it'll take a few weeks to get here."

"Good idea," I said. "We can do that after dinner." Hopefully, he had a big enough credit card for us to order all this stuff. He'd bought a large house, which meant we needed a lot of furniture to fill it.

Jax had inhaled two of his tacos while Finn and I spoke. "Damn, these are good. Where'd you learn to cook?"

Finn shrugged. "With experience."

"So, what do you do for a living?" Jax followed up with another question, barely taking a break from his food to ask it.

"I'm a doctor." Unlike when Finn spoke to me, he hardly made eye contact with Jax, like he was just some annoying person he had to deal with. Finn wasn't the warmest person in the world, but he seemed to be putting Jax at a distance on purpose.

"Cool," Jax said. "What kind of medicine do you practice?"

"Emergency medicine," Finn answered as he picked up another taco. "I work at the hospital down the road from here." With both arms on the table, he kept eating, his large hands working to hold his food as he ate. It was strange to see him stretching his shirt as he moved because I was used to seeing him without a shirt on. Now it was just strange to see him completely clothed. "I did my medical training in the military. I was just recently honorably discharged so now I'm pursuing a career in medicine."

"You were in the military?" Jax asked in surprise. "That's awesome."

Finn turned cold instantly, just like any other time this topic was mentioned. He hated talking about his time serving in the armed forces. It was surprising he'd mentioned it to me at all.

"How long were you in for?" Jax asked. "What branch did you serve? What was the—"

"Finn doesn't like to talk about it." Now that I understood Finn better, I knew he was emotionally scarred by his experiences. He never actually said it, but I knew he'd seen war firsthand. He was a strong man who carried himself with pride, but his demons clearly ate at him every single day. The last thing he wanted to do was talk about it like it wasn't a big deal.

Finn's eyes softened slightly as he looked at me. Then he gave a slight nod in my direction.

It seemed like we had our own connection, our own relationship.

Jax backed off. "Sorry, man. I should have been more sensitive."

Finn didn't accept his apology. "What do you do?"

"I'm a Realtor," Jax said. "I've been in the business for ten years. I know pretty much everything about all the homes in Seattle. Makes me friends with almost everyone. What Realtor did you use?"

"Tim Coonce," Finn answered.

"He's good," Jax said. "He's an honest guy. Some Realtors are two-timers, will bring you to an overpriced house just to make you think about raising your bid on a different house. But in reality, that first house is purposely overinflated and not really on the market."

"Are you one of those Realtors?" Finn asked bluntly.

"Me? No," Jax said quickly. "I wouldn't be in the business this long if I were pulling tricks like that."

"When am I going to see the place?" Colton asked. "Does it have a basketball hoop?"

"Actually, it does," Finn said. "In the driveway."

"Awesome," Colton said. "I don't like to watch the sport, but I don't mind playing it. What about a pool?"

"No pool," Finn said. "But there's a hot tub."

"Ooh...that will be fun." Colton always ate his food

quickly, so his plate was wiped clean. Anytime a hot meal was placed in front of him, it wasn't there very long. The exception to that was my cooking—because I wasn't very good at it. His mother was a homemaker, so she knew her way around the kitchen like a badass. Must have been where he picked up on it.

"That neighborhood has an excellent school system," Jax continued. "It's not even private."

Finn finished his food then focused on his scotch. He was the only one drinking hard liquor at the table, and he seemed like the only one that could handle it. "I bought it because it's a quiet neighborhood. I'm not a big people person."

"You don't say," Colton teased.

Jax nodded in agreement. "It's definitely quiet, so you picked the right place. But good thing we aren't neighbors, because when the guys come over, we get a bit loud. We usually play ball in the driveway every weekend."

The longer the conversation continued, the more annoyed Finn seemed to be. He didn't care for Jax—it was written all over his face. Finn turned his gaze on me, and while Jax talked his ear off about the neighborhood, he kept his concentration on my face. He focused on my silence instead of Jax's words. Colton was oblivious to the heated connection between our eyes because he was listening to everything Jax had to say too.

I probably should have been listening to Jax, but instead, I found myself stuck in the trance between Finn and me, falling into those blue eyes and whatever thoughts burned behind them. I found myself more affected by his presence than Jax's. He said so little with his words but so much with his eyes. Maybe it was just his persona, but his mysterious-ness made him even more interesting. I told myself I was only attentive because he was Colton's brother, but now I started to wonder if there was something more there.

Something that had been there since the moment we met.

⌇

"You said no?" Stella asked in surprise. "I hate condoms. Why subject yourself to the torture if you don't have to?"

Tatum sat across from me with her beer on a coaster. We were gathered at our favorite bar, and Colton and Zach were on the way. "I agree. They slow everything way down. A romantic moment could be totally shattered when you have to strap something on."

"It just seems so intimate." The only man I hadn't used a condom with was my husband. It seemed strange going commando with a guy who wouldn't be around forever.

"Since when did you become a prude?" Stella asked. "If it's the two of you, what's the problem?"

"Because it'll get more serious," I argued. "I don't want anything serious right now. I feel like Jax is trying to push it on me without being obvious about it. I don't understand why. It seems like most guys are about hitting it and quitting it, but he's been stuck to my side since we saw each other at the lingerie party."

"And you're complaining?" Tatum asked with a raised eyebrow. "Do you have any idea how many guys I've hooked up with that I wished would stick around? All the hot ones never want to commit because they don't have to. They just find the next sexy woman and keep going."

"And Jax is hot," Stella said. "He's so into you."

"I have no idea why," I said honestly. "When I told him I was divorced, I expected him to dump me."

"Uh, you're a bit dull," Tatum said. "You're super gorgeous. Men everywhere are rejoicing that you're on the market again. Jax is excited to have scooped you up. He's not gonna care that you're divorced. He's *relieved* you're divorced."

My friends were always so good to me. "Well, that's a nice thing to say—"

"It's true," Stella said. "Jax wants to grab you while he can. Of course he's doing everything to keep you. Can't blame him."

That would be insanely romantic if I weren't still so broken. I still hadn't felt that distinct pull that I did with Colton. I liked Jax and was attracted to him, but my feelings didn't stretch beyond that. I found it unlikely that a few more months of good sex would change much.

"Do you want to keep playing the field?" Stella asked.

Finn's handsome face popped into my mind right away, but I had no idea why that happened. "I'm not sure."

"If you aren't sure, then you probably want to keep dating Jax," Tatum said. "He's such a catch, so you should keep trying. Give it more time."

I did like him. I just didn't love him. "Alright."

Stella changed the subject right away. "Has Finn said anything about me?"

"He's not really the kiss-and-tell kinda guy." He only talked about Stella when I prompted him to.

"Well, there was no kissing," Stella said with attitude. "Unfortunately."

"I asked him why he didn't go for it," I said. "He just said you weren't his type."

"Wasn't his type?" Tatum hissed. "If Stella isn't what he's looking for, then what exactly is he looking for?"

"Thank you, girl." Stella clinked her glass against

Tatum's. "What the hell is his problem? I hear he sleeps with anything that moves, but I don't make the cut?"

"I don't know," I said honestly. "It didn't make a lot of sense, but he shut down the conversation."

"Whatever," Tatum said. "You don't need him."

"I don't," Stella said. "But it sucks to get rejected... I've never been rejected before."

Tatum narrowed her eyes. "Don't rub it in, alright?"

"I wouldn't read too much into it," I said. "Finn is a peculiar guy. He's very quiet and withdrawn...says he's not a big people person."

"Well, I didn't ask him to dinner and then a party," Stella said. "I just asked for sex. Last time I checked, there's not a lot of talking during sex."

"Depends on who you ask," Tatum said. "I was with this one guy that did talk a lot. We didn't date very long."

Colton and Zach walked into the bar, both looking handsome in their t-shirts and jeans. They hit the bar first before they joined us in the booth.

Zach scooted into the seat beside Stella. "So...I heard through the grapevine Finn turned you down."

Stella gave him a mean look then grabbed her drink. "You want me to throw this drink in your face?"

He gently placed his fingers against her wrist and slowly lowered the glass back down to the table. "No. But since it didn't work out with him, I wanted you to know I was available. I know my way around a bedroom. I've got great references. Colt, tell her." He nodded to Colton.

Colton made a disgusted face. "No, I don't!"

"You know what I mean," Zach said. "Tell her what Katie said about me after we broke up."

"Ohh..." When Colton understood what he meant, he

relaxed. "She said she missed the sex most of all. Had pretty good things to say about him."

"See?" Zach waggled his eyebrows at Stella. "You don't need Finn, not when you've got me." He pointed his thumb into his chest.

Stella had been ambushed with a sexual invitation, but she kept her cool. "Don't you think that would be weird since we're friends?"

He shrugged. "Doesn't have to be weird if we don't make it so. And we were never very close anyway."

Stella's lips lifted into a smile. "You really want to get laid, don't you?"

"Oh, I can get laid," Zach said. "But I want you to be the one to lay me."

She turned back to her drink and pressed her lips to the glass, smearing her lipstick against the edge. She took a long drink.

The rest of us sat there and watched the soap opera unfold.

Stella finally gave an answer. "I'll think about it."

"Ooh...that's not a bad answer," Colton said.

"I'll take it." Zach clinked his beer against Stella's.

I watched as my two friends played a very dangerous game. They didn't seem compatible, but Stella was still recuperating from her rejection so she probably needed a pick-me-up. And Zach wanted to have sex with the most beautiful woman in the bar that night.

IT WAS toward the end of the night, so I allowed myself one more beer before I cut myself off. If I had too much alcohol after midnight, my stomach would hurt all through the night.

Tatum was talking to some guy on the other side of the room, and Stella was watching Zach flirt with a woman across the room. Colton had disappeared somewhere, maybe finding someone he liked.

"You think I should go for it?" Stella asked, still staring at Zach.

"If you want to."

"But do you think it's a bad idea?"

"Of course, I think it's a bad idea," I said with a laugh. "He's your friend. That could get messy."

"Yeah, but Zach is hot...I just never gave him a chance before."

I viewed Zach like a brother since he was Colton's best friend. He'd been off-limits since the very beginning. Even if I wanted to be with him now, Colton would never be okay with it. It would be seen as a betrayal. "Then go for it. That woman is gonna sink her claws into him any minute."

"You think he's playing hard to get?" She kept drinking from her glass even though it'd been empty for the last fifteen minutes.

"No. He just wants to get laid."

She did it again, lifting the glass to her lips and wiping off the last of her lipstick. "I want to get laid."

I finally pulled the glass away from her. "Alright... enough of that."

"You know what? I don't like Finn."

"Yeah..."

"He's a dumbass who's too stupid to know what he's missing." She flipped her hair over one shoulder.

I was surprised she was taking his rejection so personally. "Yeah..."

"I think I'm gonna go over there." She grabbed my beer, took a drink, and then slid to the end of the booth to stand up.

Finn appeared out of thin air, looking sexy as hell in his denim jeans and gray V-neck. His ink made him a bad boy, and his dog tags hanging from his neck made him a badass. With dreamy eyes and a hard body, he was gorgeous—from head to toe.

Stella got to her feet and flashed him a menacing look. "You aren't even that hot anyway," she blurted, so drunk she didn't even realize what she was saying. "You think you're so sexy with your tattoos...and your military tags...and those blue eyes." Her hand reached up to his bicep, and she started to feel him up right in the middle of the bar.

Finn watched her and let her do whatever she wanted, his eyebrow slightly raised as he looked amused.

I had to save Stella from this humiliation. "Stella, weren't you going to talk to Zach?"

"Oh yeah." She stopped feeling up Finn and slapped his arm instead. "He wants this." She pointed to her tits. "All. Of. This." Then she walked off, her heels tapping against the hardwood floor as she stormed off.

Finn watched her go and couldn't wipe the smirk off his face. He slid into the booth across from me and helped himself to my beer. "That was interesting."

I watched her move into Zach and block the woman he was talking to. "I should probably get her home. I haven't seen her this drunk in a long time."

"I'm sure Zach will take care of it."

"Well, she's in the process of throwing herself at him."

Finn turned and watched the scene, seeing the way she could barely walk in her sky-high heels. "I don't think you need to worry about that."

Zach hooked his arm around her waist, and with the aid of Colton, they helped her outside and into a cab.

As much as Zach wanted her, he wouldn't take advantage of her when she couldn't even walk in a pair of heels. "At least it's not my problem. When Stella is really drunk, she gets frisky."

He continued to hold on to my beer, his interest piqued. "Yeah? She's put the moves on you?"

"More times than I care to admit."

His eyes smoldered. "Yeah?"

I nodded. "It always happens when I'm putting her to bed. She takes off her clothes and then tries to kiss me."

Now he was absolutely still, not even breathing, and his eyes were about to pop out of his skull. He couldn't process what I'd just said, so he sat there idly. His beer was forgotten, and even his heart seemed to stop beating.

I chuckled at his reaction. "Painted you a picture, huh?"

"Did you let her kiss you?"

"God, no," I said with a laugh. "I know she doesn't mean it."

"And if she did mean it…?"

"I'm definitely, absolutely straight. So no, I wouldn't have let it happen."

As the disappointment faded from his eyes, he took a drink of my beer. "How's your night been?"

"Good. We just came out for a few drinks."

"Pick up any dates?"

"Me?" I already had one man in my bed. I didn't need two. "No."

"Are you and Jax exclusive, then?"

"No," I said quickly. "We're just fooling around."

He nodded slightly then took another drink of my beer. "And he knows that?"

"I've told him many times. He wants more."

"Can't blame the guy. You don't like him?" He sat forward, resting his powerful arms on the table as he looked at me. His ink was still noticeable under the dim lighting, and his thick arms could never disappear in the shadows. He had a lot of wonderful qualities, but his best features were in his face. Those eyes were startlingly blue, and that bone structure was too masculine for even Clint Eastwood.

He asked me a lot of questions about my personal life, diving deeper and deeper into a subject I only shared with Colton and my friends. "I like him. I'm just not looking for something serious. I haven't even been divorced a year. It's way too soon to start a relationship."

"It doesn't seem like he cares."

"He doesn't know the whole story..." I lifted my beer from his hand and took a drink, not caring that we were sharing fluids with each other.

"What part of the story is he missing?" He could go up to the bar and order his own beer, but he chose to sit across from me, splitting a beer that was already at room temperature.

"He doesn't know Colton is my ex-husband."

"So he thinks he's just some random dude?"

I nodded.

"Which means he doesn't know why you got divorced."

"Exactly." If I didn't confide that important piece of information to Jax, I didn't see how we could start a real relationship. "If things get serious, I'll tell him. But I'd rather keep that piece of information to myself as long as possible."

"You shouldn't be embarrassed about it."

"Well, I'm a human being. And yes, I'm embarrassed about it." Telling the world my husband left me because he liked other men hurt my desirability. It ripped me in half, made me less of a woman. Not all people thought that, but most people did.

He shook his head slightly. "A real man isn't going to care, baby. So you may as well tell Jax to figure out what kind of man he is."

"Why do you keep calling me that?" He only called me baby when we were alone together. It was an intimate nickname for two people who were just friends. There was a chemistry in the air between us, but sometimes I wondered if that was just his mysterious persona and my attraction.

He pulled the beer back toward him. "Because I like it."

The more time we spent together, the more I felt our connection deepen. It didn't seem platonic, but it didn't seem sexual either. But it certainly wasn't the kind of relationship I had with Zach or any other guy friend. A simple explanation could be he was Colton's brother, so I naturally felt a pull toward him. Or maybe that connection was deeper than that, more carnal than that.

I really didn't know what to think anymore.

13

PEPPER

I t was Sunday morning, so I went across the hall to see what Colton was doing. Knowing him, the football game would be on, and he would have beer and snacks. Most of the time when I stopped by his apartment, I was foraging for food rather than seeking his company.

But that was fine since he'd divorced me. I considered it to be reparations.

I walked inside and heard the sound of the game on the TV. The Seahawks were playing the Niners. It would definitely be a good game.

Finn was sitting on the couch alone, in his signature sweatpants and his hard-as-a-rock chest. A beer sat on a coaster, and his knees were wide apart.

I glanced around the apartment in search of Colton, but he didn't seem to be in sight. "Colt here?"

"No." Finn stood up and turned around to look at me. His tanned skin covered prominent muscles, making him look like a photoshopped model rather than a real person. "He went to Zach's place."

Probably because there was no food in the kitchen and he was too lazy to go to the store. "That cheap ass."

"I've got a sandwich in the fridge. We can split that."

"That's nice of you, but—"

"Come on, I can't finish it at all anyway." He entered the kitchen and pulled out the sandwich. It really was too big for a single person. It was an ultimate deli sandwich, sixteen inches long and stuffed with produce, meat, and cheese.

"Wow, you weren't kidding."

He sliced it into pieces then placed it on a couple of plates. "Beer is in the fridge."

I grabbed one and twisted off the cap.

Everything was carried back into the living room, and we sat on the couch together. We both watched the game, him sitting on one side of the couch while I stuck to the opposite side. The limited distance between us wasn't enough for me to stop thinking about how sexy he looked shirtless.

I could never stop thinking about it.

"You know, it's cold in Seattle," I said. "You should put on a shirt."

He kept his eyes on the TV. "I run hot."

Hot was an understatement.

Whenever the game became really intense, he sat up and rested his elbows on his knees. He wasn't afraid to call out the ref for the fouls, and he only seemed to make conversation during the commercials.

"Good game," I said.

"It's gonna be close." He finished the rest of his sandwich before he sat back against the couch. Even when he was sitting, his stomach was perfectly flat. He just ate a huge sandwich and he was on his third beer, so I didn't have a clue where he stored the calories.

"Do you work out a lot?" I blurted.

He turned to me, a cocky grin on his face. "Yes. Why?"

"Look at you." I pointed to the table. "Three beers and a large sandwich. Where does it go? You have no body fat."

He chuckled then turned back to the TV. "I run every morning then lift weights in the afternoon."

"That doesn't sound too crazy."

"It's about two hours a day of work."

"Whoa…" I couldn't do anything for two hours—besides nap. Walking to and from work was the only exercise I got. "That's commitment."

"I've been doing it for the last ten years, so it's routine at this point."

"Well…that's a really good routine to have." I lifted boxes in the back of the store and was on my feet all day taking care of customers. By the end of the day, I was tired—and I hadn't really done much.

The commercial ended and we returned to the game. We were both Seahawks fans, so there was no issue with who we were rooting for. If you lived in Seattle and you weren't a Seahawks fan…you were in trouble.

Finn moved on to his fourth beer.

"No scotch today?"

"It's Sunday," he said with a shrug. "Trying to take it easy."

"By drinking a six-pack by yourself?"

He turned to me, a slight smile on his lips. "You're one to talk. You've already had three."

"That's only half a six-pack—and I'm stopping for the day."

"Come on, you can do more than that. You strike me as a woman who can hold her liquor well."

"I can hold it better than most…"

"I would love to drink a bottle of scotch with you." His arm moved over the back of the couch, and instead of watching the game, he had eyes for me instead. His playfulness slowly subsided, and a dark gleam emerged in his eyes. As always, he stared at me with an intensity that rivaled the sun. No man ever looked at me that way. Not Jax or even my ex-husband. But Finn did it flawlessly, like it was the most natural thing in the world.

My pulse quickened in my neck, and I felt a thrill creep down my spine. My breathing changed slightly, but hopefully not enough for him to notice. He suffocated me without touching me, invaded my space without even leaning in close. Finn had a paranormal effect on me. He took the path through my eyes to reach my body and soul. Zach and I never had these staring contests. Even Colton and I didn't.

But Finn and I certainly had something.

It'd been there since the beginning. Was it lust? Was it infatuation? Was Finn just bored and wanted something he couldn't have? Or was there a genuine connection between us, a synchronization of our bodies, hearts, and minds. "Am I the only one who feels something here?" It was a bold thing to say, to blurt that out right to his face. But I felt comfortable with him, like I could say anything at all with no repercussions. I'd just asked my former brother-in-law if he felt the chemistry between us, and if he said no, it would be humiliating. But if he said yes, that might be even worse.

He set his beer down without watching his movements. Then he slowly shifted on the couch closer to me, his eyes unblinking throughout the entire exchange. He stopped right beside me, and the only time he pulled his eyes away from mine was when he glanced down to look at my lips.

I stopped breathing.

He held my gaze again, searching my expression for my permission or denial.

I had no idea what my expression looked like, but I could easily get up if I wanted to. I could just say it was a bad idea. I could have not brought up the subject in the first place. I didn't realize how much I wanted this until our eyes were locked like this.

"No." His voice was deep, masculine, and so sexy it didn't sound real. "You aren't the only one." He brought his face close to mine as his hand moved to my thigh. His large fingers squeezed me through my jeans, his grip tight and his veins protruding. His other hand snuck up on me and gently pulled the strands of hair away from my face. For a man so rough, he was so gentle. His fingers dug into my hair and pinned it back from my cheeks, just so he could get a better look at me.

He hadn't even kissed me yet, and it was the best I'd ever had.

He directed my head against his and rested his forehead against mine. He was dead silent, his warm breaths falling over my cheek. Pine needles were even more fragrant in my nose. It was the closest I'd ever been to him. I hadn't even hugged him before. Now I was cradled against him like he owned me.

He stretched it out as long as he could, teasing both of us with the unbearable wait.

It only made me want to kiss him more. The logical woman inside me knew this was wrong. He was Colton's brother—and there was no way he would be okay with this. But that reasonable woman wasn't available at the moment.

She was too busy waiting for that kiss.

Finn finally went in for the kill and pressed his lips to mine. The landing was soft and gentle, his full lips fitting perfectly against mine. His hand tightened around my hair, and he released a moan so quiet I wasn't sure if I heard it. It resembled the quiet growl of a bear, a carnal sound that emerged deep in his throat.

My eyes closed, and I felt the static of electricity between our lips. When he gently pulled my bottom lip into his mouth, I nearly forgot to breathe. My hand immediately went to his shoulder, and I flinched when I felt how strong he was. There were rocks under his skin, not muscles. My other hand moved to his chest, feeling the searing-hot skin that made my lips tremble.

Jesus.

His hand fisted my hair tighter as his movements became more aggressive. He breathed into my mouth deeper before he took control of my mouth. They opened. Closed. Sucked. Licked. He gave me his tongue and breathed into me again.

There wasn't a single thought in my head. I fell into the kiss, experiencing a high that was borderline Zen. My fingers explored his body freely, tracing the outline of the muscles of his shoulders all the way down to his hard chest. My palm pressed against him, and I could feel his beating heart. Slow and steady, it was a beautiful drum. My fingers fell farther and savored the grooves of his eight pack. He was a beautiful man, but he felt even more beautiful by touch.

"Pepper." My name had never sounded so sexy on a man's lips. His voice was full of desire, full of lust and unbridled longing. He suddenly ended the embrace then grabbed my legs. He pulled them down the couch, forcing me onto my back. Then he moved on top of me, his heavy weight making me sink into the cushions. He yanked one leg over his hip and held himself on top of me with one arm as he kissed me again.

My head was in the clouds, and I savored the greatest kiss I'd ever received. My fingers slid into his short hair, and I moaned into his mouth. Our lips continued to move together like this wasn't our first embrace, like we'd been doing this our entire lives. His tongue danced with mine before he pulled it away and sucked my bottom lip hard into his mouth. I was smothered with his heated kisses, his sexy physique, and the lust that made us both pant.

When he changed his position on top of me, I felt it.

All of it.

Thick. Long. Unmistakable.

I gripped his lower back and pulled him harder into me, wanting to feel that length right against my clit.

Oh god, that felt nice.

His hand cupped my face as he continued to kiss me, showing me the moves he must have put on so many other women. It was no surprise he got action whenever he wanted it.

Who would turn him down?

Poor Stella. She had no idea what she was missing.

The sound of the doorknob turning was audible over our heavy breathing, and then the door swung open.

Finn stopped kissing me but remained absolutely still. The back of the couch blocked us from view from the doorway. Maybe if we were really quiet, we would get lucky and Colton wouldn't spot us.

Oh god, Colton. He would flip if he saw this.

A betrayal—from both his brother and his best friend.

"Finn?" Colton called into the apartment as his footsteps tapped against the hardwood floor.

Finn kept his eyes on me, but he didn't move.

Even now that we'd been caught, I wanted to keep kissing him. What was wrong with me?

Colton's footsteps disappeared down the hallway.

Finn quickly hopped off me and helped me to my feet. He took me by the hand and guided me to the front door. Then he opened it and closed it like we'd just walked inside. "Follow my lead."

My heart was beating so fast. I was terrified Colton would figure this out and storm out of the apartment. I'd never been a good liar, and I wouldn't be able to start now.

"Oh good." Finn spoke a little louder as he walked into the apartment. "The Seahawks are still winning."

"Oh yeah," I said in forced agreement. "Look at that."

He walked to the fridge and opened the door. "You want a beer?"

Yes, I needed alcohol. "Please."

Colton walked back into the living room. "Oh hey. Did you just get here?"

"Yeah." Finn twisted off the cap to both beers. "We went down the hall to get more beer from Pepper's fridge."

Colton bought the story instantly. "Good. She mooches off me all the time, so it's nice to get something from her." He grabbed one of the beers that had already been in the fridge and twisted off the cap. "Were you guys watching the game?"

"Yeah. I came looking for you, and then we just started watching it." I felt the heat rush to my cheeks as the guilt suffocated me. I felt like he could see right through me, and now that the heated moment had passed, I realized how wrong it was.

I couldn't believe it happened at all.

"I was watching the game at Zach's," Colton said. "But then his TV kept cutting out, so we decided to come back here."

"Where is he now?" I asked.

"Picking up more beer," he said.

Good thing they didn't walk in here together. Zach would have headed right for the couch, and we would have been caught in the act.

"You guys wanna order a pizza?" Colton asked as he pulled out his phone. "I haven't eaten lunch today."

"Yeah, sure," I said weakly, even though Finn and I already split a sandwich—and a kiss.

"You can invite Jax over too if you want," Colton said. "I just like to watch the guys in the tights, but I'm sure he actually appreciates the sport."

I hadn't thought about Jax once in the last few hours. All I'd been thinking about was Finn, and now I knew the exact definition of his package. A single afternoon could change your life so permanently. "I think he already has plans..."

Colton walked to the couch and sat in front of the TV. "I wish they didn't have to wear all those pads. Their muscles would be easier to see."

Now that Colton's back was turned to us, Finn stared at me with the same heated expression—along with a dash of relief.

I still didn't know how we'd managed to pull that off. Colton was either really dense, or he trusted us so much that the thought didn't even cross his mind. I grabbed my beer and joined my best friend on the couch—wanting to put as much as distance between Finn and me as possible.

14

PEPPER

F inn and I didn't cross paths for a few days.

I was busy at work, and when I wasn't at work, I didn't stop by Colton's apartment.

I wasn't necessarily avoiding Finn, but I wasn't going out of my way to see him either. At some point, we'd have to talk about what happened, but it seemed like neither one of us was in a rush to make that happen.

How would that conversation even go?

What exactly did he want from me? Just an easy lay? Did he want something more?

I really had no idea.

Jax asked me out a few times, and when I couldn't dodge his calls anymore, I agreed to have dinner with him tomorrow night. There was no reason to feel guilty for kissing Finn when Jax and I were just fooling around, but I still felt like I'd done something wrong.

I hadn't decided if I was going to tell him or not. It wasn't like I'd slept with Finn.

Would I have slept with him if Colton hadn't come home?

I'd like to believe I would have put a stop to it, but at the time, I couldn't even recite the alphabet if someone asked. My mind was completely filled with the sexy half-naked man on top of me. The second I felt his long length pressed against me, all I could think about was having that monster cock inside me.

I was sitting on my couch staring at the TV without really watching it when someone knocked on the door. It was a single knock, loud and distinctive. If it were Colton, he would just walk inside the way I welcomed myself into his apartment.

That meant it was Jax or Finn.

But I suspected it was Finn.

I was just in my sweatpants and a loose-fitting sweater, but I didn't have time to change and make myself more presentable. There wasn't a drop of makeup on my face because I'd been in a hurry that morning and hadn't had the chance.

It was biting me in the ass now.

I opened the door and came face-to-face with the man I'd been expecting.

Finn was dressed in his blue scrubs with a stethoscope around his neck. His satchel was hooked over one of his large shoulders. The deep cut in the front of his scrubs showed some of the muscles of his chest—along with a hint of his ink.

I kept my hand on the doorknob and stared at him, unsure what to do next. Once those blue eyes were fixed on me, it was hard to think logically. At least I wasn't jumping into his arms and wrapping my legs around his waist.

Wordlessly, he invited himself into my apartment. He dropped his satchel on my couch then turned to look at me, his hands resting on his narrow hips.

I shut the door and faced him, surrounded by the silence that alerted us we were completely alone together. I crossed my arms over my chest, like that would somehow protect me from this powerful man.

He still didn't say anything.

I didn't say anything either. Where were we supposed to start? We'd spent the last four days ignoring each other, but dodging each other couldn't last forever. Neither one of us wanted to lay our cards on the table—because we both had terrible hands.

Finn went first. "I'm not going to apologize for what happened. You were the one who provoked me."

That was the last thing I'd expected him to say. "Whoa...excuse me?"

"I never would have kissed you if you hadn't asked that question. You were begging me for it."

"Begging?" I asked incredulously. "Asshole, if I wanted a kiss, I would have just kissed you."

"Are you saying you didn't want me to kiss you?" He stepped closer to me, crossing his arms over his chest as he cocked his head to the side. He wore his authoritative expression, his eyes narrowing on my face. "What did you think was going to happen when you asked that question?"

"I...I don't know." I got a hit of his cologne when he came that close to me. Seeing him dressed in his scrubs and stethoscope only added to his sexy persona. The tattoos just made it worse. "I wasn't thinking when I said that."

"And I wasn't thinking when I kissed you."

"So maybe we should give each other a pass." There'd always been this electric chemistry between us, but I'd never thought we would combust like that. It wasn't just a short kiss, it was full of tongue, and I'd ended up on my back with his dick pressed against my clit.

"I guess. But are we going to do about Colton?"

"I don't know..." I felt like I'd betrayed him by fooling around with his brother. I preferred to come clean about my actions and not harbor any secrets, but I also wasn't entirely sure what telling the truth would achieve. "I'm all about being honest, but it was just a kiss. It's not like we slept together."

"And it would just piss him off."

"Then he would feel uncomfortable being in the same room with both of us."

He stared into my eyes, his expression still just as hard. "And he would always worry about it happening again."

"Yeah..." I could understand why.

"I know Colton would be furious with me if he knew. He doesn't want me involved with you."

"He said that?" I asked.

"Pretty much. I was asking about you, and he asked if I had a thing for you. Because if I did...he wouldn't like it."

When I thought back to my previous conversation with Colton, he'd said something similar. "Yeah...he said the same thing to me, that it would be the weirdest thing in the world if something happened."

"I'm the kind of guy that doesn't give a shit what anyone thinks. If I want something, I go for it. If there's a woman I want, I take her. But...you're off-limits. I believe in loyalty above all things...and I felt like I betrayed my loyalty to my brother. That's not the kind of man I want to be."

"I understand." I felt like I'd betrayed him too.

"So maybe we should keep this to ourselves and move on."

Now the situation had been resolved, but it seemed like so much was left unsaid. "Yeah..." There was still this combustible energy in the air between us. Even now, I could feel the magnetic pull in his direction. That kiss we shared was phenomenal. Were all his kisses like that? The second his mouth was on mine, all logic went out the window. I wasn't myself anymore, just some woman who only had one thing on her mind.

He continued to stare at me, like the conversation wasn't over.

It didn't feel over to me. "What is this, exactly?" I pointed back and forth between us, wishing my fingers could graze his chest once again. He was so hard, it was like feeling up a wall. "Are we just attracted to each other?" Because I'd felt something deeper from the moment we'd met. I'd experienced lust before. It was exactly how I felt for Jax when I first saw him. But that emotion was superficial and one-dimensional. What I felt for Finn seemed deeper.

"I have no idea, Pepper. And I don't think it really matters."

It mattered to me. "Did you just want to sleep with me and forget about it? A one-night stand like all the others?" If that was how he felt, I wouldn't be offended. I'd understand that was how he was, how most men were.

"I'm not sure."

"Then what are you sure about?" I should just let this conversation die because nothing could ever happen between us again. One heated embrace had almost been discovered by Colton because we were stupid enough to make out on the couch in his apartment. Clearly, neither one of us could think straight when we were in the same room together.

He slowly dropped his arms to his sides then released a quiet sigh. He didn't seem annoyed, just uncertain. "I can't explain it. The second I laid eyes on you...I felt something. Was it lust or attraction? Maybe. I'm not sure because I've never had an experience like that. As time passed, I didn't just find you just beautiful, but also interesting and strong. What my brother did to you was wrong, but you refused to let it define you. You carried on with grace. Not many women could do that. It's very difficult to earn my respect, but you've definitely earned mine—a million times over."

My eyes softened at the compliment. "That's nice of you to say."

"I've never been close with a woman before. Any time I interact with them, sex is usually involved. Even when I was in the military, that was the kind of relationship I had with the other female officers. But since I couldn't sleep with you, I was forced to have a friendship with you...and that just made my feelings more complicated."

Now my feelings for him were more complicated, after hearing all of that.

"What about you?" he asked, his voice deep.

"They're just as complicated as yours. I'll leave it at that."

His eyes remained glued to my face, hardly blinking. "None of this matters because Colton would never be okay with it, and I don't blame him. There're millions of women out there, and I decide to fool around with his ex-wife...not cool."

"It wasn't just you, Finn. I never should have said what I said."

"No, I'm glad you did. There's always been this heat between us. Now that we've talked about it, maybe it'll die down and we can be real friends. We've seen the end before the beginning...and it doesn't end well."

"No...it doesn't." Colton would be livid if I started fooling around with his brother. He'd encouraged me to keep seeing Jax and he wanted me to be happy, but Finn was one person he wouldn't want me to be happy with. Zach would be the next worst person.

He moved his hands into his pockets and released a long sigh. "So...friends?" He extended his right hand to me.

Shaking his hand felt anticlimactic. If we really were friends, we should start acting like it, not like strangers. I ignored his extended hand and moved into his chest. My arms wrapped around his muscular torso, and I rested my face right in the opening of his shirt. I could smell him even better now, and the warmth his body emitted was so comfortable.

He tensed before he reciprocated the affection. His arms locked around my waist, and he rested his chin on my head. He squeezed me a little tighter, bringing me hard into his chest so there was no opening between our bodies. One large hand moved up the center of my back until his fingers stopped above my bra. He lightly played with my hair as his chest slowly expanded against me with every breath he took.

The second I was in his arms, I didn't want to leave. It was inherently comfortable, like walking into my home after a long day at work. It was my safe place, where I could drop everything and find peace. With my face pressed against his chest, my lips felt his warm skin. It tasted like his mouth— like a man.

"I've never hugged a woman like this." He rested his lips against my forehead.

"And I've never been hugged like this." Colton and I had a happy marriage, but now that I felt this level of affection, I realized it'd been missing in our relationship. We didn't have this kind of innate heat. It was all friendship—and nothing more.

He slowly pulled his hands away, dragging them down my back until the moment he had to let go. He'd procrastinated as long as he could, but once he ran out of space, it was over. He stepped back, his eyes filled with disappointment and longing. "Not a good way to start off our friendship."

I chuckled, but it was forced and fake. "Yeah…"

He placed an extra step between us, like anything closer than that was a betrayal to his brother. "Jax is a good guy."

The surprise stretched across my face because I hadn't anticipated that statement coming from him.

"I know I was an ass to him. That was only because…you know."

I crossed my arms over my chest again.

"He's successful, good-looking, and not arrogant. But more importantly, he adores you."

I couldn't believe I was getting love advice from someone like him.

"There's a lot of jerks out there. A lot of assholes like me. He's not one of them."

"You aren't an asshole, Finn." He was rugged and cold sometimes, but definitely not an asshole.

"Not to you. But ask most of the women I've slept with, and they'll tell you otherwise." He grabbed his bag and moved to the door so he could leave.

"I don't believe that a man who's served our country for ten years could be an asshole. I don't believe a man who saves lives every day at work could be an asshole. And I don't believe a man so supportive and loyal to his gay brother could be an asshole."

Finn stopped before he crossed the threshold. He didn't

turn around, and his shoulders stiffened in reaction to my words. He stalled for nearly thirty seconds, as if he might turn around and acknowledge what I said. When he made up his mind, he walked out without turning around, leaving the door wide open.

15

COLTON

I stepped inside Mr. Robinson's office with the folder tucked under my arm. In his late fifties, but looking more like he was in his late sixties, he was the top partner at the firm, the one who called all the shots. My original boss who had hired me left eighteen months ago, so I'd been stuck with this conservative jerk ever since. "Mr. Robinson?"

He glanced up from his paperwork with a look of loathing. He didn't try to be professional. His judgments of my lifestyle were written all over his face. Once I divorced Pepper and the truth of my orientation came out, everything changed. We were never close to begin with, but the environment hadn't been hostile either. "Yes?" he said, his voice full of impatience.

"I wanted to talk to you about the Hamilton case." I'd been taking on the smallest projects possible because that was all I'd been assigned, but working on the same thing every day had started to make my job so boring I fell asleep at my desk. "With my background, I think I would be a really good candidate—"

"I've already given that case to Steve." He turned back to his work like the conversation was finished.

"Yes, but I'm from New Jersey," I insisted. "I have a better understanding—"

"Look, the jury decides everything." He threw his papers down on the desk. "And if they take one look at you, it could sway them in one direction or another."

"Look at me?" I asked, my anger brimming. "Because I'm going to walk in their dressed like a woman and act all flamboyant." This man signed my checks every two weeks, so mouthing off to him might be stupid, but I didn't care. Ever since this asshole took over, I'd been completely defined by my orientation. I was a damn good lawyer and graduated at the top of my class. I was far more qualified than anyone else in the office.

Mr. Robinson never answered my question. "Get out of my office if you want to keep your job."

The hatred built to a new level, and I stopped caring about my rent, my health insurance, and my career. Nothing else seemed important besides my pride. I deserved better than this, and I wouldn't put up with it anymore. If that meant I had to move in with Pepper or Finn, so be it. "I don't want to keep my job."

Mr. Robinson looked up again, unable to hide his look of surprise.

I tossed my folder in the air, and the papers scattered everywhere, like flakes of snow that filled his office. I turned on my heel and walked out, letting the asshole worry about the mess. As I marched down the hallway past my peers, I felt my heart pound hard in my chest. The adrenaline was so strong, I thought I could tear down the building with my own hands.

I made it to my office to grab my things. I left the rest behind, making it someone else's problem.

Then I marched out of there with my head held high.

WHEN I STEPPED inside the apartment, Finn was sitting on the couch. He usually worked the night shift at the hospital, so he lounged around the apartment all day while I was at work. It was a good system for us because it allowed us both to enjoy our space while the other was gone.

I slammed the door behind me and tossed my keys on the counter.

Finn turned around to get a look at me. "Stop by for lunch?"

"No." I tossed my bag on the kitchen table and ripped off my jacket. I tossed it over the back of the chair then yanked my tie loose, not caring about keeping it unwrinkled.

When Finn realized something was wrong, he rose to his feet and walked toward me. "Everything alright, man?"

"No. It's not alright. Nothing is alright." I gripped the back of the chair because I was so livid. I wanted to pick it up and throw it out the window.

Finn watched me closely, his pretty eyes shifting back and forth as they looked into mine. "Is this about Pepper?" He brought his hands together and slowly massaged his left knuckle. "Because it was just—"

"No, Pepper had nothing to do with this." I should have listened to her and quit my job a while ago. I shouldn't have waited until the straw broke the camel's back. My temple was thudding because I was reliving my mistreatment. For a place that practiced law, it was laughable how they broke the law every day by mistreating me. "I quit my job. I told Mr. Robinson to fuck off before I stormed out."

Instead of reacting like most people would, Finn remained calm. His eyes continued to take me in without judgment or prejudice. "What happened?" Finn and I had little experience interacting with each other, but in the short time he'd been here, our relationship had changed so much. It didn't matter how masculine or macho he was, he never made me feel bad for being on the softer side.

"My boss and the entire office have ostracized me since I came out. I've always been given the shitty cases because my boss didn't want me to see court. When I offered to take on a higher profile case because of my background, he shot me down...because the jury wouldn't like me."

Finn didn't visibly change, but his eyes took on a darker look. They burned with rage that slowly filled the entire room. Like heat from a fire, it made the room feel like a furnace. He could be hostile without saying a single word, could be ferocious without raising a hand.

"I got fed up with it and—"

"You should have left a long time ago."

"Yeah...Pepper said the same thing."

"She knew about this?" he hissed.

"She knew I didn't like my job. But she didn't know why."

He stepped back and crossed his arms over his chest, his visage full of fury. "You could sue them for that, Colton."

"I know. But I don't have the resources the firm does. Plus, I don't have any money saved. I can't even pay my rent now."

"You can live with me, Colton. My place will be ready any day."

"Really?" I asked, surprised by his generosity.

He cocked an eyebrow, like he couldn't believe my surprise. "You think I'm gonna let you live on the street?"

I shrugged. "I thought you might suggest I live with Pepper."

"No. I'm your family."

"She's my family too." Even when she changed her last name, she would still be family.

"But I'm your brother." His hand moved to my shoulder, and he gave me a gentle squeeze. "That house is too big for one person, so it's perfect."

"Then why did you buy it?"

He shrugged. "I wanted to get a dog."

"Really?" I asked in surprise. "You don't seem like a dog person."

"I am a dog person. We had canines in the field with us all the time. It'll be nice to have a partner around."

"I wouldn't be your partner?" I asked.

"No. Just my brother."

"Well, I'll take it." All the frustration from the afternoon seemed to fade away once Finn comforted me. We'd missed the last ten years, but now we were reconnecting in a way I never expected.

"You want a drink? I think a scotch is in order."

"I don't drink scotch—"

"Come on." He retrieved the bottle from the kitchen along with two shot glasses. "Don't be a pussy."

"I'm not a pussy. It's just not even noon yet."

He poured the two glasses and handed me one. "In the military, we always commemorated every single event. Whether it was a victory, a fallen soldier, or a saved soldier." He clinked his glass against mine. "Because you don't know how many more chances you're going to get. So let's celebrate this moment."

"Celebrate?" I asked.

"Yes. Because you're moving on to greater things." He tilted his head back and downed the scotch in a single gulp. "Drink with me."

I held my breath before I brought the glass to my lips. I downed it one gulp so I could ignore the fire as it burned down my throat. It moved all the way into my belly, burning throughout the entire journey. "Geez, that's strong. You drink this every day?"

He chuckled and clapped me on the arm. "Like water."

AROUND DINNERTIME, Pepper stopped by. She knocked this time, getting used to the fact that Finn was also a resident in the apartment.

"It's open." I rose from the couch and ignored the show on the TV.

Finn was in the kitchen, finishing up dinner.

Pepper walked inside, dressed in black boots, black tights, and a long-sleeved green dress. Her hair was pulled back in a ponytail, and her earrings dangled as she moved. A small freckle was in the corner of her mouth, an area I used to kiss almost every single day. "Just here for my mail." She found the pile by the door and flipped through it. "Junk. Junk. More Junk."

"All spam?" I asked in surprise.

"No. Just bills." She picked up what she needed and tucked it under her arm.

"And you call that spam?"

"Pretty much."

Finn carried the serving dish to the kitchen table. "Hey, Pepper. Would you like to join us for dinner?"

She sniffed the air and slowly came over. When she spotted the platter of freshly made lasagna, she made up her mind quickly. "Hell yeah. That looks delicious." She fanned the smell toward her nose. "That's the best thing I've smelled all day."

"And you sell panties," Finn said. "So that's a compliment." He winked at her before he set the plates on the table.

I was relieved Finn and Pepper got along so well. My brother usually screwed any pretty woman he came across, but obviously, my ex-wife was off-limits, and we didn't even need to have a conversation about it. But they'd clearly developed a friendship, and that was nice to see. I needed the two most important people in life getting along—that way, all three of us could be one group.

She rolled her eyes before she grabbed a beer from the fridge and sat down. "They're new panties...so they don't smell like anything."

"Not true." Finn handed out the silverware before he sat down—with his glass of scotch. "They smell like women's perfume. And that's pretty sexy."

I sat between both of them at the round table and scooped a piece of lasagna onto my plate. "How was work today, Pepper?"

"Uneventful. I had a few customers, but most of the time, I just read my book." She sliced her fork into the pile of pasta and cheese and placed a small bite in her mouth, careful not to ruin her lipstick.

"What are you reading?" Finn asked.

"A new Jodi Picoult book," she said. "*Small Great Things*. Do you read much?"

"I read a lot of James Patterson," Finn asked. "He

releases so many books a year, I always have something to look forward to."

"I didn't know you read," Pepper said, even though she didn't know him well enough to guess what his hobbies were.

"I didn't know that either," I blurted. "You just don't seem like a reader."

"I have a degree in medicine," Finn said sarcastically. "It's not that crazy."

"You know what I mean." I ate my dinner as my muscles started to relax. I was surrounded by my two favorite people in the world, and the horrible day I'd had seemed to vanish. Losing my job didn't seem to matter, not when I had this waiting at home for me.

"How was the office?" Pepper asked me, her eyes on her food. She seemed to ask me that question while already knowing the answer. Her tone always dropped a bit, as if she expected that same sadness to echo back at her.

Finn looked at me as he chewed his garlic bread, waiting for me to tell her the truth.

"Well…I had a really great day." Now that the burden was off my shoulders, I felt better than I had in a long time.

"Really?" she asked. "That's good to hear. It always seems like you're unhappy at the office."

"You're dead on about that," I said. "But the reason why I had a good day was because I quit."

She dropped her fork onto her plate, the clatter echoing in the small apartment. "What? Are you serious?" Her shock was mixed with happiness, already relieved that I'd left the firm even though she didn't know why. "That's great. You should never work somewhere that makes you so unhappy. Everyone may not love their job, but they shouldn't hate it either."

"I do feel better." Like a heavy weight had been removed from my chest, I felt a million times lighter. It would always haunt me that my boss and the rest of the staff turned their noses up at me, but if that was how they really felt, I didn't want to be associated with them anyway. "It was the right decision, and I shouldn't have waited so long to make it happen."

Finn drank his scotch then cleared his throat. "Are you going to tell her why you quit?"

Pepper studied him for an instant, reading the meaning in his eyes before she turned back to me. "What aren't you telling me, Colt? Did something happen at your office?"

I wasn't going to keep it from her because she would find out anyway, but I didn't want to tell her the truth either because she would get so worked up over it. "Well...the reason it was always such an inhospitable atmosphere was because they had a problem when I came out of the closet."

Pepper's face deepened into a wary look, like she couldn't believe what she'd just heard. "You're serious?"

"They weren't giving me the good cases because they didn't want me in court. It just kept getting worse and worse until I confronted my boss about it. It became more intense, so I quit on the spot and marched out."

"Hell yeah." She slammed both of her fists onto the table and made all the dishes shake. "That's absolute bullshit. Come on, this is Seattle in the twenty-first century. Who the hell does that asshole think he is?"

"His loss," Finn said. "He lost the best lawyer in his office."

"He didn't use me anyway, so he didn't lose much," I said.

"I can't believe this," Pepper said. "I can't believe there's such evil in the world."

I shrugged. "Whatever. I left, so we'll put it in the past."

"I guess," Pepper said. "But I'm marching down there and giving your boss a piece of my mind."

Pepper didn't kid about stuff like that, so I knew she was being serious. "Whoa, hold on—"

"I was thinking the same thing," Finn said. "First thing in the morning."

"No." I set down my fork. "Guys, no. I'm serious. I appreciate it, but really—"

"Too bad," Pepper said. "I don't give a shit who he is. No one treats another human that way. This isn't even just about defending you. It's about all of us."

"But for me, it's mainly about you," Finn said. "If he wants to act like an asshole, he'd better be prepared to face the consequences."

That was the last thing I wanted. "Guys—"

"Too bad," Finn said. "Consider it done."

Pepper changed the subject because she knew I would keep arguing for the rest of the night. "Are you going to keep living here while you look for a new job? You could always move in with me."

It didn't surprise me at all that she offered.

"He's moving in with me," Finn offered. "It's a big house, so there's plenty of room."

"Oh, that's a good idea," she said. "Well, the offer always stands if you want to crash with me. I only have a one-bedroom apartment, so we'd have to share a bed and that wouldn't be fun."

"That wouldn't work," Colton said. "Where would Jax go?"

"He hasn't slept over yet," Pepper said. "And if he did, he'd be on the floor." She turned back to her lasagna and ate most of it within a few bites.

"What's going on with Jax anyway?" I asked. "I haven't seen him in a while, and you don't talk about him much."

"I've just been busy," she said. "And we're still taking it slow."

"Do you even like him?" I asked bluntly. "Because I can't tell if you do."

Her eyes immediately moved across the table to Finn. She held his gaze for a heartbeat before she looked down at her food again. "I do. I guess I just haven't really let him in…"

"You should," I said. "He seems like a really nice guy, and he's been patient with you. Whenever I see you two together, he only has eyes for you. If you keep being distant with him, you might lose him forever. I don't know Jax that well, but I wouldn't want you to lose a great guy because you're too scared to give him a real chance."

Pepper stared down at her food, and she swirled her fork through the globs of cheese. She usually had a comeback to everything I said, but this time, she was speechless.

"I agree with Colt," my brother said. "There are a lot of dogs out there. Jax isn't one of them."

She spun her fork around for a long time before she got a massive bite on the end. Then she placed it into her mouth and chewed slowly, prolonging the continuation of the conversation. "You're right. He's a good guy. I guess I just… purposely kept him at a distance. I already married a great guy, and the possibility of finding another great guy seemed so unlikely that I didn't even bother."

I hated myself for what I did to Pepper. She said she didn't regret anything, but I certainly did. While I cherished our relationship now, I would go back in time and erase all of it. The memories of her tears during our divorce would haunt me every single day. If I'd just been honest with

myself sooner, I could have spared her the pain and humiliation. But I fucked all that up. What I wouldn't give to take it
all back.

"I just don't want to get hurt again," she admitted. "So I
was expecting to have a bunch of one-night stands with guys
I wouldn't remember. Instead, the first guy I find turns out to
be pretty great...caught me off guard."

Finn looked down at his plate and kept eating.

"Then go for it," I said. "And give him a real chance."

"Yeah," Pepper said with a sigh. "I think I might." She
took another bite before she washed it down with her beer.
"How are things with Aaron?"

I hadn't thought about him once today. "We text on and
off. Sometimes when I text him, he doesn't text me back for
two days. I can't tell if he's really interested or not. Sometimes I wonder if he's just throwing me a bone because I'm
new at this."

"He's sleeping with someone else," Finn blurted.

My head snapped in his direction. "What?"

"If a guy doesn't text you back all the time, it's because
he has other prospects." Finn didn't lay it on me easy. He
made his point and didn't sugarcoat it. "Trust me on that. If a
guy wanted you to know you were the only one, he would
answer all your text messages. He would be there all the
time. If he's not...then you know he's playing the field."

"Didn't realize you knew anything about gay relationships," I said.

"I don't know anything about gay relationships," Finn
countered. "But I do know men. We aren't hard to read. If
we're into you, we'll make it blatantly obvious. If we don't
give a damn, you'll have a relationship with our voice mail.
Just want to be straight with you so you don't get your heart
broken."

"Well, thanks for laying it on me so gently." I chuckled at the end of my sentence, but my heart was actually full of dread. Coming out of the closet was hard enough, but finding the right guy to spend my life with seemed even harder. A part of me still wished I was straight so I could live happily ever after with Pepper.

Finn shrugged. "Relationships are hard. Why do you think it's so rare to find a good one?"

I turned back to Pepper, remembering the night I gave her a ring it took me a year to save for. "I miss being married to you. I was a lot happier then than I am right now." A confession like that probably didn't make her feel better, but at least she knew I was suffering too.

She gave me a slight smile then rested her hand on mine. "I know. We were great together."

"Yeah...we were." I squeezed her hand and sighed with sadness. There were a lot of things I missed about our marriage, like coming home from work and seeing her smile at me. I missed going to brunch every Sunday, going out on the town with her hand held in mine. I missed picking out the perfect gift for her for Christmas and then opening it under the tree first thing in the morning. We were still close, but we would never have a relationship like that again.

Finn watched our joined hands before his eyes moved to Pepper.

Pepper pulled her hand away. "But you're going to find someone who makes you happier than I ever did. And I believe I'm going to find someone too."

16

PEPPER

Being with Finn and Colton at the same time only reminded me that being with Finn romantically wasn't an option.

We could only ever be friends.

The attraction I had for him would have to disappear, be locked away deep inside my chest so I wouldn't think about it ever again. Even if Colton were ever okay with it, I doubted it would ever go anywhere. Finn was a one-night stand kinda guy. Always had been and always would be, it seemed. I wouldn't want to be his guinea pig.

After thinking about it, I realized they were both right. Jax really was a great guy. Maybe I didn't appreciate that at the time, but now I did. Instead of taking things slow because of my divorce, I should be living life to the fullest—not being chained to my past.

It was a slow day at the store, so I texted Jax. *Hey, have plans tonight?*

No response.

Hours went by, and I didn't hear from him. It was unusual because his responses were usually instantaneous.

He was either pissed at me or had moved on to someone else.

No one to blame but myself.

At the end of the day, I went home to my empty apartment and pulled a beer out of the fridge. I stood at the kitchen counter as I drank it, unsure what to do now. I blew off a nice guy I could have had something with. Now all I could do was sit around and drink.

After a few beers, I found the courage to call him. I wasn't going to ask him out again. Instead, I was going to apologize for the way I behaved. All he ever did was try to get close to me, and all I ever did was push him away.

I got his voice mail.

That was fine. It was easier this way. "Hey, Jax. It's Pepper. Look, I know you're either pissed at me because of the way I've been toward you...or you're seeing someone else by now. Either way, that's fine with me. I just wanted to apologize for keeping you at a distance. After my divorce, I wasn't in a hurry to find the next guy to start dating. I just wanted sex and some time. Meeting a nice guy like you wasn't in the cards...but I did meet you. I know I'm realizing this too late and you've moved on with your life, but it's never too late to say you're sorry. So...I'm sorry. Goodbye, Jax." I hung up and tossed my phone on the counter. It was a bummer I'd lost a good catch, but now that I'd apologized, I had some closure.

I grabbed another beer and parked my rear on the couch —where it belonged.

~

KNOCK. Knock. Knock.

My head turned toward the door in surprise. It wasn't

Colton, but it wasn't Finn either. He had a distinctive knock, a single sound that announced his rough presence to the entire apartment. That left either Girl Scouts selling cookies...or Jax.

I hoped it was the second one.

I opened the door and came face-to-face with the handsome man who had entered my lingerie shop. Lean and toned, he had a tight physique and the height to boot. He was in a long-sleeved gray shirt with a black blazer on top, probably having just finished showing a house to someone. He didn't wear his happy smile that I'd become used to seeing. His eyes were heavy lidded with anger, like my hunch about his resentment had been right.

"Hi..." Now that I was looking at him, he seemed like all he wanted to do was yell. He sure didn't appear happy to see me.

He invited himself inside and shut the door behind him. "There're a few things you should know about me." He towered over me with his height, his shadow crossing the apartment to the opposite window. "I pick up women in bars all the time. I fuck them at my place, and they leave. Sometimes I ask them to stay, but most of the time, I don't. When I met you, it was different. I instantly liked you, instantly wanted you. But you've been dragging me along on your hook for weeks now, and I'm not doing it anymore. I don't put up with that shit. I'm not a nice guy. I just happened to be a nice guy to you because I actually liked you."

I stayed quiet as he finished his speech, knowing this anger had built up inside his chest. Every time he'd tried to be more serious with me, I'd kept him at a distance. I'd hardly treated him like a friend. I picked him up at the bar, used him, and hadn't really paid attention to him since. Men had treated me that way more times than I could count, and

I'd hated every second. Now I did it to someone else—and I didn't like that. "You have every right to be upset. But the most I can do is apologize—which I've done." He could keep yelling at me if he wanted, but it wouldn't change anything. If this was over, we should just go our separate ways and forget about it.

His nostrils flared slightly as he continued his elevated breathing. His hands moved to his hips. "I slept with someone. I was showing her a few houses, and it happened—a couple times. It didn't seem like anything was happening here, so I moved on."

I didn't expect that to hurt as much as it did. Instead of spending my time on a guy who could actually be something, I'd wasted more time on the wrong guy. First, I married a gay man, and then I made out with his brother. Clearly, I had serious issues. "You had every right to, Jax. We were never serious." I saved face by brushing it off. Besides, I'd kissed someone else anyway. It wasn't like I was so innocent.

His anger slowly started to simmer. "I don't like her, not the way I like you."

"Yeah?" I whispered.

"Yeah."

I crossed my arms over my chest, feeling the tension sink into my skin. He kept staring at me with those pretty green eyes, and I felt like I might burst into flames under the heat. "I kissed someone. A few days ago."

To my relief, Jax didn't ask who the recipient was. "Are you dating this guy?"

"No. It was just a one-time thing." I wanted to call it a mistake, but it wasn't. A kiss that good couldn't be a mistake. Finn was an incredible man and probably an incredible lover, but it just wasn't possible. He would be the perfect person to sleep with and get my mind off everything that happened, but it would also cause a lot more problems.

Jax didn't ask for more details. "You want to have dinner with me tonight?"

Was he giving me another chance? "Depends."

His eyes narrowed.

"Will you sleep over tonight?"

The aggression left his eyes, and a slight smile formed on his lips. "Yes, I'd love to."

"When is Sasha getting married?" We went to an Italian bistro a short walk from my apartment. It was usually quiet during the weekdays, so we got a table without an issue. A low-burning candle was between us, and we both enjoyed the cheese ravioli.

"In two weekends." When he sat perfectly straight, his shoulders and arms looked more defined in his shirt. There was always a light in his gaze when he spoke about his sister, even when he tried to pretend he was annoyed with her. "Can't wait until that moment comes. My bachelor pad will be back."

"Are you giving her away?"

He drank from his wineglass before he responded. "Yes."

"Aww...that's sweet."

He shrugged then took a bite of his dinner.

"You love her."

"Of course I love her. But that doesn't mean I like her."

"Whatever," I said as I teased him. "You love her, and you like her."

He deflected the statement by changing the subject. "You don't have any siblings, right?"

"Only child."

"You're lucky."

"No...I'm really not." I didn't have a single family member in the world. I was the last of my line and the only member of my line.

Jax looked apologetic when he realized what he'd said. "I'm sorry. I didn't mean it that way."

"It's okay," I said quickly. "I know you didn't."

"Do you mind if I ask what happened with your parents?" He'd never asked me that before, probably because the question was too intimate for people who were barely dating.

"Of course not. It's a pretty short story. My mother was really young when she had me. About fifteen or sixteen at the time. She didn't want to have an abortion, so she gave me away for adoption. Unfortunately, a family never picked me, so I stayed in the system for a long time before I legally declared myself an adult at sixteen."

He stared at me with a baffled expression, like he hadn't expected me to say that in a million years. "I don't know what to say...I'm sorry."

"There's no need to be sorry. I've had a great life. When I got older, things got easier. Please don't feel bad for me."

"You seem to be in a good place now."

"Yes, I am." Minus being divorced from a gay man. "So, I probably do have siblings out there somewhere. At least my bloodline continues."

"You've never considered contacting your mom?"

"No. Her information is protected, and even if it weren't, meeting her isn't on my bucket list. She was so young at the time that I don't judge her for what she did. She was just a child. And in the end, it worked out fine. I don't want to be with someone who doesn't want to be with me."

Jax continued to look at me, slightly sad.

"Stop." I gently placed my forefinger on the tip of his nose.

He chuckled at my touch. "Sorry. I don't mean to do that. I really admire your attitude. You don't throw yourself a pity party, and you don't want anyone else to pity you either."

"Unless it's the kind of pity that will get me sex." I made a light-hearted joke to change the subject.

When he smiled, I knew it worked. "In that case, I feel *really* bad for you."

JAX HELD his weight on top of me with his muscular arms. They were resting on the mattress on either side of my chest, and he moved his hips in the sexiest way as he rocked into me. The condom separated us, but after another clean exam, I was prepared to remove it.

Instead of kissing me, he kept his eyes focused on mine. When he showed such intensity, he looked so undeniably sexy. His jaw was tight, and his eyes were focused with a beautiful smolder. Sweat glistened on his chest and shoulders, and he made the deepest moans in the back of his throat.

I fingered the sweaty strands of his hair and locked my ankles together around his waist. "You're going to make me come, Jax." Sex with him was easy because I almost always had a good climax. One of my biggest fears was being the reason Colton was gay, but with Jax, I wasn't worried about the past repeating itself. A man couldn't make love to a woman this well without enjoying every second of it.

"Come, sweetheart." He ground hard against me, hitting me right where I needed it most.

My nails sank into him, and I came all around him, slathering his length with my come and tightness. My thighs squeezed him harder, and the rush I experienced was so powerful, my toes curled and my body nearly turned rigid. "Jax."

He watched my performance with those smoldering eyes before he hit his own climax. "Yes..." He made his final pumps with aggression, hitting me deep and good every time. He finished with a groan, full of satisfaction and a hint of never-ending arousal. "Just as good as I remember."

"Yeah..." My nails stopped digging into his back, and I slowly dragged them down his sweaty skin. I could feel him softening inside me.

Jax got off me and disposed of the condom before he came back to bed. "Here's an idea. I got another test done, and we skip the condoms."

There wasn't anything I disliked about Jax, so I decided to move forward. If I stopped dating him and put myself back on the market, I wouldn't find anyone else I liked more. Maybe I wasn't ready for a relationship, but I wasn't ready to lose something good either. "Good idea."

"Yeah?" He cuddled into my side as he wore a handsome grin. "Good. I would much rather come inside you than a piece of latex."

The last man to do that was my ex-husband, and at the time, it felt erotic to me. But now that I knew nothing was ever truly real, it didn't seem sexy anymore. Maybe the intimacy with Jax would be a lot more fulfilling. "Me too."

He rubbed his large hand across my tummy. "I probably shouldn't rush this, and you can say no if you want, but would you want to—"

"Yes." He'd just invited me to his sister's wedding. I had a good hunch about it. "I would love to come as your lady."

His grin widened. "Great. I look forward to it. After I give my sister away, I finally get to have some fun. There's no one else I would rather have fun with than you."

"That's sweet."

"And you can stay at my place—because she'll finally be gone."

I TRACKED down Aaron at his work and helped myself inside to his station.

He clearly wasn't expecting to see me, but he wore a genuine smile. "Hey, Pepper. What brings you to this side of town?" He wore a tight t-shirt over his fit physique, and his green eyes looked even brighter under the salon lights.

"Colton."

"Yeah?" he asked. "Is he with you?" He remained aloof, like there was no possibility he was doing anything wrong. That was the truth—he wasn't. But Colton was a special case.

"No. He doesn't know I'm here—and it's going to stay that way."

He raised an eyebrow. "Okay..." His smile slowly slid off his face.

"Look, I don't know how much Colton has told you about himself, but this is his first time on the scene. He was married to me for three years before he came out. He's nervous, self-conscious, and vulnerable right now."

"No...I didn't know he was married to you."

"It ended on great terms, and we're still just as close as we were before. The last thing I want for him is to get hurt. So this is my point, Aaron. If you don't like him and don't see it going anywhere, tell him that and stop texting him. If you do actually like him, be more responsive to him. He's just in a really vulnerable place right now."

Aaron stared at me for a while, clearly unsure how to process that much information in thirty seconds. "You're looking out for him. I respect that."

"Good. So figure out what you want—and stick to it."

"I do like him, Pepper. But I'm also at a stage in my life where I'm just having fun. I like to go out with different men and have a good time. We were never exclusive, so I'm sorry if he ever thought we were."

"No, he didn't think you were exclusive. He's just having a hard time figuring out why you aren't texting him back."

He shrugged. "I was busy. You know how it is when you're single."

No, I didn't. I was only single for a short time, and I wound up in a relationship I wasn't ready for. "You aren't doing anything wrong, Aaron. But Colton is delicate. If you aren't looking for a relationship, just break it off. There's nothing wrong with that. But don't keep him on your hook either."

He nodded before he gave me a slight smile. "You're a good friend, Pepper. I like the way you have his back. Makes me like him more. It's not easy to be married to a woman, realize you're gay, and then keep that same kind of relationship. He must be an incredible man."

"Yes...he's the best." I loved him with all my heart —forever.

I was at the shop when Finn showed up.

But I wasn't ready for what I was about to see.

Dressed in his military uniform with his captain's rank

on his shoulder, Finn walked inside as his heavy boots thudded against the hardwood floor. Wearing a serious expression that would terrify any enemy that he came across, he was all man—from head to toe.

I'd never cared about a man in uniform—but my jaw was practically on the ground right now.

He headed for my desk, his eyes locked on me while he kept his stoic expression. He seemed even taller in his uniform, more muscular, and more regal. I'd seen him without a shirt, and that was a beautiful sight—but this was even sexier.

He stopped at the counter and stared at me.

My brain was scrambled, and I couldn't say a single word. All logic left my mind, just as it had when we kissed last week. A more handsome man had never stepped foot inside my store—or my life. My eyes trailed up and down, taking in his perfection with a suddenly dry mouth. "Uh...if you're trying to bring more customers into the store...I think it's going to work."

Finally, the corner of his mouth rose in a smile. "I was going to stop by Mr. Robinson's office and give him a piece of my mind."

"Right now?" I blurted, still thinking about how that uniform fit his perfect body. "What's your goal? To turn him gay?"

His smile widened even more. "Women always love the uniform..."

"Can't blame them." My eyes continued to scan his body as I reminisced over our kiss.

"I was planning on threatening him instead."

My eyes flicked back to his. "I don't think threatening a lawyer is a good idea."

"And I don't think discriminating against someone based

on their orientation is a good idea either," he countered. "You coming with me or not?"

No good would come from this, but I wasn't going to let some asshole put Colton down. "I'm in."

"I knew you would be."

WE IGNORED the protests of his secretary as we barged into his office.

"You really can't go in there," she said as her heels clapped on the floor behind us.

"Shh! Go away." I shut the door in her face.

Mr. Robinson was on the phone, and he looked at Finn with a raised eyebrow as he continued his conversation.

Finn snatched the phone out of his hand before he slammed it back down on the receiver.

Mr. Robinson took a second to respond because he was shocked by the audacity. "Who the hell do you—"

"Finn Burke—captain and physician in the armed forces. That's who the fuck I am, asshole." He placed both hands on his desk and leaned forward, invading Mr. Robinson's space like it was land about to be claimed. "You discriminated against my brother and harassed him for being gay—and I don't need to remind you that's illegal."

"You know what else is illegal?" Mr. Robinson challenged. "Breaking in to someone's office and harassing them."

Finn kept his cool. "What about assault?"

Mr. Robinson froze at the insinuation.

Finn made good on his word and punched him in the face, making his nose bleed.

I covered my mouth to stifle my scream.

Mr. Robinson covered his nose then examined his bloody hands. He didn't make a single sound before he looked up and met Finn's gaze, too shocked to speak.

I couldn't believe Finn had done that.

"I could strip you of your merits and bring your ass into the courtroom," Mr. Robinson threatened.

"I hope you do." If Finn was bluffing, it didn't seem like it. He continued to control the situation with his authority, towering over Mr. Robinson like he was a little girl. "I'm sure the world would love to hear about a captain defending his brother's basic rights. I'm sure they would love to hear about my tours in Afghanistan and the number of soldiers I've saved on the battlefield. And I'm sure they would love to listen to me rip you apart. So it's up to you. I don't give a shit what you do." He stood upright and straightened, his massive shoulders tensing with rage. "Don't fuck with my brother, asshole." To top it off, he spat on his desk, right on a pile of documents.

I was there to defend Colton too, but I didn't get a single word in—not that I needed to.

Finn turned for the door and walked out with me. The hallway was silent as the lawyers and clerks watched us go. Only the footsteps he took in his heavy boots were audible —along with the sound of my pounding heart.

WHEN WE WALKED inside Colton's apartment, he wasn't home.

Finn immediately removed his boots and left them by the door.

I was still shocked by what had just happened. "That was amazing. It looked like he was gonna shit his pants."

"I'm sure he did." Finn brushed it off like it was nothing. "Asshole gets what he deserves—including pants that are full of shit."

That could have gone much worse, but it seemed to work out in our favor. "The way you punched him…"

"He's gonna be in pain for a while." He stood upright and slowly walked toward me, his muscular arms hanging by his sides. "I never thought I would wear this uniform again. I'm glad I could put it to good use."

"Yeah…and it looks great on you." My eyes moved up and down as I smiled. Now that he knew I had the hots for him, I didn't feel the need to hide it anymore. Nothing would ever happen, so it was harmless.

He grinned. "Thanks."

"Are we gonna tell Colton?"

He shrugged. "Maybe later. I think the wound is too raw right now. He might get upset."

"Yeah, you're right."

"We'll wait until he starts his new job." Just like any other time we were alone in a room together, the tension escalated. Like heat from the floor that rose to the ceiling, I could feel it brush against my skin. Sometimes it seemed like it was just lust that existed between us, but I suspected it was more than that. Exactly what it was…I didn't know. But it was always there no matter what. "What's new?"

"With me?" I asked.

"Yeah. We haven't really talked much lately." He turned to the fridge and grabbed a beer. "You want one?"

"Sure."

He twisted off the cap and left the bottle on the counter. Instead of joining me, he went for the scotch.

I shouldn't have expected anything else. "I talked to Aaron today."

"Yeah?" He brought the glass to his lips as he stood at the counter. He was usually shirtless whenever he was in the apartment, so seeing him fully clothed was rare. Seeing him in uniform was even rarer. "You just bumped into him?"

"No. I tracked him down at work."

"Bit stalker-ish," he teased.

"I told him to be sensitive to Colton since he'd been through so much. I said it's fine if you don't like him, but don't keep him on your hook. If you do like him, be more transparent about it."

He set down the glass. "That was sweet of you."

"I just don't want Colton to get hurt. I understand heartbreak is a part of life, but...I don't want him to go through that right off the bat. He's nervous and self-conscious. He's really vulnerable right now. I just want the world to go easy on him for a while."

Finn watched me as he took a drink, his blue eyes drilling into mine. "He's lucky to have you, Pepper. Not too many people would do that for their ex-husband who lied during their marriage and wasted their time."

"That's not how it was..."

"I know my brother didn't mean to hurt you. But that doesn't excuse his behavior. It wasn't right—and we both know it."

"What's done is done. No point in being angry about it." I loved him too much to be angry.

"I know. But it's still surprising that you would bend over backward for him."

"It's not surprising at all." We were very happy together, even if it didn't last forever.

"He's a lucky guy—having you look out for him."

"You look out for him too, which means he's even luckier." Colton had both of us to defend him even if he didn't realize it. I guess that justified the kiss we'd shared behind his back. We made a mistake, but we made up for it in every other way.

"I think we've established he's a lucky bastard," he said with a chuckle. He unbuttoned the jacket and then peeled it off his body to reveal the olive-green t-shirt underneath. His muscular physique made his uniform so formfitting, but once he peeled it away, all that hardness was visible. "Colton's life is definitely on the rise. When he gets a new job, he'll be much happier. And maybe Aaron will be more serious or leave him be."

"I hope he's more serious. Even if it doesn't last forever, it'll give Colton some experience and confidence. Then he can play the field and have fun with it. I know Colton isn't looking to settle down right now anyway, but he needs to get out of his awkward phase. He's a good-looking guy with a lot to offer."

"He'll get there eventually." He folded the jacket neatly then placed it on the dining table. With his other clothes, he tossed them aside and seemed indifferent, but his uniform was obviously special to him.

I stared at the uniform and noticed a medal pinned to the front. I wasn't familiar with the different ranks and medals along with their meanings, with the exception of the Purple Heart. This metal in particular hung from a red fabric rectangle with a blue line down the middle. "What medal is this?" I stood next to the table and pointed at the one I referred to without actually touching it.

He came to my side, and his eyes followed my finger. "Bronze Star Medal."

"What does it mean?"

"It's a medal given for an act of heroism in a warzone."

I turned back to him, my eyes examining the painful memory in his eyes. "What was your act of heroism?"

Finn stared at the medal for a long time, his body absolutely still and his eyes unblinking. The silence stretched for so long that it seemed like he was reliving every moment of his past, thinking about the day he'd earned that medal. "I don't want to talk about it." Our conversation had been positive a few minutes ago, but just like any other time his tenure in the military was mentioned, he shut down completely. He picked up the jacket and carried it to his bedroom.

When he didn't return, I knew he wanted to be left alone.

I t was nice not having a job.

I didn't miss the office, and I loved sleeping in every day. By the time I woke up in the morning, Finn had already showered, hit the gym, and ate breakfast. If he brought a woman over, I didn't see her at all.

I entered the kitchen when it was almost eleven.

Finn sat at the kitchen table with his paperwork spread around him. He used his cell phone to dictate his medical records after spending twelve hours in the ER the night before. He finished up one folder then hung up. "It's almost noon."

"It's not like I have anywhere to be." The coffee in the pot was six hours old, so I made a new batch then joined him at the dining table. I wasn't in a rush, so I sipped my coffee and relaxed in the chair, watching the steam rise from the surface of the hot liquid.

Finn flipped through his paperwork and organized his next dictation.

"What are you doing?"

"I have to do a bunch of paperwork for every patient I see. It's for billing purposes."

"So you work for twelve hours and then have to keep working?"

"I have to dot the I's and cross the T's to get paid." He was in his sweatpants, and like always, he was shirtless. He made a few notes before he leaned back in the chair and examined me. "Colt, I can't hide it anymore."

"Hide what?" I asked blankly.

"I need to tell Mom and Dad I'm here. Once I do that, we're going to have to see them. And when we see them, you're coming clean."

I'd never dreaded doing something so much in my entire life. When I told Finn the truth, I wasn't sure how the military captain inside him was going to respond, but even then, I wasn't nearly as afraid of telling the truth. The idea of disappointing my parents made me sick to my stomach. "I'm going to tell them I'm divorced, gay, and unemployed in the same sitting?" I asked incredulously. "You want me to give them both a heart attack?"

"We can skip the job part. That's not important."

I rubbed the back of my neck, turning anxious when I'd been so relaxed just minutes ago.

"Suck it up," Finn said coldly. "You can hold your head high and be brave, or you bow your head and act like a pussy. Which one do you want to be? Before you choose, keep in mind I'm not letting you pick the second one."

"Then you don't leave me much choice…"

"Exactly. I'll call Mom and set up a dinner Friday."

"This Friday?" I asked with a sigh. "How about—"

"Friday." Finn gave me that no-bullshit look. "The sooner you get it over with, the sooner you'll be free. If they disown you, whatever. That means they disown me too. At the end of the day, you always have me and Pepper. If they can't accept you, then we don't need them."

"Do you think they'll disown me?" I whispered.

Finn shook his head slightly. "I don't know. But I do know they're going to be surprised and upset. They aren't going to brush it off and be supportive a second later. This conversation will be painful. No way around it."

"Thanks for making me feel better…"

"I'm not trying to make you feel better. I'm trying to prepare you."

This dinner would be a nightmare. Mom would cry, and Dad would be disappointed. I would have to sit there and be pelted with questions left and right. Finn had just come home from the military, but my news would overshadow it. But that was probably exactly what he wanted. He hated to be the center of attention—especially when it came to my parents. "Well, consider me prepared."

PEPPER SAT beside me on the couch with a glass of red wine in her hand. "So, Friday?"

"Friday." I took a long drink of my wine, sitting there with my ex-wife as I prepared to announce the news to my parents. "Sometimes I think about breaking my own foot just to get out of it."

"That wouldn't stop anything. Finn would just pick you up and carry you. Then you would be in even more pain for no reason."

Sometimes I hated having a buff older brother. He wouldn't allow me to be cowardly, and if I tried, he would just force me in the direction I didn't want to go. "Yeah...he's an asshole."

She chuckled before she drank her wine. "If that war hero is an asshole, then our society is in big trouble."

"War hero?" I asked.

"I noticed he had a medal on his uniform. When I asked him about it, he said it was the Bronze Star Medal. I looked it up when I got home, and I guess it's a pretty prestigious award, given to a soldier that does something heroic in battle."

I lowered my glass and gave her a blank stare. "He never mentioned that to me. I don't think he mentioned it to our parents either."

"That doesn't surprise me. When I asked him about it, he said he didn't want to talk about it."

He never wanted to talk about his decade in the military. "Wait, why were you looking at his uniform?"

She brought the glass to her lips and took a long drink, smearing her lipstick against the rim. "He had it out when I stopped by. So, are you excited to live with him?"

"Well, I already live with him. It probably won't be much different."

"Are you going to take an Uber to work every day?"

"Hmm...didn't think about that."

"It's probably a good thing that we won't be across the hall from each other anymore, but I'm definitely going to miss it."

"Only because you'll starve."

She chuckled. "True."

"And you're too cheap to buy your own coffeemaker."

"Well, you took ours in the divorce," she countered. "And I'm too stubborn to buy another."

"You want it?" I asked. "I'm sure Finn will have his own coffeemaker."

"No, it's okay. You aren't going to live there forever, and you'll need it eventually."

"So his place is nice? I still haven't seen it."

"Oh, it's gorgeous." She set the wineglass on the coffee table because only a shallow pool remained in the very bottom. The glass was smothered with her dark red lipstick everywhere. "It's so quiet and private. So many large trees everywhere. It's unfortunate that it's a drive from the city, but it'll be worth it."

"Hmm...maybe I'll hold off on getting another job and milk it as long as I can."

"It'll definitely impress your dates."

I hadn't seen Aaron in a while, so I suspected he wouldn't get to see it. "So what's going on with Jax? Is that over?" I really liked the guy, so it would be bum me out if she let him go. Most men were assholes, and it would be a while before Pepper found someone decent again.

"No...we made up."

"You did?"

"I apologized to him, and we talked it out...so we're gonna give it a go."

"Like, you're in a relationship?"

She shrugged. "We're exclusive, I guess."

"That's great." I patted her thigh. "I like Jax. He's sexy, has a nice smile, he's successful. And the most important reason of all, he's got it for you bad. That guy can go out and catch tail every night, but he'd obviously rather be with you."

"I know. He's great." She smiled, but it was the forced kind of smile that didn't reach her eyes.

"What's wrong?" I asked. "Do you not like the guy?"

"No, I do like him." She pulled her knees to her chest, and her eyes shifted to the TV, looking at nothing in particular as she considered the question. "It's just... Doesn't it seem too soon for me to have a boyfriend? We've been divorced for only eight months. Isn't that kinda fast?"

"Eight months is a long time, Pepper. And we weren't even sleeping together toward the end. It's been more like... a year."

"I'm just afraid this is happening too fast. And the reason it's happening so fast is because he's rushing it. But he basically gave me an ultimatum. We're either exclusive, or we don't see each other at all."

"He said that?"

"Not in those exact words..."

"He's just eager to make you his. But that doesn't mean you need to move in together or talk about marriage. He just doesn't want you to sleep with anyone else. If anything, it's romantic."

"Yeah...I guess."

I wanted Pepper to be happy, and sometimes I didn't understand why she wouldn't allow herself to be that way. "Why do I feel like you aren't telling me something?"

Her eyes shifted back to me. "What makes you think that?"

"Because it seems like a piece of this story is missing. After what I did to you, you could have moved on the very next day, and no one would have judged you for it. I wasted years of your life, so you're entitled to be with someone whenever you want."

"Not wasted," she whispered. "Don't say that again."

"Fine...but you don't owe me or our marriage anything. So, what's the real problem? Is it Jax?"

She looked away again. "No. He's wonderful."

"Then is there another guy you have in mind?"

She kept her gaze away from mine, avoiding eye contact as much as possible. She was quiet for so long that it seemed like there was something missing. But then she looked back at me and finally answered. "No."

18

PEPPER

Jax lay beside me, naked in my bed with sweat still gleaming on his chest. His bag was on the armchair in the corner, and his outfit for the following day was hanging up in my closet. Now he slept over at my place on a regular basis. Until his sister was officially out of the house, it made more sense to enjoy our privacy in my apartment.

"I want you to come out with me and the boys on Friday night. What do you say?"

I hadn't met his friends, but he was well acquainted with mine. Just like I didn't want, we'd jumped into a relationship. He wanted me to meet his friends and come with him to his sister's wedding. Since he was such a great guy, I shouldn't focus on the speed of the relationship. As long as he didn't tell me he loved me or ask me to move in, there was nothing to worry about. "I can't on Friday night. I'm having dinner with Colton and his parents."

"And why are you doing that?" he asked with a laugh.

I knew I should tell him Colton was the man I was married to. He was a gay man so there was nothing to feel threatened by, but if we really were in a relationship, it was something Jax should know. I would tell him—just not tonight. "Basically, he's coming out to his parents. He wants me there for backup. His brother too."

Jax raised an eyebrow, somehow looking even sexier when he appeared quizzical. "Colton hasn't told his parents?"

"He's put it on hold for a very long time."

"That's too bad. So he's had to lie about who he is this entire time?"

I shrugged. "Basically. His parents aren't conservative or anything, but he thinks they'll be disappointed. Finn is so masculine and successful, and he's afraid that'll just make him look worse."

"That's stupid. No way." He shook his head.

"I know they'll love him no matter what, but I think when he confesses, they're going to be upset. Not necessarily disappointed, but overwhelmed. They won't see it coming, so it'll be a shock."

"I don't know...parents understand their kids pretty well. They've probably wondered why their son has never been seen with a woman or had a girlfriend."

It was wrong to keep my mouth shut, but I did it anyway.

"It's nice of you to be there for him. I'm sure that'll be hard."

"What are best friends for?"

"I like your relationship." He turned on his side so he could cuddle closer to me. His arm hooked around my waist, and he brought us closer together. "You guys always have each other's backs, and you're so close. I have my boys, but I've never had a friend that close."

"Well...sometimes it just happens."

"How about tomorrow night? As long as I'm buying the rounds, the guys will come out anytime."

"I can't tomorrow either. We're all having game night. Colton considers it the last night of his life he'll ever be happy."

Jax couldn't hide his disappointment.

I didn't want him to think I was yanking his chain, so I made an offer. "I'm free Saturday night if you want to do it then."

"Yeah?" he asked, that charming grin coming across his lips. "That should work."

"And you're welcome to hang with us tomorrow. We basically just drink and play games until we're too drunk to play. Stella gets really competitive, so that will turn into a shitshow. And Zach will let her win to make her happy. I'm not sure if Finn will play. He seems too serious to do something so normal."

He chuckled. "Yeah, that guy is pretty intense. Never smiles. Seems like he's pissed most of the time."

He probably was pissed most of the time. "I think it's been difficult for him to adjust to civilian life. He's used to being so hard and serious all the time that he doesn't know how to relax. Every moment in the military was about discipline and life and death. Now that he's home, he doesn't know how to unwind."

"If he doesn't want to unwind, why did he leave?"

"I don't know. He doesn't want to talk about it."

"He's probably seen some pretty gruesome things..."

And lost people he cared about. Saw how evil humans could be. "Yeah..."

"I'd love to participate in your game night. But I have to warn you, I'm pretty competitive." He grabbed my leg and hooked it over his hip. Jax had gotten retested, and now we were screwing without condoms. It was weird at first because Colton was the only man I'd been that intimate with. But now it was comfortable, so much better than feeling the latex slide in and out of my channel.

"Yeah? Well, I'm not competitive. But I tend to win."

STELLA SIGHED as she stared at the Monopoly board. We all had houses and hotels, and almost all the property had been purchased. "Guys, this game is soooooo boring. Colton, why do you like it so much?"

"Finn and I used to play it all the time." He rolled the dice then moved his silver boot around the board. He passed GO and collected two hundred dollars.

"Because you were kids and had nothing else better to do." Stella downed her beer then tucked her hair behind her ear.

Zach had barely taken his eyes off her. "Don't drink too much tonight, alright?"

Her eyes turned into two tiny bombs. "Excuse me?"

Tatum shook her head. "You said the wrong thing, man…"

Stella held up her glass. "I'll drink as much as I want, asshole. That's what Uber is for."

"And who's gonna ride in the Uber with you and help you get inside?" Zach asked. "And put you to bed? Plus, you took off your top last time and stuck your tongue down my throat."

Stella raised an eyebrow. "Are you complaining?"

"I'm complaining because there was nothing I could do about it," Zach countered. "I can't screw a woman when she's that wasted, unless it's my girlfriend or something."

I nudged Jax in the side. "Your turn."

Jax grabbed the dice. "Sorry, their little debate is distracting."

"You get used to it," I said with a sigh.

Jax moved his piece to Park Place.

Finn snapped his fingers. "Pay up. Fifteen hundred bucks."

Jax rolled his eyes. "Damn." He counted the cash and handed it over.

Zach kept arguing. "You always do that. Anytime someone tucks you in, you throw yourself at them. Such a tease."

"I do not," Stella said in offense.

"Uh, yeah, you do." Zach turned to me. "Doesn't she try to make out with you every time she's drunk?"

"Well, when she's super drunk," I said. "Not like when she's drunk like this."

"Whoa, hold on." Jax raised his hand. "Did you ever let her?"

I rolled my eyes. "No. It doesn't mean anything. She doesn't know what she's doing."

Stella shrugged. "Alright...maybe I'm a little frisky when I've had too much to drink. But who isn't like that?"

Jax placed his beer in front of her. "You can have mine. How about I get you a scotch?"

Stella rolled her eyes. "I'm not going to make out with you."

"I was hoping you'd make out with Pepper." He nudged me in the side. "So how about that scotch?"

"Men are all the same." It was Stella's turn, so she rolled the dice. "It doesn't matter how drunk I am. This game is sooo boring. Let's play something else."

"How about you stop drinking? That way I can take you

home and finally get some action?" Zach asked. "Every time I try to put the moves on you, you're too drunk to function. I need a fair chance."

Just to be spiteful, she grabbed Jax's beer and took a drink.

Zach sighed.

"I'm down to play something else," Tatum said. "This game could go on forever."

"How about Pictionary?" Stella asked.

"Ooh." Tatum clapped her hands. "I love that game."

"We'll play in teams," Colton said. "But there's an odd number of us playing."

"I'll sit out," Finn volunteered. "Not my game anyway." He took a drink from his scotch. He was the only one drinking hard liquor because we all drank beer like normal people.

"Great." Stella moved into the living room and started setting everything up. "Let's pick the teams."

I knew I should partner with Jax, but I'd prefer Colton. We were always unbeatable because we could practically read each other's minds.

Stella set up the whiteboard along with the colored markers. "And Colton and Pepper can't be on a team together ever again. You're officially banned."

"Yeah," Tatum said. "It should be a rule that you can't be teammates with someone you were married to." She didn't realize what just came out of her mouth because she moved into the living room and got the cards ready.

Stella paled slightly, like she knew that information shouldn't have slipped out.

Everyone at the table went quiet.

Colton's eyes immediately shifted to Jax, waiting for his reaction.

Finn was the only one who kept drinking like everything was normal.

Jax stilled once the information fell on his shoulders. His first instinct was to look at Colton before he turned to me. His gaze was full of accusation as well as confusion, like he hadn't heard Tatum's words correctly.

I knew this information was delicate, and this was not how I wanted him to find out.

He kept staring at me, the playfulness in his eyes long gone.

When Jax didn't say anything, Finn tried to disrupt the tension. "Let's get this game going. Otherwise, we'll be here all night."

JAX DIDN'T COMMENT on the revelation. He played the game as my teammate, doing the best he could to figure out what I was drawing. But his buoyant mood had been destroyed by Tatum's words, so he looked visibly angry the entire time. He had the class not to blow up in front of my friends, but I knew I would get an earful once we were alone.

Colton and Zach won the game.

Finn sat in the armchair with his glass in hand, watching us all make idiots out of ourselves.

Zach high-fived Colton. "We got it, man. You and I have one mind."

"Yep." Colton did a little dance. "We kicked everyone's ass. Wasn't even a contest."

"That's what happens when you've been best friends for so long," Zach said.

Jax tossed the cards on the table, his mood souring even more now that the game was over. "I'm done for the night.

Let's go, Pepper." He wouldn't ordinarily tell me what to do, but he clearly wanted to talk to me in private. At least he didn't tell me off in front of all my friends.

"Alright." I exchanged a look with my friends before I headed to the door. Finn was the last person I looked at. Even though his expression appeared exactly the same as it usually did, there was a hint of sympathy.

Jax walked into the hallway, and I followed behind him.

We didn't even make it to my door before he rounded on me.

"Colton was the guy you were married to?" His voice immediately exploded like a bomb, bouncing off the walls as if it was projected with a microphone. If he was going to be this angry and yell this loudly, we might as well have stayed in the apartment. There was no doubt they could hear everything anyway.

"Yes. But I—"

"But what?" The vein in his forehead was visible now that he'd lost his temper. "You didn't think that was something I should know? You live ten feet away from the guy, for fuck's sake. And you spend every waking hour with him. Were you too much of a coward to tell me? Did you think it was better for me to hear it from one of your drunk friends?"

I knew he would be upset, but I hadn't anticipated this. "Jax, I'm sorry. I was going to tell you, but I was waiting for the right time."

"I've been hanging out with you and your friends like some kind of idiot. How do you think it makes me feel to be the only one who doesn't know your best friend is your ex-husband?"

"I never meant to embarrass you—"

"Well, you did." His eyes were wide open, his neck tight with his rage. "This is bullshit."

The door opened, and Finn stepped into the hallway, surpassing Jax in height by a meager inch. He shut the door behind him and faced Jax. "Stop yelling at her. I get you're pissed, but knock it off. Pepper didn't want a relationship with you in the first place because of this reason. She wasn't ready to talk about it. She wasn't ready to share that piece of her life with someone. You were the one who forced her into something more serious. So cut her some goddamn slack, or I'll drag you out of this building and put you in a cab."

I didn't need a man to fight my battles, but I was relieved Finn made such a strong argument for me. It was a valid point. I didn't want a relationship because I wasn't ready, and the reason I wasn't ready was because of my marriage.

Jax stared at him with the same rage, his chest rising and falling with his deep breaths.

"If I hear your voice again, I'll come after you." Finn walked back inside the apartment and shut the door behind him.

We were left alone in the hallway, and I wondered if Jax would take Finn's threat seriously. He should, because I suspected Finn could demolish a dozen men entirely on his own.

"He's right." I kept my voice low, trying to defuse the situation so he would calm down. "When I said I wasn't ready for a relationship, I meant it. I didn't want to share that piece of my life with someone...just yet."

Jax stared at me, his anger slowly abating.

"I'm sure you've figured out the reason we got divorced... because he realized he was gay. We were happily married until he dropped the bomb on me. It's embarrassing...and not something I want to share openly. I was afraid of what you would think of me, that you would think I was less of a woman. I didn't want to project my insecurities before you even got a chance to know me. We're going to see his parents because they still think we're married...and we're going to them the truth."

He put his hands on his hips and stared at the floor.

I knew my friends all had their ears pressed against the door, listening to every single word like they were witnessing a soap opera.

Jax still said nothing, staring at the floor as he collected his thoughts.

"I'm sorry...I don't know what else to say." I suspected this relationship had been killed the moment Tatum opened her mouth. There was no point in fighting or making an argument. Jax would probably be too uncomfortable hanging around with me and my ex all the time.

"You blindsided me." He lifted his gaze to look at me. "I didn't see that coming so I just exploded..."

Was that an apology? Sounded more like an excuse.

"When did you get divorced?"

"Eight months ago. But our relationship fell apart months before that...so it's been almost a year."

"Why do you live across the hall from him?"

"When we were going our separate ways, this apartment opened up, and I just took it."

He raised an eyebrow. "And you don't think that's inappropriate?"

"As you can see, we ended on great terms. He's still my best friend. Maybe we weren't meant to be married, but we're still meant to be friends. I have to cut him out of my life on principle?"

"No, but can you really get over someone when you see them every day?"

"You aren't friends with any of your exes?"

"No."

"Have you ever had a girlfriend that could be an ex?" We should move this into my apartment, but the moment was still too intense for a location change.

He took a while to answer. "No."

"Jax, this is exactly why I wanted to take things slow. I didn't want to owe you an explanation, but you pressed me into a corner I couldn't get out of. You gave me an ultimatum. I didn't want to lose you, so I caved. Now I'm having a conversation I didn't want to have, defending myself over something I wasn't prepared to handle, and you're pissed at me in the hallway. Maybe this was a bad idea—"

"Maybe all of that is true, but you still should have told me."

"Well, I didn't. And here we are…" I threw down my arms.

He stared me down, still angry. "Are you still in love with him?"

"No."

"It seems like women are always in love with their gay best friend."

"Stereotype," I snapped. "And I will always love him because he's the closest person in the world to me. He's my family. But no, I'm not in love with him. For the first three months of our divorce, we didn't talk to or see each other. I needed that space to get over him. When I finally did, we became friends again. We needed that time to let go of our past relationship and start a new one. I waited a long time before I put myself out there again. When I picked you up at the bar, I was totally ready. So, no, I'm not in love with my ex-husband."

The fire in his eyes slowly dissipated.

"If I were, I would probably move. If I couldn't get over him, then I really would have to cut him out of my life. But thankfully, that didn't happen." It was ironic that Jax accused me of still wanting my ex-husband when there was someone else I was attracted to—his brother. A single kiss with him left me reeling. It was the best I'd ever had—and it only lasted a few minutes. Jax's paranoia was completely off the charts. "I kissed someone else and you didn't care, but my gay ex-husband turns you into a psychopath. That makes no sense."

"Kissing someone and being married to someone are totally different. You know it."

I crossed my arms over my chest. "I don't know what else to say. I'm sorry I didn't tell you..." Jax would either let it go, or we would go our separate ways then and there. The only reason I was still there was because I believed I could have something great with Jax if I gave it enough time. Right now, everything was still so messy.

He sighed then stepped closer to me. "I know I rushed this relationship when I shouldn't have. The only reason I did was because I didn't want someone else to have you. That doesn't happen to me very often...when I meet a woman and feel this way. But when I realized you were married to Colton, I lost sight of everything we agreed on. You did tell me you were married and you weren't ready for something serious...so that's my fault. Honestly, this sounds so complicated and I should just walk away...but I don't want to. I really like you, Pepper. I don't want to lose you."

My eyes softened, and I remembered why I liked Jax to begin with. He was sweet, affectionate, and understanding. "So...we can let this go?"

He nodded. "Yeah. Now let's go inside your apartment. I'm sure all of your neighbors are tired of listening to us."

I smiled. "Or they're munching on a bowl of popcorn

and hoping we'll have make-up sex right here in the middle of the hallway."

When he smiled, he showed his pearly whites and the pretty brightness in his eyes. When he smiled like that, he looked even more handsome. It was no surprise that he sold prime real estate and made a great living. No one could resist those good looks and natural charisma. "How about we have make-up sex on the couch then eat a bowl of popcorn?"

"Ooh...that sounds like my style."

19

COLTON

I sat at the dining table with a mug of coffee in front of me. I was shirtless and in my sweatpants, attire I used to wear all the time, but now that my brother's frame was constantly in my line of sight, I felt self-conscious.

I had a trim body with muscles, but my physique paled in comparison to his. Plus, he had all those badass tattoos that made him look even more dangerous.

Finn worked on his paperwork, oblivious to my stare.

I finally got up and put on my shirt, losing the contest we weren't actually having.

I sat down and sipped my coffee again.

"How's the job hunt?" Finn flipped through his notes, examining lab work and scans for his patients. He seemed to read their file before he picked up the phone and did his dictation for the medical chart.

"I haven't even started looking."

"Why not?"

"You don't want me to live with you?" I countered.

He raised his eyes to meet mine. "Not forever. I'm not looking for a permanent roommate."

"How long can I stay?"

"As long as you want—within reason."

"Maybe I can just marry a rich guy and never work again…" Wouldn't that be nice?

Finn continued to stare at me, his shadowy beard starting to come in because he hadn't shaved yet. "Everyone should work. You'd be unhappy if you didn't."

"What about housewives?"

"That is work. They keep up the house, run all the errands, raise the kids, do the cooking…it's a job."

"Well, I can do that."

"But do you want to do that?" he countered. "You got a law degree because you wanted to be a lawyer. Don't let one bad experience sour your motivation. That office wasn't a good fit, but you'll find something better. Every man needs a purpose. Without a purpose, we fade away."

I knew he made his bed every morning, kept up perfect hygiene, and always cleaned up after himself like an inspection would happen at any moment. Of course, he had a strict perspective on what men should be doing with their time.

"Do you like being a doctor?"

He set his paper down and grabbed his mug of coffee. "It's the only thing that interests me."

"But do you like it?"

"Sometimes."

"When do you like it?"

"When I save someone."

"And when do you not like it?"

His eyes turned cold. "When I don't save someone." He sipped his coffee then set it down.

"So, are you going to buy a car? Your place is a drive from the city."

"Yes. A truck."

"Can I borrow it?"

He continued to wear that annoyed expression. "What's wrong with Uber?"

"Nothing but it's expensive."

"Another reason you need a job."

"You're home during the day, and I'll be at work. So I could take the truck and have it back before you go to work."

"And what about when I want to leave the house during the day?"

"And do what?" I countered.

His eyes narrowed. "Does it matter? I can already tell living with you is going to be a pain in the ass."

"You live with me now, and it's fine."

"Yes...because I'm the guest. I've been a great roommate, so I expect the same courtesy from you."

"So I should parade my dates around the house naked? You know, since you're straight?"

He shrugged. "I don't care. Just pick up after yourself and be clean. Make me ask more than once, and I'll kick you out."

"You'd kick out your own brother?" I asked incredulously.

His only response was a threatening look.

"Alright...maybe you will kick me out."

Finn turned back to his paperwork.

"I'm glad Jax and Pepper worked things out. I really thought that was going to be the end of them, which would have been a shame because I like the guy."

"If he was actually threatened by a gay man, then he didn't deserve Pepper anyway."

"I'm not just a gay man...I was married to her. I shared every day with her. I slept with her."

"Doesn't matter." He flipped through his papers. "A real man isn't threatened by a former lover. A real man erases the memory of every guy she's been with. A real man doesn't know jealousy because he's too secure to be jealous."

Sometimes Finn talked about relationships like he'd been in one, but I knew he'd never been close to a woman. But he had distinct opinions on how relationships should be, how a man should treat a woman. "I think Jax had the right to be upset because he found out in such an insensitive way."

"Maybe. But he should have gotten over it quicker."

"Do you not like Jax?" I asked, my eyebrow raising.

He read through his notes and never answered the question.

Pepper walked inside, dressed for work in skinny jeans, heels, and a teal blouse. Her brown hair was straight, and she had hoops in her ears. She smiled sincerely as she stepped inside, like last night had ended on good terms. "Morning."

"You look happy." I drank my coffee.

"Well, I survived a hurricane," she said with a laugh. "So I'm feeling pretty good."

Finn's eyes followed her as she crossed the room, not blinking as he took in her frame. "There's leftover egg whites in the pan."

"There is?" I asked. "Why didn't you tell me?"

Pepper scooped the leftovers onto her plate and made a cup of coffee. "Because he likes me more than you."

I glared at my brother. "Clearly…"

Pepper took a seat beside me and added cream to her coffee. "Ready for tonight?"

I'd been putting all my energy into not thinking about it. I lowered my forehead to the table and sighed. "No…"

Pepper rubbed my back. "Nothing is ever as good or as bad as you think it will be."

"Is that supposed to make me feel better?" I asked, my eyes closed and my torso sprawled against the table.

Finn spoke. "When I spoke to Mom on the phone, she was practically crying. Said it's been so long since she had both of us in the same room at the same time. She might be so happy that she may not care about your news."

"Yeah, right." I sat up and pulled my mug in front of me. "She's going to be crushed when I tell her she lost Pepper."

"But she didn't lose me," Pepper said. "I'll always be around. Even when I'm married, we'll still come over for holidays and stuff. Nothing has to change. When your parents see that, they'll feel better."

"Maybe..." But would they feel better knowing they had a gay son? "That means I'll never have kids, and since Finn won't have kids either, Mom will freak out about that."

"You can have kids," Pepper argued. "You know I'll always be a surrogate for you."

"Really?" I asked, shocked by the offer.

"Why wouldn't I?" she asked, dead serious. "There are plenty of ways to grow your family. You have options. And who knows what the future holds for Finn. Maybe he will have a family someday. The future isn't set in stone."

"No," Finn said as he looked down at his newspaper. "No kids for me."

"Really?" Pepper asked. "Never?"

He lifted his gaze and met her look. "Never. I prefer being an uncle. Someone will have to teach Colton's kids how to throw a ball, drive a stick, and punch a bully in the face to break their nose in four different places. That's where I come in."

Pepper didn't hide her look of disappointment at his answer.

"What?" Finn asked. "You judge me? Is there something wrong with not wanting kids?"

"Not at all," she said as she shook her head. "No judgments. I just think it's a shame...because you would be a good father."

Finn ignored his paperwork altogether and stared at her. With unblinking eyes and a stature so still he seemed like an inanimate object, he looked at her like it was the first time he really took in her features. Finn made any expression seem intense, but the look he gave her now reached new levels.

She sipped her coffee as she looked at him, seemingly unaffected by that penetrating gaze. When she couldn't withstand his look any longer, she turned her eyes into her coffee.

Sometimes I felt the energy between the two of them. The temperature rose by several degrees within just seconds. Sometimes the air was hostile, so saturated with emotions, it was difficult to breathe. Maybe that was because Pepper was one of the few people confident enough to withstand his intensity. When I'd asked Finn if he had a thing for my ex-wife, he'd said no. And he was too honorable of a man to cross the line like that. There was an endless supply of beautiful women in the city he could enjoy. There was no reason to focus on Pepper. Maybe the entire thing was just a product of my imagination.

20

COLTON

"Ugh, this is gonna suck." I walked beside Finn as we headed to the front door.

"Hold your ground." Finn wore a gray V-neck and black jeans even though it was a cold evening. He hardly wore a jacket because he claimed he ran hot all the time. "Mom hates my tattoos, but I'm not going to cover them up."

"Being gay and having a few tattoos is not the same thing," I said. "If only it were."

Pepper walked behind me. "It may take a while for them to come around, but the sooner you do it, the sooner this will be over. Think of it that way."

"And it could be the end of my relationship with my parents..." Coming out was difficult for anyone who had been in my position. But the hardest part was the way it ostracized people from their families. Maybe some members of the family would approve, but others wouldn't. That was the scariest part of all. "Just give me a second before you—"

Finn rang the doorbell. "No. When the bombs are going

off, you don't hide away and wait until you're ready. You rush into the fray and try to survive. Because you'll never be ready for the most difficult phases of your life."

My parents' footsteps could be heard approaching the door. "Oh my god, they're here," Mom said. "Our babies are here."

Pepper smiled. "How cute…"

I knew I couldn't run from this, but there was nothing I wanted to do more than jump back in the truck and drive away.

MOM HAD ALREADY HUGGED Finn when he first walked inside, but now she wrapped her arms around him and held him tight, burying her face in his chest and closing her eyes. "I'm so glad you're home…you have no idea."

Finn didn't push her off when the affection lasted longer than thirty seconds. His arm wrapped around her shoulders, and he rested his chin on her head. "I know, Mom."

"I worried about you every single day. Most nights, I couldn't sleep. I knew you were doing what you wanted…but it was so hard. You're a grown man, but you're still my son… my first boy."

Finn was the least affectionate person I've ever known, but he let Mom do whatever she wanted. She was the one person he wouldn't push away, insult, or ignore. "I know, Mom. But I'm home now."

"Home for good?" she whispered.

"Yes." He rubbed her back.

She pulled away and cupped his cheeks, staring into his face with tears in her eyes. "I love you so much, honey. More than you could ever understand."

He kept his patience. "I love you too, Mom." He squeezed both of her wrists then lowered her hands back to his sides. "My life in the military was difficult at times, but it was exactly where I was meant to be. I couldn't imagine spending the last ten years of my life doing anything else."

She gripped his biceps and squeezed them. "And we're so proud of you, Finn. I don't know what we did to raise such a strong man...but we did something."

"Give yourself more credit, Mom," he said. "Strong parents raised me. It's no surprise I turned out the way I did."

Her eyes softened. "We're so lucky to have you as our son."

I watched the interaction with Pepper beside me. "And I'm supposed to follow that?"

Pepper didn't hear me because she watched the interaction with tears in her eyes.

God, I was so screwed.

Dad hugged Finn next, holding him for a long time. "I'm very proud of you, son. But I'm happier that you're home now."

"Promise us you'll never reenlist," Mom said.

Finn stared at her then shook his head slightly. "I can't make that promise. But I don't think I'll ever go back."

I whispered to Pepper, "Maybe I should do this another time..."

She turned to me, finally focusing on what I said. "You're doing this tonight. You either do it, or Finn will do it for you."

That wasn't so bad since they adored Finn. "Hmm..."

"No, Colton," she said. "You need to do it yourself." She walked away from me and joined Finn with my parents. "I'm sure Finn is gonna be angry with me for telling you this, but I saw his uniform and he received the Bronze Star."

Finn didn't seem angry, but he took a deep breath like he hadn't been expecting Pepper to throw him under the bus like that.

Mom turned to Finn, shock in her eyes. "Why didn't you tell us?"

"Son, that's amazing." Dad squeezed Finn's shoulder, pride in his eyes. "When did this happen?"

Finn looked at Pepper for a moment, but he didn't seem angry with her. He didn't seem pleased either. "About a year ago."

"What happened?" Mom asked.

Finn never talked about his time in the military, but he didn't deny our parents anything. He respected them too much to sidestep their questions. "We were in the field when our team was hit by gunfire. One of my guys had been shot in the stomach, close to the aortic artery. I couldn't reach him because there were too many enemies, but if I didn't do something, he was going to die. So I grabbed a gun and went to him. Stopped the bleeding and stabilized him while my men covered me. And he made it..."

I listened to every word and felt my jaw slacken in shock. My brother was a trauma physician, so I'd assumed he was at a safe location and the men were brought to him. I had no idea that my brother literally put his life on the line to save others.

Pepper's expression changed too. She'd been smiling a second ago, but now she gave him a new look entirely. Surprise mixed with awe stretched across her features.

Mom and Dad were speechless too.

When no one said anything, Finn changed the subject. "I'm starving. Let's get dinner started." He left the room and walked into the kitchen so he could retrieve the hot dishes Mom had prepared.

Mom turned to Dad. "Can you believe he's our son?"

Dad shook his head. "No...I can't."

WE SAT TOGETHER at the dining table and enjoyed the pot roast Mom made.

"Are you liking the hospital?" Mom asked Finn.

"Yeah," he answered. "It's a different environment from what I'm used to, but I like it. It's a lot of the same thing over and over again. Whenever a code happens, I have a whole team of nurses to help me, so that's a nice change. I usually have to do everything by myself."

I'd never heard Finn talk so much, but he couldn't be the cold and indifferent man around my parents. He had to be kind and responsive. Otherwise, it would be rude. It allowed me to learn more about him, which was nice.

The entire evening had been centered around Finn, which was a weight off my shoulders. Maybe I would never have the opportunity to tell my parents the truth, and I could just get out of the situation altogether.

"Are you seeing anyone?" Mom asked. "Maybe now that you're settled, you can find a nice girl."

Finn looked at his plate as he stabbed a piece of carrot with his fork. "Yeah, maybe."

Mom turned her attention on me, and that was when I knew my turn was up. "What's up with you, sweetheart? How's work?"

I didn't want to discuss the ordeal with my job. That would just get us off topic. It also wouldn't make any sense because I couldn't tell them what the problem was unless I told them I was gay first. "It's fine. Nothing too interesting going on there."

Pepper shot me a glare.

Finn did the same.

"Have you guys considered starting a family?" Mother asked. "You've been married long enough now. You've gotten to enjoy each other for many years. When your father and I got married, we started trying a year after we were married. We kinda rushed it, but we were so eager to start our family."

Finn stared at me, his eyes glued to me with aggression.

I pushed my food around on my plate, stalling as long as possible.

When I didn't say anything, Mom examined me harder. "Something wrong, Colton?"

"No," I blurted. "I just..."

Pepper looked at me. "Come on, Colt."

Mom exchanged a look with Dad. "You're starting to worry me, honey. Did something happen? Are you having a difficult time conceiving? There are so many other options out there that you don't need to stress about it."

She got the completely wrong impression. "No, it's not that. There's something I need to tell you, actually..."

"Alright." Mom set down her fork and glanced at Dad.

Dad rested his elbows on the table, preparing for bad news.

"This is gonna come as a shock. I know it's gonna be hard to understand. This is really difficult for me to say..." I glanced at Pepper beside me, remembering that I would always have her through this ordeal. "Pepper and I split up a few months ago."

All the life drained out of my mother's face. She even

cupped her mouth with her hand to silence herself as the cry emerged from her throat.

Dad's eyebrows rose, like he couldn't believe what I'd said.

"We divorced eight months ago," I said, knowing this would break my parents' hearts.

"Eight months ago?" Mom asked, heartbroken. "Eight months? Why didn't you tell us? What happened? You guys are so perfect together. I don't understand..."

"We are perfect together," I said. "We're best friends, and we'll always be best friends."

"Then I understand this even less," Dad said. "If you're still close, then why...?"

This was the hardest part. "Because I'm gay."

Finn's expression didn't change, but he gave me a slight nod in approval.

Mom's mouth dropped open, and the confusion in her eyes was mixed with pain.

Dad seemed even more shocked.

Neither one of them said anything.

I guess their silence was preferable to their rage.

It was quiet for a long time. No one said anything, and it became more and more uncomfortable. Pepper patted my hand affectionately, and Finn took a drink of his wine even though he didn't like wine.

Mom stared at Dad.

Dad stared at the table, gathering his thoughts.

"I know this is a shock," I said. "It's a lot to process. But I realized it a while ago, and that was why Pepper and I decided to divorce. She was really supportive about it, and I'm lucky we're still so close. I'm sure it'll take you some time to swallow this because it's so unexpected, but take all the time you need."

Mom eyes watered, and she wiped away a tear.

Oh god. This was bad.

Finn was sitting beside her, so he patted her back gently.

Mom turned to me, and instead of giving me that look of unconditional love, she looked broken. "How could do you that to Pepper? How could you waste so many years of her life and live a lie? This woman is like a daughter to me, and I don't accept this betrayal."

That wasn't what I expected her to say. "I didn't know at the time. It just kept creeping up until it was undeniable. I feel terrible for what I did to her. I really do—"

"I'm not angry with him," Pepper said. "We were really happy together while we were married, and we're still best friends now. I wouldn't go back in time and trade those years for anything else. Colton and I will still be together for the rest of our lives...but as friends."

Mom shook her head. "That's unacceptable, Colton. Just because Pepper has class and compassion doesn't right the wrong."

This was much worse than I expected. "Like I said, I didn't know—"

"How do you not know what you prefer?" Dad questioned. "It's pretty straightforward. If you're gay, then you've always known you were gay. You could have come forward about it before you married this wonderful woman and wasted her time."

Instead of being supportive of this news, they were protective of Pepper. Pepper was close to my parents so I knew they cared about her, but I didn't expect them to gang up on me.

"Really, it's fine," Pepper said. "Colton and I are in a very good place. There're no hard feelings."

Mom shook her head slightly. "Colton, I don't know what you want us to say."

Finn looked at his plate, disappointed by Mom's reaction.

Dad wouldn't look at me. "Gay or straight, we don't care. But you've never seemed gay. There was always porn on your computer, and you had girlfriends in high school. Are you sure this isn't a phase? Just an excuse to get out of a marriage?"

Whoa...that was harsh. "No...not an excuse." My voice came out weak because I was so hurt. "I loved being married to Pepper. I wish I could still be married to her. This isn't some lame scheme to get out of my responsibility. You have no idea how hard it was to come here tonight and tell you the truth. Cut me some slack."

"Cut you some slack?" Mom asked incredulously. "Our oldest son is finally home from the military, finally back in our lives, and you choose tonight to tell us that you're divorced and gay?"

Finn interceded. "Mom, I told him to tell you. He'd been dragging his feet, and it was time to come clean. He'd been dreading this dinner for weeks because he was afraid of how you would take the news. Now I don't blame him because you're handling this without a hint of compassion."

Dad turned to him. "Finn."

"I won't take back what I said," Finn barked. "You need to be supportive. Maybe Colt should have figured out how he felt sooner, but we can't change the past. We can only change the present. We're turning a new page in this story. We're starting over. Your son just told you he was gay, and now you need to tell him it's okay and you love him just the same."

Mom was silent.

So was Dad.

I actually felt like crying.

Mom rose to her feet to excuse herself. "My oldest son just came home with a uniform decorated in medals. He risked his life for our country, risked his life to save his men."

Finn closed his eyes and sighed.

Mom kept talking. "He served a decade in the armed forces and has returned home as a hero. And you tell me that in that same amount of time you couldn't figure out who you were? That you had to hurt this wonderful woman before you got what you wanted? Colton, your father and I don't care that you're gay. But we do care that you hurt our daughter, a young woman who is as much a part of our family as you are. That's unacceptable—and you won't get our support for that."

THE DRIVE HOME was long and quiet.

We didn't talk about what happened at the house.

There was nothing to talk about.

My parents were disappointed in me. They despised me. They hated me for mistreating Pepper.

Not that I could blame them. I hated myself for what I did to her when I first told her the truth. It was a difficult few months, lots of tears and lots of fights. But we worked through it and had a new relationship.

Now those old wounds had been reopened.

We walked into the apartment building and headed down the hallway. I moved my feet but felt like a zombie. There was no feeling inside my chest. I felt nothing at all, nothing but emptiness.

Pepper turned to me to say goodnight.

I ignored her and turned to Finn. "I'm gonna stay with Pepper tonight. I'll see you later."

Finn was rarely affectionate, but he wrapped his arm around my shoulders and gave me a gentle squeeze. "It'll be alright, man. Maybe not tomorrow or the next day. But eventually, it will." He unlocked the door and stepped inside my apartment.

I walked with Pepper to her door. "Do you mind if I stay with you tonight?"

"You don't even need to ask." She got the door unlocked, and we stepped inside.

I kicked off my shoes and went into her bedroom. I used to sleep with her every night, and for the first few months after our divorce, I missed it. I missed the way her hair made the sheets smell like lavender. I missed the way she would hog the covers all night, but she would still be cold so she would smother against me. Her presence always comforted me, made me think of happier times.

We went into her bedroom, and she changed into a long t-shirt before she got into bed. I stripped down to my boxers then lay beside her, like we were going back in time to the height of our marriage.

Side by side, we faced each other under the sheets, her face still visible in the darkness.

I didn't shed a tear because I was too empty to actually feel anything.

"They'll come around, Colton."

"Maybe. Or maybe my relationship with them will never be the same."

"It will be the same. It'll just take some time."

"Finn is the hero...and I'm the screw-up." They basically

said Finn was their favorite, that they were proud of him and ashamed of me.

"That's not true."

"It is true."

"Things are really bad right now. But they won't always be bad. You hit them with a lot of information at one time. They will come around, Colton. It'll just take lots of time and lots of patience."

"Maybe..." Or maybe not.

21

PEPPER

When I woke up the next morning, Colton was smothered into me, cuddling me just the way he did when we were married. Last night had been a difficult night for him, so when he asked to sleep over, I didn't object.

A part of me thought it was wrong because of my recent fight with Jax.

But Colton was going through a really difficult time, and it would have been wrong for me to say no.

I carefully snuck out of bed and headed into the kitchen so I could make breakfast for Colton. I was no chef, but pancakes were easy to whip up. All I had to do was put the bacon in the oven and scramble some eggs on the stovetop. Anyone could do that.

I tried to stay quiet as I prepared everything, making sure not to disturb Colton as much as possible. The dinner had gone much worse than any of us expected. I knew his parents well enough to understand they wouldn't be thrilled by the news, but I didn't expect them to be so cold either.

And I didn't expect them to be so personally offended by what he did to me.

I'd been close with his mom since I met her. We went shopping together often, had lunch several times a month, and she'd been the mother I never had. Maybe she was particularly kind to me because she knew I didn't have a family of my own. Or maybe she just really adored me. Whatever her feeling was, she'd been so compassionate, and I would never forget that.

That made this situation so difficult because I didn't outright hate her for her reaction. I knew she was struggling with the pain that her son lost a woman he loved. She wanted us to be together, and she couldn't comprehend a reality where we weren't. His father felt the same way.

She was protective of me like I was her own daughter, even when I wasn't her daughter anymore.

It only reminded me how painful our divorce was. I didn't just lose him as my husband, but I lost his family as my in-laws. I still wished Colton wasn't gay. I still wished we could have a family, grow old together, and die together.

But that would never happen.

We were just friends now—and we would only be friends.

A knock sounded on the door.

I was dressed in an oversized t-shirt that I probably stole from Colton a long time ago. The only person who could be at the door was Finn. He was always up early, so he probably wanted to check on his brother.

I cracked the door open and hid most of my body from view. "Hey..." My mouth closed when I came face-to-face with Jax, who was holding a handful of red roses. "Ooh... what a surprise."

"I've been thinking about my behavior a lot lately...and I

wanted to apologize." He held the roses out to me. "I yelled at you when I shouldn't have. I rushed things when I shouldn't have. I know we already made up, but I'm still sorry."

"Thank you..." I took the roses from his hand and released the door. It automatically crept open and revealed the apartment behind me. The roses were a touching gesture and closure to that terrible fight, but all I could think about was the fact that Colton slept in my bed last night—and he could wake up any minute.

Jax watched me smell the roses and then sniffed the air. "Are you cooking?"

"Yeah, I was making breakfast."

"You?" he asked in surprise. "I thought you didn't know how to cook."

"I don't," I said. "But I can make some pancakes and stuff. I just thought—"

The universe conspired against me, and Colton stepped out of the bedroom. Thankfully, he put on all his clothes, but since I only had a one-bedroom apartment, it was obvious where he came from. "Something smells good." He stepped into the living room, noticed Jax in the doorway, and smiled. "Hey, man. Roses...nice touch." He gave a thumbs-up before he kept walking and entered the kitchen.

Jax's contrite attitude immediately disappeared. He glanced at my bedroom, looked at what I was wearing, and then looked a million times more pissed than he had during our last fight. His eyes bored into mine like plumes of lava were about to erupt.

Shit.

He shook his head slightly then stepped back. "Good-bye, Pepper." He headed down the hallway and didn't look back.

I didn't chase after him because I wasn't dressed for it, and I also didn't see the point. Jax just saw me in my worst light. Anyone else would have reacted the exact same way— and I couldn't convince him not to be angry.

I shut the door and tossed the roses on the coffee table.

Colton took over the stove and flipped the pancake before scooping it onto a plate. "You didn't have to do this."

Normally, I would tell Colton everything that had just happened, spill my heart out to him. But I couldn't do that, not after what he was suffering through. It would be selfish. Plus, it would make him feel worse if he thought he was responsible for Jax dumping me. "I wanted to. But now that you're up, you're going to help me."

"I figured. We want this to be edible, after all."

AFTER COLTON WENT BACK to his apartment, I tried to make things right with Jax.

I showed up at his doorstep around five in the evening, taking an Uber to his neighborhood. It'd just started to rain, and thankfully, he had a patio cover over his front doorstep. I rang the doorbell and hoped he would answer.

Footsteps sounded through the foyer, and judging by the distinct sound, they carried a man's weight.

There was a long bout of silence that followed. Jax probably looked through the peephole and debated whether he should open the door or not. I was the last person he wanted to see right now.

But he opened the door anyway.

He stared at me with the same coldness, the same hatred. He kept one hand on the doorknob like he considered shutting it in my face. He didn't say a word, the vein on his forehead doing all the yelling.

"Let me explain, okay?"

He raised his hand, silently giving me the floor. "Go ahead. Explain to me why your ex-husband slept over last night and you were wearing pretty much nothing. Explain to me why you cooked him breakfast this morning, like you're still that married couple you used to be. Yes, I'm curious how you're going to spin this."

I already knew this was going to end terribly. When I left his house tonight, it would be for the last time. Jax was too angry to forgive me this time. Since I didn't really blame him, I didn't see the point in fighting. "We had dinner with his parents last night. He told them the truth, that he was gay and we've been divorced for a long time—"

"Not long enough, apparently."

I kept going. "When we came home, Colton was in a really dark place. He asked to sleep over, and I didn't say no."

"That's what a couch is for."

"Well, he didn't want the couch. All we did was sleep."

"Even if that's the truth, it's still completely inappropriate. You say you don't love this guy, but you obviously do."

"I never said I didn't love him. I'm just not in love with him."

His jaw clenched. "Same difference."

"It's not the same at all. I'm sorry that it happened, and I understand why you're so angry. I don't blame you."

"I don't blame me either."

"But...he's my best friend. He needed me last night, and I'm not going to turn him down. It's not like this happens often. It's never happened at all, actually. It wouldn't be any different if he were Stella or Tatum."

"But you weren't married to either of them."

"So?" I countered. "I know you don't understand what it's like to have a best friend the way I do. There will always be love between us, but it's not romantic love. I don't feel bad for being there for him, not when he's my family. Colton is definitely gay, so there's no reason for you to feel threatened."

"Maybe you'll never hook up again, but I don't want my girlfriend to be in love with her ex-husband while she's seeing me."

"Well, I'm not...and that's all I can say."

He lowered his hand from the doorknob, but not because he was less angry. "It's completely inappropriate, and I won't change my mind about that. When I saw him walk out of your bedroom, I was so angry."

"I know. I don't blame you."

He stared at me, his eyes still angry but slowly waning.

"I wanted to explain what happened. I didn't want you to think I just sleep with him for the hell of it. It was an unusual circumstance. I just...wanted you to know that."

He shifted his gaze to the floor as he crossed his arms over his chest.

It seemed like the conversation was over, so there was no reason for me to say. "Goodbye, Jax. I'm sorry...about everything." I turned away and prepared to stand in the rain until another Uber could pick me up. Good thing I had my umbrella.

"Pepper."

I turned back around, hoping he would give me another chance, not that I deserved one.

"I can let this go if it never happens again."

If I explained to Colton why it couldn't happen again, he

would understand. He wanted me to move on and be happy. "That's fair."

"But I can't let this go unless you stop seeing him."

I looked into his green eyes as I heard what he said. The rain poured into the driveway and the street, the sound of the heavy raindrops surrounding us. This man just gave me an ultimatum, that I had to drop Colton if I wanted to keep him. "That's—"

"Take it or leave it. No compromise. If you really want to move on with your life, you need to let him go. If you think I'm the only man who's going to have a problem with this, you're wrong. Being this close to your ex-husband will sabotage every relationship you ever have. Get a new apartment, cut him out of your life, and be with me. Or continue to live across the hall from your ex-husband, continue to have your sleepovers, continue to have this deep and intimate relationship with him instead of finding a new man to spend your life with. It's your choice."

I couldn't picture my life without Colton, but I couldn't argue with Jax's reasoning. If I continued to have this close relationship with my ex, every man I met would be scared off by it. It was definitely a turnoff. Jax wasn't the psycho jealous type of man. He was easygoing and reasonable, but he couldn't look past this.

"Pepper."

I lifted my gaze to meet his, feeling so much pain in my heart. "I can't live without him…" I wanted to move on and find a man I would fall deeply in love with. I wanted to have a family, to live in a beautiful house just like this. But I also wanted Colton to come over for Super Bowl Sunday, for the holidays, and for game night. I needed a man who accepted Colton as my past, present, and future. The odds of that were slim, but I had to try.

Jax sighed to himself as my words stung him. His nostrils flared with annoyance, and his eyes shut like I'd insulted him. He grabbed the doorknob again and prepared to shut the door in my face. "Goodbye, Pepper."

DESPITE THE USE of my umbrella, I was still pretty wet from the rain. But the damp coldness didn't affect my mood.

I was too bummed out to care about the rain.

My feet immediately carried me to Colton's apartment, the place I used to live when I was married. Talking to Colton about this was a bad idea, but I didn't know where else to go. I didn't knock before I stepped inside.

Finn sat in the armchair, reading a thick book on his lap. His eyes glanced up, and he looked at me. "What were you doing in the rain?"

I set my umbrella in the sink then came back to him. "Colton here?"

"No." He shut his book and set it on the end table. "He's at Zach's."

"Oh…" I could use the company right now, but I felt awkward running to Zach's place when Colton already had his own pain to deal with. I stayed rooted to the spot instead of leaving, not sure what to do.

Finn stared at me for a while before he rose to his feet and came toward me. Like always, he was in just his sweatpants, his ink acting as his t-shirt. He stopped in front of me and examined the hurt in my eyes, absorbing my pain like he could physically see it. "What's wrong, baby?"

I didn't even care about the use of the nickname. I didn't care about anything at that moment. Losing Jax wasn't the worst part. It was the terror that I might never find a man I loved, a man who could compete with Colton. "It's a long story..."

"Well, I'm off tonight, so I've got the time." He stepped closer to me. "Talk to me." His blue eyes shifted back and forth as he looked into mine, his look soft for once. He was normally cold and hostile, the last person you would want to confide in, but when it was just us two, he seemed like the most understanding man in the world. He soothed my pain with just his presence. He made me feel safe when I wasn't scared in the first place.

"Well, Colton slept over last night as you know. When I woke up in the morning, I made some breakfast. I didn't change my clothes, so I was just wearing a long t-shirt with my hair in a bun."

He was a foot away from me, his eyes glued to my face like every word was more interesting than the last.

"Then Jax stopped by....and watched Colton walk out of my bedroom."

His eyes narrowed slightly, immediately understanding the problem.

"He'd brought me roses to apologize for the night before, but when he saw Colton...he left."

His eyes softened in sympathy.

"I just went to his place to explain what happened. He was understanding, to a certain degree. But he said he couldn't make this work unless I stopped seeing Colton altogether. As in, permanently."

Finn sighed quietly and rubbed the back of his neck. Even with just the slight change of expression, he was so sexy. Whether he was angry, indifferent, or concerned, he looked handsome no matter what. This caring side of him was particularly attractive. "What did you say?"

"The only thing I could say...no."

Finn didn't look surprised by my answer.

"I wanted to make it work with Jax...but I can't live without Colton."

Finn moved into my chest and wrapped his arms around me. His thick arms cradled me with the strongest support in the world. His chin rested on my head, and he blanketed me with his smell, of body soap from the shower.

I rested my cheek against his chest, listening to his strong heartbeat.

His hand moved into the back of my hair. "I'm sorry, baby."

"I know..."

His lips tilted down, and he pressed a soft kiss to my forehead, his full lips soft and warm to the touch. His fingers cradled the back of my neck as he held me against him, carried the burden of my weight with no effort.

That kiss chased away most of my pain. Being in his arms was the most comfortable place for me, a safe haven where no one could ever touch me. Something about Finn made me feel like I was home, made me feel like I was surrounded by unconditional love. I'd never felt this safe, not even with Colton.

That was exactly why I pulled away. Last time we were too affectionate, bad things happened. After the night I'd had, I couldn't afford to get myself into more trouble. Finn was my weakness, a man I couldn't have. I shouldn't tempt myself, not even with something as innocent as a hug. "Let's keep this to ourselves, okay?"

"Why?"

"I don't want Colton to know."

"But you tell him everything." He let me step back, but he kept his hand on the back of my neck, touching me even when I didn't want him to.

"Because he'll feel terrible. He'll know he's the reason Jax left. He's going through so much right now that I don't want to make it worse. It doesn't matter anyway...it's not going to change anything."

Finn shook his head slightly, like he didn't agree with that statement.

"Promise me?"

He shook his head again, this time more decisive. "Real men don't make promises. Their word is good enough."

My eyes softened. "Thank you."

"Then what are you going to tell him?"

I shrugged. "It just didn't work out."

He gave a slight nod. "Alright."

The conversation was over, so we just stared at each other, the longing burning inside us both. Anytime we were alone in a room together, the heat rose like the thermostat had been cranked up high. It could be freezing cold, but I could feel the sweat drip down the back of my neck. This man made me illogical, made me disloyal. He was the one man in the world who was off-limits, and I'd just ended a relationship with a great guy for Colton. It didn't make sense to throw that relationship away. "I should go..."

Finn didn't try to dissuade me.

When I was vulnerable like this, I wanted to lie on that couch with his arms around me. I wanted those lips against my forehead...as well as in other places. Maybe it was just because I was upset that I felt that way. Until I felt better, I should be alone.

He didn't argue with me, probably because he felt the same way. "Alright. You know where I am if you need me."

I turned to the door and felt his eyes drill into my back. I could feel the heat of his gaze, that he wanted me and wanted to hold me at the same time. Jax was an attractive man with a lot of qualities, but I'd never felt this intensity with him. I'd never felt it with anyone, not even Colton. I finally got into the hallway and shut the door.

The spell was broken. The temperature decreased. His stare was interrupted, so I felt myself breathe again once more.

Until I saw him again.

ALSO BY E. L. TODD

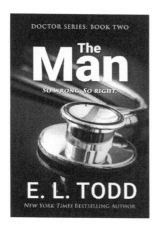

Now that Jax is gone and I'm single once again, I'm supposed to be finding Mr. Right.

But Finn is the only guy I want.

Every time we're in the same room together, the heat is explosive. We can barely look at each other without our hands shaking. As days turn into weeks, our resolve softens.

And then we can't fight it anymore.

Order Now

Made in the USA
Columbia, SC
02 August 2020